To Live With A Stranger

Mary T. Bradford

Published by Cregane Publishing, 2021

Cover Art: Wild Girl Covers
Editor: Christine McPherson

Table of Contents

Dedication

The setting in this novel is based on my Nana's home in Cregane, Churchtown, in north County Cork. Her name was May Egan neé Sheehan. Raising six children there with Grandad, five boys and one girl (my mother), Nana played a big part in mine and my siblings' lives. Sadly, Grandad died a young man, six months before I was born.

It is set in a quiet rural area and I have always thought it would make a wonderful retreat centre for artists of all talents. The local village is weaved in too to the story.

I believe I had to write a story about the cottage. It had to be recognised in some form and so, To Live With A Stranger came about.

It is wonderful that this home which holds many memories for so many is still owned by family.

May Egan 11/12/1909 – 27/01/2002

Chapter One

Cathy Reed hopped from one foot to the other with excitement, the phone receiver clamped against her ear. Her chestnut-coloured curls bounced on top of her shoulders as she abandoned her breakfast to read the letter over and over, while the rain lashed against her apartment window. The heating was on the blink again and she shivered in her pyjamas and fluffy socks, yet could not contain the elation that flowed through her curvy body, wobbly bits and all.

'Calm down, tell me again what you said. No, I've not had a letter from any solicitor,' her sister Gemma replied.

'Are you not listening?' Cathy squealed.

'You've news about some inheritance? From whom? A letter?' Gemma's words continued to tumble out. 'And you got this when, today? Yesterday?' As always, Gemma needed facts. This unexpected news appeared to have thrown her as much as it had Cathy.

'But who died recently in the family?' She kept the questions coming. 'Look, I'm coming over. You're not making any sense, and you seem to be in cuckoo land. I'll read it for myself.' Gemma hung up.

Bingo, thought Cathy. Why had she phoned Gemma? *Think before you act*, Cathy scolded herself.

• • • •

The two women sat speechless on the worn, cloth-covered couch. The formal letter stated that Cathy had indeed been mentioned in a will, and that she was required to visit the named solicitors for further instruction.

'It sounds so formal for Great-Aunt Lizzie: Elizabeth Marion Sheldon, neé Reed. Very fancy, indeed, don't you think?' Gemma still had her coat on; she couldn't understand why her sister put up with the broken heating in the apartment. Her tone made it clear that she was put out – not just with being omitted from their great-aunt's final wishes, but that Lizzy had died and they had not been informed. 'Dead and gone without a goodbye. So sad,' she said mournfully. 'It says here she died of a heart attack, but had chosen to donate her body to medical research and did not want a funeral or any kind of memorial service.' She pulled the collar of her coat up and sighed. In contrast to her sister's soft curls, Gemma maintained a tight, pixie-style haircut, sleek but short.

Cathy took the letter from her sister's hand and re-read it. She had not seen Great-Aunt Lizzy since their father's funeral. Those few minutes they'd spent together suddenly rolled into her mind. Lizzy's voice had been soothing; Cathy remembered a charming, caring woman. 'Why, Cathy, so good to see you. Just a pity it's a sad occasion,' she'd said. 'Your father was a good man. You make sure to mind yourself, and call out to see me some time. I'd love a visit.' Elizabeth had rested on her walking stick, and her gloved hand had held Cathy's tightly for a brief moment, acknowledging the younger woman's tears and encouraging her to cry it all out. And as they'd parted that day, Cathy had leaned in to share a warm, comforting hug with her aunt.

Now she recalled thinking how frail her great-aunt had been as she held her, and Cathy marvelled at the old lady's insistence to attend her nephew's funeral. A sad occasion, yet gentle memories. She wished she'd made more effort to take the bus out to Ballybawn to see her elderly relative, but now it was too late. Suddenly she remembered the boots Lizzy had worn that day and sniggered.

'What's funny?' Gemma snorted with distaste. She disliked nothing more than being kept out of the loop.

'Lizzy. We saw her last at Dad's funeral, remember? And she had on a pair of red ankle boots with purple tights. The boots even had pom-poms swinging from them. Totally eccentric but colourful, funeral or not.'

'Oh goodness, yes, she was a disgrace. Still, Dad did have a soft spot for her. He said she was mad as a hatter but had a heart of gold.' Gemma's tone softened at the memory of their father, then she turned to Cathy, her manner becoming more business-like. 'Let's phone this solicitor and get an appointment. Better not to wait around.'

Cathy was aware that her sister was struggling with the cold apartment; she was almost shivering. 'Look, you go home and check your post,' she suggested. 'I'll make the call and then phone you.' She stood and lifted her sibling's bag. She felt mean making it so obvious, but being in Gemma's company for too long always made her unsettled. Cathy was always waiting for the next put-down, the snarky comment; never a compliment. And she really didn't want her sister there when she spoke to the solicitor.

Once Gemma left, Cathy grabbed the letter once more. Had she really inherited something of value? Knowing odd Aunt Lizzy, maybe she had left Cathy her red boots – after all, she *had* admired them that day!

• • • •

Three days passed and Gemma did not receive any letter, so it appeared that she had not been in Aunt Lizzy's thoughts when she made her will. Cathy knew her sister would never admit to being put out, but she could hear the annoyance in Gemma's sharp attitude when they spoke. Even if Aunt Lizzy had just left her a small trinket, it would have been something to soothe Gemma's grievance, Cathy was sure.

Gemma's hints about accompanying her sister to the solicitor's appointment fell on deaf ears, but Cathy did promise to call to the house for dinner afterwards and fill her in. She would even bring a bottle of wine for the occasion.

The night before the appointment, Cathy flung her clothes on her bed in dismay. What the hell should she wear? She had no option; she would have to ask Gemma. Her sister was bound to know the protocol of how to dress for such an occasion. 'It's a late afternoon appointment, so what should I wear?' she wailed down the phone. 'Should I be in funeral garb, do you think, since it's to do with a will and that?' Her bedroom was in chaos; a bit like her life at the moment. Clothes were scattered on the floor, across the bed, and a pair of tights draped the nightstand lamp in a messy twirl.

'From what we said of Lizzy, morbid mournful colours are the last thing you should wear. Just go casual but smart,' Gemma snapped.

She was not taking being excluded from the reading of the will too well, Cathy recognised. But she didn't feel guilty. Gemma rarely thought about others and how or what they felt, and she'd never visited or cared much about their relatives, generally opting out of family gatherings on some pretence or other. It was always Cathy who had accompanied her parents on visits, so she wasn't really surprised that Lizzy had ignored her sister.

Returning to the task of picking an outfit, Cathy rummaged in the wardrobe for over an hour before settling on some black pants and a grey wool jumper. Her red earrings would be a pop of colour, in recognition of Aunt Lizzy.

Chapter Two

The abstract paintings dotted on the walls were in perfect symmetry to the framed legal degrees, Cathy noted, before dragging her eyes away to focus on the man in front of her. *Had she trouble hearing, or did he just say what she thought he did?* The potted plant in the corner fluttered as though it could not believe the solicitor's words either.

'Can you repeat that, please?'

'Repeat what?' The solicitor, Roman O'Driscoll, glared at her from behind his desk.

'What you just said about a clause.' Cathy turned to look at the other man in the room. She and this person – a complete stranger that she had never met before – were expected to what? Live together? What on earth had Aunt Lizzy been thinking?

The man sat in the chair beside her, apparently calm and unmoved by what he was hearing. *Had they even been properly introduced?* Cathy wondered. The uppity solicitor had mumbled something when she arrived, but she'd not caught what he'd said.

'Your great-aunt's will states that for you to inherit her country cottage, you must live in it for the next two years. After two years, if you decide to sell it, then you can do so. But you must both do this together.' He looked pointedly first at Cathy and then at the man beside her.

The young man's pallor had changed, as though Mr. O'Driscoll's words were finally sinking in. They'd inherited the cottage... together!

Definitely crazy. Cathy's thoughts filled with words to describe her father's aunt, and they were all connected to a lunatic asylum. The deep green wall behind the solicitor's desk seemed to close in on her. It seemed as though it was quietly but steadily moving nearer, and she was trapped. Her breathing quickened, and her knuckles glowed white as her hands gripped the arms of the chair, and a jumble of thoughts ran through her head. *She must be in the wrong office. How could she possibly live with a stranger?*

'Are we clear, Ms. Reed?' The solicitor, in his polished tan shoes and smart navy suit, continued to look at her. His fingers splayed out on his desk as he loomed over her.

He would be perfect in the role of a judge, Cathy reckoned. *Sitting above his minions and doling out jail sentence after jail sentence.*

'Ms. Reed?'

'Yes, yes, thanks, thank you.' She swallowed. If only she could hide behind the large potted plant. Sitting here brought back memories of being called to the school principal's office.

'Excuse me, I'd like to ask a question.' The stranger's voice was gentle, almost pleading in tone. Cathy turned immediately to listen.

'Of course, Mr. Daniels, what can I help you with?' The judge-to-be turned his attention to her new housemate.

'What if we say no, or one of us says no? What then? What happens to Cregane Court?'

Cathy smiled in support of Mr. Daniels' excellent question, holding her breath for the answer.

'Because you both have inherited Cregane Court, if either of you says no to the conditions laid down, then the other cannot inherit the property on their own. After that happening, well, I'm not at liberty to divulge. Suffice to say that, if such a thing happens, the situation has been catered for.' Roman O'Driscoll tapped his pen on the desk and glanced at his watch. No doubt he had other appointments to attend to.

'I shall let you know once I've thought about it, Mr...' she floundered at his name.

'O'Driscoll, Roman O'Driscoll. And you both have one month from today to give me your answer.'

Cathy looked at Mr. Daniels, smiled, and wondered what on earth she had been dragged into. *Whatever had Lizzy been thinking?*

• • • •

It was Mr. Daniels' idea to go for a coffee together. After all, they had a major decision to make. And if they both said yes, they would be living together and sharing lots of cups of coffee, he'd joked. As they left the stuffy office, he held his hand out in friendship and apologised for not hearing her first name earlier. When Cathy admitted that she hadn't heard his name either, the ice had been broken.

Over coffee, Mark suggested it would be better if he told her a little about himself. He worked in finance but enjoyed carpentry, was single, with no intentions of changing that anytime soon, and was also on the wrong side of 30. 'Though not by much,' he added, and winked.

In response, Cathy shared her story – recently unemployed, single, over the fence of being thirty. Now more at ease with each other, the pair settled back in their chairs and ordered two more coffees.

'I'm sorry. I feel like an imposter,' Mark told her. 'And I'm really sorry for all this grief with your great-aunt's will. I had no idea that I was going to be in it. I mean, I liked Elizabeth – she was fun and quirky, and a darling to spend time with.' He chuckled. 'That sounds so shady, doesn't it? But the truth is, she and my grandmother were the best of friends for many years.'

He was such a dear; all apologies, Cathy thought, as she studied him closely. There was a touch of Colin Firth about him – long, lean, and soft wavy hair. Hmmm... handsome, too.

'Stop apologising. I mean you didn't twist my aunt's arm to write you into her will, did you?' she laughed lightly, then wondered whether maybe he had. *Perhaps this nice guy was an act.*

'No. Of course not.'

Cathy thanked the waitress as she placed their fresh drinks on the table.

Mark continued, 'My grandmother, Diane, and Elizabeth were great friends, and they played bridge and other card games at Elizabeth's house every Tuesday evening. I was sent to my grandmother's a lot – my parents liked to offload me to her during all the school holidays, too – so I met your aunt fairly often. My grandmother died a number of years ago, but I kept in contact with your aunt; she was like a surrogate grandmother. Unfortunately, I hadn't seen her for a couple of months as I have been on secondment to our office in London, and only learned that she'd died when I got back.' His face clouded over, and he sighed. He appeared genuinely saddened at Lizzy's passing.

'Ah, Diane.' Cathy nodded. 'I do recall that name. So, she was your granny? It seems to me,' her voice was soft, 'that you are more deserving of Cregane Court than I am. I knew my great-aunt, of course. She was my father's aunt, so I usually went with him to visit her when I was young. Not as much once I left home, I'm sorry to say. But every time we did meet, we had fun. She had a wicked sense of humour and a great love of life.' It was Cathy's turn to sigh.

'Well, you obviously left an impression on her.' Mark smiled as he picked up his cup and sipped.

Lizzy's bright yellow cottage, with the rose garden to the side and the white iron bench on the front lawn facing up to the house, slipped into Cathy's thoughts. Prompted by happy memories there, she broke their comfortable silence.

'So, what are we going to do about our predicament?'

Mark shrugged. 'I don't know. I don't think I've really grasped the reality of it.'

'What's your gut reaction, Mark?'

'Um... yes, go with it.' He looked over at Cathy with his head tilted to the side, waiting to see her reaction.

'You think we should do this? Are you not going to take the month offered to us to think it over?' Her tone was incredulous.

Noise from the coffee shop broke her thoughts on the subject, and she glanced away from his gaze. A customer disputing the bill was shouting about poor service, and the young waitress who'd served them looked terrified. When Cathy turned her attention back to Mark, he was staring at her.

'It's my gut reaction, like you asked,' he said quietly. 'I take it yours isn't the same.' A shadow of sadness crossed his face.

'No, I don't think it is,' she admitted. 'I mean... Well, to be honest, this is a momentous decision that can't be fixed over two cups of coffees. How can you be so sure so fast? Look, Mark, I don't know what to say or think.' She slumped down in the chair.

Cathy hated pressure. She watched him, unsure of what to say next. Again, they slipped into silence. If one said no, then the other one lost out. It was a monumental task to arrive at an answer that would keep them both happy and also fulfil Aunt Lizzy's wishes. Cathy's mind was a whirl of questions. She didn't know where Mark lived or worked. Moving in together would mean changes to their daily living. *How would they share the property? The cottage was small, she knew; what if their tastes differed widely?* She sighed heavily. Aunt Lizzy had really thrown a spanner in their lives, but she decided she would give it her best shot.

'Tell you what, let's take a few days to get our heads around this, meet up, and talk again,' she offered. 'What do you think?'

'I agree. It's Friday now, so maybe Wednesday week? Here? Two o'clock?' He handed her a small card. 'Here's my number.'

'Perfect.' Cathy stood and put her jacket on then reached out to shake Mark's hand.

What a crazy few hours it had been, she thought, as she headed out of the café. When she'd first opened the letter from the solicitor's firm, she hadn't known what to expect. But she would certainly have never predicted how this afternoon's meeting would turn out!

• • • •

Gemma had pulled out all the stops for dinner. She was desperate to know what her sister had inherited. *If it was money, maybe Cathy would treat her to a few bob*, she thought as she placed the cutlery on the table. A stab of envy pierced her at the idea of Cathy coming into cash, just as the doorbell announced her sister's arrival.

'So, that's it,' Cathy said, having explained the outcome of the solicitor's meeting. 'This Mark and I must meet up now and see what we are going to do.' She smiled at her sister. 'The roast beef is delicious, Gemma.'

Cathy was sitting next to her young nieces at the dinner table. The girls were anxious to finish their meal and get back to their games, probably hoping their aunt would keep their mum busy for the evening and allow them a late bedtime.

'But this fellow, Mark Daniels, do we know him at all? I mean, was Lizzy in her right mind when she made the will?' Gemma dabbed at her mouth, frowning. As far as she was concerned, Cathy's description of the meeting was strange, and dinner had been eaten amidst a flurry of questions... with very few answers.

Chapter Three

Cathy looked out of the large window of her apartment. Three floors below her, those scurrying around on the busy city streets looked more like spiders than ants. The evening light shed shadows across the room, and the heavy rain outside did little to help Cathy's dark mood. She opened the window slightly to hear the street noise: buses sliding by, taxis hooting horns, the splish-splash as cars manoeuvred their way through dirty puddles. Cathy glanced up at the darkening sky and sighed heavily. She still had not come to any decision about Lizzy's cottage. Right now, her life had been turned upside down, and having to decide her future within a month had her seriously stressed.

Feck this! She moved purposefully away from the window. *I'm not going to waste another evening worrying about tomorrow or even the next week.*

• • • •

Umbrellas poked her head and shoulders as she dashed between people to reach the little café. Shaking her wet hair and slipping out of her jacket, she smiled at the waitress behind the corner counter and sat at the nearest vacant table. The place was almost empty. Everyone outside was in a rush to get out of the dreadful weather; there was no loitering this evening over a cuppa or evening drink.

Having got her breath back, Cathy ordered a coffee and pastry. She was glad she'd decided to get out of the apartment. Staying in would only add to her confused feelings, and she really was trying not to worry. Her phone jumped into song as she saw her sister's name flash on the screen. *No, not now. Please not her,* the words screamed in Cathy's head.

Realising the waitress was watching her, Cathy blushed and picked up the phone. 'Hello.'

'You took your time. What are you up to?' Gemma snapped.

'What do you want, Gemma?'

'Are you out?'

'Yes, having a quick coffee.'

'Great for some. Easy to see you don't have my responsibilities. Getting two kids settled for bed is exhausting.' Gemma loved to exaggerate and complain about her life.

At the mention of the children, Cathy smiled. 'How are my two beautiful nieces? Did Ava go to her princess party?'

'Oh, they're grand, and she did go to her party – but as a pirate. She insisted, and wouldn't change her mind.'

Despite the disgust in her sister's voice, Cathy was thrilled to hear that young Ava had stuck to her guns and suited herself.

The silence between them grew. Cathy knew Gemma was going to pounce with a dozen questions about what Cathy was doing to solve the inheritance debacle or, God forbid, to invite herself over for a heart-to-heart. Somehow, that always ended up as more of a lecture than a chat. Her sister liked to voice her opinion, but wasn't so keen to listen to others. Before Gemma could bring up the inevitable, Cathy decided to end their conversation.

'Well, Gemma, I shall let you get on with the girls' bedtime. Like you said, you're busy. Chat soon. Bye.'

She put the phone on silent immediately, in case Gemma decided to call back. Cathy was sure that she would have no place in Gemma's life if they weren't related, and she found it tiring and frustrating to be the one who always tried to keep the peace. She'd contacted her sister as soon as she received the solicitor's letter, but Cathy wondered if Gemma would have done the same if the tables had been turned. Stirring her coffee, she gazed at the street outside through the rain-lashed glass. *Damn!* She suddenly realised she hadn't closed the window in her apartment before she came out. The place would be even colder than usual when she got back. Her spirits drooped. *Why was she always the one who did the stupid things?* Cathy wondered. *Never Gemma. Never anyone else.*

It was eleven months since their father had died, and four months since Cathy had lost her job. Since then, her savings had quickly and steadily been eaten into. *Could she really afford to turn down this unexpected inheritance?* She heard the café door being pushed open.

'Any change?' A young man held out a soggy paper cup towards her. Behind him, the open door allowed the bitter cold evening to sweep inside. Menus ruffled on the nearby tables.

'Close the fecking door, will you, and stop annoying customers,' the cafe assistant shouted over, but smiled to soften the blow of her words.

'Join me altogether,' Cathy said to the young man.

'What?'

'Sit and join me. My treat.' She smiled as she gestured to the waitress for another coffee and the menu. 'Miserable outside, isn't it?' she said.

'Not as bad as three nights ago; it was freezing. At least the rain will stop, but the cold gets into you and it shivers your bones for days.' The man dragged a chair out and sat down heavily. Water dripped from his jacket, and he rubbed his hands together to warm them. He was young, maybe early twenties, but his green eyes were dull; there was no sparkle, no life in them, as he stared back at her.

'I'm Cathy.'

'Luke. Thanks for the food.' He had a nice smile.

'Have you a place to stay at night?' Cathy often wondered about the homeless when she looked out of her window and saw them below on the street.

He shook his head but looked unconcerned about his plight. He wasted no time in tucking into a plate of breaded fish and chunky-cut chips, doused with loads of vinegar, then followed with a slab of lemon cake and a large mug of tea. They ate without any further conversation, both staring out into the wet world, lost in their own thoughts. After a while, as he'd predicted, the rain stopped. The night was just beginning as he thanked her again for the meal and left.

••••

Back in her one-roomed apartment, Cathy quickly closed the window. The street below glistened, cleaned by the earlier downpour, and the streetlights lit the pavements and made the puddles shine. *At least I've got a roof over my head*, she told herself. She might have lost a lot in recent months, but not as much as many others out there. She went to the kitchen and filled her hot-water bottle.

In her bedroom, she paused to think about her evening. Something in her had changed, though she didn't quite know what. As she heard the rain starting up again, pounding her windows, Cathy thought of Luke. She cuddled under her duvet, cosy and dry, thankful for her lot in life for the first time in ages.

••••

The café waitress closed up the diner and pulled her jacket around her tightly. It was cold and wet again, so she grabbed a forgotten umbrella. How she hated this job. But that old cliché 'beggars can't be choosers' shot to mind as she strode to her bus stop. What that lady had done for the young homeless lad had been kind. *The world could do with more like her*, she reflected, as she stepped carefully to avoid the puddles.

••••

Luke huddled in a doorway in an alley not far from the café. Earlier, he had hidden a few pieces of dry cardboard in some empty rubbish bins, and now he spread them out on the ground. He squirmed into his shabby sleeping bag on top of the cardboard and pulled his hood up to keep warm. The alleyway was quiet; he wouldn't be disturbed or picked on. He had a full belly and a quiet spot to rest. *It's a good night,* he thought, as he drifted to sleep.

Chapter Four

Mark Daniels lay in bed. It was 7am, and he listened to his housemates out in the kitchen singing along to the morning radio. Yesterday had been the craziest day ever in his life. When he'd arrived at Roman O'Driscoll's office, he'd certainly never expected that he would walk out an hour later having co-inherited Cregane Court. But why him? He had wonderful memories of evenings filled with fun and mischief when he'd visited Elizabeth with his grandmother. And after Diane died, he'd happily continued to call on her closest friend out of affection, not duty. Elizabeth had been more of a comfort to him than his parents.

So, how was he going to handle this? Chatting with Cathy over coffee had been pleasant. *She seemed agreeable, with a hint of naughtiness*, he thought with a smile, *not too unlike her great-aunt.* He had a feeling that living with her could be eventful.

Stretching his long body, he grabbed a towel from the floor and jumped from the bed, heading for the shower. The office awaited.

• • • •

The day passed quickly, and Mark had plenty to deal with at work. Being a finance advisor in an accounting business kept him on his toes. His Master's in Business had helped him climb the promotional ladder, but he wasn't sure that he wanted to aim for the top position in the firm. He was not a big socialiser within the company and preferred to spend his weekends in his workshop – or that's what his housemates called it. In truth, it was just a glorified shed at the end of the garden, damp and cold, but big enough to house his tools and the timber he worked on.

• • • •

That evening after work, Mark sat alone, a bottle of red wine open on the coffee table. A glance towards the window showed another evening of rain – the staple of Irish weather. Sighing, he flicked through the channels on TV, but nothing caught his interest. As he sipped his wine, his thoughts turned again to Cathy. *Was she older than him, maybe by a couple of years? Imagine inheriting a house; a house with a stranger, no less!*

He had surprised himself with his answer to Cathy's question about them sharing, but his gut reaction had genuinely been yes, and still was. It itched him as to why that was, but he really liked the idea of Elizabeth's challenge. He would be 32 later in the year and wondered if this opportunity was the kick in life he needed. His beloved grandmother's best friend had remembered him in her final wishes, so he felt he owed it to her to agree.

Evenings at Cregane Court had always been great fun, with Elizabeth and his grandmother drinking sherry or a hot port, sharing secret jokes, a wink here and a nod there, and the pair would howl with laughter during their many card games. As a child, he had loved to sit quietly in the corner and observe their petty quarrels over cheating, or listen to the village gossip about an affair or the priest's drinking hours in the pub. Simple lives, simple pleasures.

That's what Mark yearned for – a simple life.

He loathed his job, wearing the business suit, making deals, working lunches... all the time working. It had been his father who'd insisted that Mark should follow in his footsteps with a solid career. 'The right connections can lead to greater things,' had always been the mantra of Daniels Senior.

Thank goodness for his grandmother, Mark thought with an affectionate smile. Diane had seen how his parents liked to offload him when he was in their way, even though he was an only child. And she'd nurtured his love for wood, encouraging him to follow the local handyman, Charlie, around when he came to carry out odd jobs for her. And Elizabeth had been there for him when he'd needed a shoulder; when the grief of losing his dear grandmother had overwhelmed him, and his parents had simply told him to grow up and be a man.

Yes, Mark owed it to both elderly women to take on the challenge of Cregane Court; the village of Ballybawn was where his happiest memories were. This was his chance to be the man he wanted to be. A man true to himself, for himself. And if Cathy Reed was anything like her great-aunt, living with her would make the journey a lot more colourful.

He could only pray that her answer would be yes when they next met.

Chapter Five

Grabbing a pen and paper, she placed it on the wonky table, reminding herself how she never got around to fixing the loose leg. Munching on some buttered toast, Cathy began to write the by now familiar columns of the pros and cons of her life. It wasn't her first attempt at this draining exercise, but she had made a promise to herself last night and she wanted to honour that. Procrastination had kept her company for the past few months, and she intended to kick it aside and be more proactive with her life.

Drawing two columns on the blank sheet of paper, she wrote the headings. She started on the pro side: one, she had a home; two, experienced in office administration; three, easy to get along with. Her sister suddenly rushed into her mind, *a pushover*, but Cathy shook her head. Her sister wasn't allowed any headspace this morning. *Concentrate!* Continuing, she wrote four, can drive but no car at present. *Couldn't see the sense of it when living in the city,* her mind once more wandered. *Anything else*? Stalling for a moment, she glanced at the other column.

The con side. This was easy. One, Dad was dead, with Mum now; two, no job. *Damn downsizing*. She buttered some more toast and freshened her coffee. Grabbing her pen, she struggled with the reality of what was facing her: three, no real friends; four, Gemma. A sister by birth, not much more. Downhearted, the soft tears dampened the paper before her. Life looked sad. Both parents gone and no home place to visit. There had been no chance of keeping it when funds had been needed for their father's nursing home care.

Swallowing hard, she straightened a little. *No self-pity*, she scolded herself. Nope, she was determined to recall and enjoy the good things, like her happy childhood, loved by both parents, marred only by the bullying of her sister. Gemma, five years older than her, had not been happy when her little sister was born. Gemma did not do sharing, and had let her sister know it at any opportunity.

Cathy put the pen down with a sigh. She'd had enough of being cooped up in the apartment. Going out and doing something would shake off the pain and the useless feeling that threatened to swamp her. *Her future demanded it,* her inside voice shouted. She would check out jobs in Ballybawn just for curiosity.

Cathy's internet was no more; she couldn't afford it. But she could use the library service. The library was some streets away so she would head for there first.

Showered and determined, she set out. She trembled a little with this bold person she was turning into. Yes, she was 34, but *not everyone blossoms at the same time.* Her great-aunt had used those words at a family function when she'd heard an overbearing relative ask Cathy in a sarcastic tone if she was not married yet. Great-aunt, what a friend!

'Sorry, you need to book an appointment to use a computer. They are in great demand, as you can see.' The librarian looked genuinely apologetic. 'I have a half-hour slot on Friday at 4.30pm, do you want to take it?' That was four days away. It seemed everyone had the same idea, as the place was busy with people waiting for their turn on the computers.

'Can I use your newspapers instead, please?' Cathy thought she may as well make use of her time while here. Directed to a collection of tables in the far corner, she made her way over to where two or three others sat; people older than herself. The quiet area was behind screens covered with posters offering courses, events, and services that were local to the suburb. Pleased she had thought about the newspapers, a smug little smile tickled her bottom lip. Life wasn't all online.

Head down, she searched page after page. Nothing. It seemed there weren't many vacancies in a sleepy village like Ballybawn, or its surrounding areas.

• • • •

The days became harder to fill, and the decision about Cregane Court sat heavily on her shoulders. She still hadn't an answer for Mark. He'd appeared calm about it after the appointment, but maybe he'd changed his mind now that he'd the time to think.

Her home became a weight. The wonky table bothered her more; the dead plants outside the window became ugly to look at. All the things that she had thought quirky before, now became nuisances. And not just her home. Life's colour was drained and empty. Dreary, solitary, is how it looked to Cathy's eyes. Her upbeat mood slid away.

• • • •

'A coffee and pastry, please.' Cathy placed her bag on the narrow countertop.

'Back again? You've become a real regular these late evenings.' The waitress chatted while preparing the order. Hot water hissed from the machine, and the clatter of a cup and saucer filled the almost silent café. Most of the tables were polished and set for the following morning, napkins and cutlery stacked neatly in a boxed container on each one.

'Is it always quiet at this hour?'

The young server nodded at first in reply. 'Yeah, the office and some shop workers are gone home and the lonely have yet to come out.' The jam-filled pastry placed in front of Cathy screamed comfort. 'Want custard on that?' the girl asked.

Shaking her head, Cathy gathered up the plate and coffee to sit over at a table. The counter was for ordering, not dallying. The young woman continued to buzz around, wiping down tables, straightening chairs.

'What you said about "the lonely", that's fair depressing?' Cathy shot the girl a look. *Did she consider Cathy one of the lonely?*

The waitress stopped what she was doing and came over to her. 'That was nice what you did for Luke.' Her statement surprised Cathy.

'Luke? Oh, the young lad. Nah. That was nothing. You know him?'

'Sort of. He comes in here for something to eat now and then. When the boss is not here, I can give it to him on the sly, but well, it's not often that others treat him to food.'

'Have you been working here for long?' Cathy squeezed her eyes a little to read the name badge pinned to the girl's uniform.

'Sno,' the waitress offered.

'Sno? That's your name? Sorry, it's a bit unusual, that's all.' Cathy smiled, hoping she didn't appear rude.

'It's okay. A conversation-starter for sure. Hang on, I'll grab a coffee and join you. No-one's gonna come in for another while. Like I say, too early for the lonely.'

Sitting across from her, Cathy watched the young girl with the unusual name sip a hot drink. 'Tell me about your name. I'm Cathy, by the way.'

She was charmed by the waitress. The inside of Sno's wrists were tattooed with what looked like Celtic designs. Her tight shave haircut made her look tough, but hearing how kind she was to Luke, Cathy knew it was only appearance – and appearances could be mistaken.

'My mother is a hippy/eccentric type. My full name is Snowflake. She said I looked fragile and perfect the day I was born, just like the falling snow.'

'That's gorgeous. Almost romantic.' Cathy clasped her hands to her chest. She thought of her own name, Catherine – named after her grandmother, that was it.

'Do you think? Try getting bullied and mocked all the way through school! A cute story won't save you.'

'True. But you didn't change it. You could have,' Cathy mentioned.

'Honestly? I like it. It's different.' She smiled.

'So, you know Luke, you said. He seems young.'

'He's a good lad. Reminds me of my brother. Wayward and stubborn. Been around here now for quite some time. Won't stay in a hostel. Says it's safer on the streets.'

'I've heard it said. Crazy world we live in.' Cathy drained the last of her coffee, but didn't make to go. She was enjoying the chat with Sno.

The women continued their conversation, with Cathy filling her new friend in on her life changes. She explained that she was searching for work, but proving either unqualified or over-qualified. Sno returned to the counter to serve a few customers that came in, but Cathy sat waiting for her until they could resume their conversation.

Time to close up came all too soon. It had passed another evening for both women, but this one was different. This evening they had bonded; unclear and unwritten but still certain, they had become friends.

Chapter Six

She was expected at 12.30 for lunch at Gemma's house. It was Cathy's own fault for ignoring her sister's phone calls and not replying to her texts. Still, she would get to see Ava and Lily, and that was always a plus.

Gemma was filled with the local gossip of her neighbours' goings-on. Cathy listened with glee to the stories, only interrupting to say, 'of course you do realise, if you are here gossiping about them, then they are doing the very same about you to someone else.'

'Cathy Reed, you always have to spoil it! Anyway, there's no gossip about me. Sure, I never go anywhere or speak about others... you know what I mean... with them, not you.' Still the older woman looked doubtful while she refilled their cups.

Cathy picked up another slice of Bailey's cheesecake. Her sister was an excellent cook and baker – a trait Cathy most definitely did not inherit. Promising Gemma she would babysit soon to let her sister go out, she hoped to soften the comments about her sister being a gossip.

But a frown burrowed in Gemma's forehead told Cathy she was not impressed with her. 'Will you stay for dinner?' The tenor indicated Gemma was asking out of duty.

Cathy felt torn. She wanted to spend more time with her nieces, but she also wanted to go for what had become her routine evening coffee and chat with Snowflake. The women had struck up a companionable friendship and it suited both of them as a nice way to end their evening.

'Another time, thanks.'

'And? Have you decided on your inheritance?' This was asked with a bitter twist of the mouth.

'Ah, not really.' Cathy knew it was time to go before she was bombarded with more questions she wasn't willing to answer.

'But you must have some idea about what you're going to do. If it were me, well, living with a stranger? No thanks. He could murder me in my bed. If I were you—'

'Well, you're not me,' Cathy interrupted, and was up and off before Gemma realised her sister was not staying to listen to her advice.

• • • •

'Hello, Luke. How are you doing? Want to get a coffee?' People weaved in and out as Cathy stood near the young lad. He was sitting cross-legged against a shopfront, a plastic bag pulled close beside him.

'Move on, will you? I'm working.' A large window stood behind him, mannequins staring out as the world passed by.

'Working?' Her voice was incredulous at his reply.

'Look, it's busy. This is my bread and butter, so move on.' He spoke from the side of his mouth, like he didn't want to be heard.

Cathy finally copped on to his distress at her presence and stealthily slipped away. She watched while he held the torn paper cup towards the passers-by for some coins. Then she made her way to the café, ordered, and took up her usual spot. There were some others in there tonight, and Sno was busy. Cathy noticed the side-glance her friend gave her towards a man in the corner. He wore a shabby business suit and was occupied with folders before him.

'The boss?' she mouthed towards Sno, and the girl nodded in reply.

There would be no sitting down and chatting tonight. After she had finished her pastry and coffee, Cathy made to leave, but turned and called out towards her friend, 'Thank you. See you again.'

Sno glanced over at her boss and saw he was looking at Cathy. 'You're welcome, and thank you,' she replied, and went about her work.

• • • •

Cathy's latest bank statement was a disaster. Her savings had dwindled and there was no longer enough to continue without a job. She needed something. Anything. Otherwise, paying her rent would become impossible. *But that would not be a problem if she lived at Cregane Court*, she reminded herself. Unless, of course, Mark said no. Then there would be no cottage.

• • • •

Luke apologised for his abruptness the next time he met her. Cathy told him she understood, and apologised, too, for not realising she had been a nuisance. He was a nice young man, and sometimes he popped into the café to chat with the two women. He filled Cathy in a little on his past.

'So, why not get a job for yourself?' she asked.

'Because I'm not a nine-to-five type of guy. It would kill me.'

'Do shift work then,' Cathy replied.

'No, no, no. I mean any job that has set hours. It would stifle my creativity.'

'What creativity?' she couldn't help but ask.

Sno chortled while she went around filling up the milk jugs on the tables, listening to their chat as she went. Those two were really getting on well.

'I'm an artist.' The lad placed his hands firmly on the table between them. He looked Cathy in the eye and continued, 'And one day I shall be famous. Mark my words.'

Cathy believed him. There was a determination in his stance – something she envied, maybe even aspired to.

Chapter Seven

'Thanks for lunch. Nice to not have to prepare food all the time.' Sno stretched as she sat at Cathy's kitchen table. She looked at her watch. She had another while to kill before her shift started. The women relaxed after their lunch and talk came easy.

'I love your scarf. The colours are so pretty,' Cathy said while clearing the table.

'Yeah, the yarn caught my eye and I treated myself to it.' Handling the garment, Sno wound it around her neck a few times.

'You made it?' Cathy was impressed.

'Ah, sure. With the creative mother I had, it had to rub off on me. And I'm glad it did, I must say. I enjoy crafting, especially crochet and knitting.' Sno walked over to the large window, looking out to the street below.

'That's wonderful. I'm not very crafty, but I enjoy dabbling in some writing. Short stories, mainly.' Cathy followed her friend to the window.

'Great view. You can see the café from here. Almost stalker-*ish* feel to it.' Snowflake laughed.

'Strange, really. When I was working, I didn't even notice it. Once I left the building, I turned right and headed to the train station, so it wasn't on my radar.' Cathy's thoughts wandered back to those days, and for a few moments nostalgia swept over her.

'Tell me about your writing. Anything published?'

'Just some stories here and there. Funny, I was standing here in this spot the night I decided to go for a coffee and get out of here, then I met you,' Cathy admitted. 'Lashing the same night, too. The place here really crowded in on me, and I needed to escape for some reason I now can't remember.'

'Well, I'm glad you did go out. It's nice that we met.' Snowflake gathered up her jacket and bag and walked to the small hallway. 'Thanks again for lunch. I've a few errands to do before my shift, but catch you soon no doubt.'

The ease between the women was comforting and promising; no expectations, just acceptance. The two friends hugged, and Cathy closed the door behind Sno.

• • • •

Her post did not make for happy reading yet again the following morning. The bills were now arriving thick and fast, and when she checked her funds, she saw she had enough to see her through two or three months if she was really careful with her spending. She decided to phone her sister. She owed her a babysitting night.

'Gemma, hi. Still want me to babysit? I know I promised you, but I've been busy until now,' Cathy lied. Her evenings were never booked up, but she really had to be in the mood to see Gemma.

Once the arrangements were made, she put on her coat and decided to go out for a walk. Maybe if she was lucky, she would see some job vacancies in shop windows.

Uncertainty about Lizzy's cottage continued to cloud her judgement, though. *Would she like the commute from the village to the city each day if she got a new job here? Would she miss the buzz of the traffic, the ease to go to a cinema, a meal, or any place of choice at short notice, if she lived in Cregane Court, Ballybawn?*

And of course, even now that she was drawn to the idea of moving to Ballybawn, it still might not happen. That would depend on Mark. Although he had been quite keen after the initial meeting at the solicitor's, he could well have decided against it now. This thought kept playing on her mind.

• • • •

At ten o'clock on Sunday night, Cathy switched off the television. Her sister and brother-in-law, Paul, were out for a few drinks and not due home for another hour or so. Curling up on the sofa, she grabbed a magazine from the oval table. Gemma was a proud housekeeper and the glass-topped coffee table gleamed. Not a child's handprint anywhere. Everything had a place, and her taste in décor was soothing and pleasant.

Cathy wondered if she would ever have children. If so, it wouldn't be happening anytime soon. Lizzy's cottage swept into her thoughts again. It would be a great place to raise a family, unlike her present apartment. Kids needed freedom to run around and play, meet other children, and have space for all the stuff that they accumulated. *Stop it, Cathy Reed, you need to find a boyfriend first*, she scolded herself.

Flicking through a magazine, all the skinny women advertising everything from a shoelace to a comb stared back at her. Cathy sighed. She looked down at her non-existent waist, and slight depression waved at her. Calling in to see Sno and having pastries hadn't helped, but her whole life needed an overhaul. She promised herself to start in the morning. She would take proper stock of her life and get active.

••••

The school rush was over, and her sister had gone home that morning leaving Gemma ready to do her housework. She and Paul had enjoyed a nice evening out together. Maybe she would ask Cathy to babysit a little more often. It's not like she was busy, and it made Gemma feel useful in her sister's life. She heard her mobile ringing but couldn't find it. *Where had she put it?* She searched behind cushions, under tea-towels, coat pockets, but it wasn't to be found. Then it went silent. Gemma hated that; she didn't like missing calls. *What if it was the school, or an emergency?*

She retraced her steps from when she'd returned, and eventually found her phone on a step of the stairs, beneath a discarded school jumper. Cathy. A missed call from Cathy. *What had she forgotten?* Gemma wondered. She shrugged; she would call her later.

• • • •

Sno, weary and quiet, sat down on a chair opposite Cathy. It was almost closing time; in another hour, she would be home.

'What's up, Sno, you seem restless?'

'Here, the job. Sick of it. But it pays the bills and, yes, I know I'm better off than you right now, so no lectures, or I shall have to call you Gemma.' She pulled a face at her friend and they both laughed.

'Why don't you ask for an early shift then, and have your evenings free?'

'Because that means getting up early, and buses are a nightmare in the mornings.' The thought of sitting in traffic and getting nowhere did not appeal to the waitress, which brought to mind it almost going home time. 'Okay, go home, we shall talk tomorrow,' she said. 'I'm closing up.'

Reaching the café door, Cathy turned. 'Any sign of Luke lately? I hope he's okay.' She had not seen the lad for some days now. When you lived on the streets, anything could happen, and attacks on the homeless were common.

'Nope, not seen him.' Sno was doing her final checks on the premises.

The friends said their goodbyes and Cathy made for home.

• • • •

Inside the apartment, she stood at her window watching for Luke. Sometimes he sat outside Sno's café before he settled for the night in the alleyway around the corner. His youth made him believe he was invincible, but Cathy knew there was danger out there and no-one was immune to it.

• • • •

Some days later, Gemma was fussing around the house before Cathy came over. They had agreed to chat about her sister's inheritance tonight – at Gemma's insistence – and as she placed the cutlery on the table, a tiny stab of envy pierced her thoughts at her sister coming into property.

Once Cathy arrived, she went to play board games with Ava and Lily, laughing and shouting at who was the winner. Cathy loved it; the girls were great fun. When they'd finished, dinner was served.

'He and I are meeting up shortly. He appears really quiet, almost shy,' Cathy explained. 'The roast beef was delicious, Gemma. That's where we are at the moment, still to meet up.'

She leaned back on the chair, twisting the linen napkin on her lap. She didn't appear to have any answers where Mark and Cregane would lead to, nor had she any idea why she had been chosen and not a different family member.

'But this Mark, it puzzles me. We don't know him. I keep wondering whether Lizzy was in her right mind when she made the will.' Gemma dabbed at her mouth, then sipped some wine. Cathy's retelling of the meeting didn't clarify anything new, which did not satisfy Gemma one bit. Her sister was so impractical with her life.

'No idea.' Cathy shrugged. 'We were both in shock. We are meeting in Ballybawn village in two days, and we are going to view the cottage then, too.' It seemed Aunt Lizzy had created a whole mountain of problems.

Now hearing again the complexities of the awful saga, Gemma couldn't help but feel a little smug that she hadn't been left the cottage. Her envy of earlier melted away. It had turned into a very complicated situation, and Gemma didn't do complications.

Chapter Eight

It was time to share her inheritance news with Sno and Luke, if the lad showed up. Maybe speaking about it with them would confirm she was doing the right thing by saying yes. An outside opinion was always helpful, especially as Gemma kept throwing doubts about it at her.

'That is intriguing. Wow, look at you, a property owner. And you were worried about losing your apartment.' Sno smiled as she poured them both some coffees. She remained standing, as it was easier to slip behind the counter if a customer came in.

Cathy sat at the café counter, having dragged a chair over.

'Jeeze, what's up with you two?' Neither had heard Luke enter the shop. Another round of pastries and a fresh coffee for their friend was served, while Cathy explained her dilemma.

'Delighted for you, Cathy, I really am. You're a nice person, and you deserve to have nice things happen to you.' The young lad spoke in earnest, his eyes sparkling with sincerity, causing Cathy to blush at the warm words.

'Oh, Luke, I don't know where to start.' Cathy, visibly tired after explaining her situation, sagged with exhaustion. 'There's more to it than just inheriting the house. There's a catch I've not yet told ye about.'

'Well, say nothing until Snowflake can sit with us.' Luke winked. Sno was settling a bill with another customer.

Ten minutes later, the waitress had made the executive decision to close the café early and listen to the rest of her friend's story. If this continued, she would be out of a job, Luke teased, which made Cathy a little anxious. But Sno egged her on to share the rest of her dilemma.

'So, there you have it,' she said eventually. 'I've got a country cottage on an acre of land or more, which I own with Mark – a man I never heard of before all this. Neither of us can sell the property, and we must live in it – together – for a minimum of two years, once we accept. Of course, we both have to say yes first.'

The three stared into their cups, a stillness covering the already quiet shop.

'Well, meet with this Mark and then we shall know if we are losing a friend to the country.' Luke stood and shuffled to the door.

'I agree,' Snowflake said, as she rose to tidy up the tables.

They agreed to meet after Cathy and Mark had come to a decision, for the big reveal. The odd trio smiled their goodbyes and went their separate ways into the cold evening.

• • • •

Back at home, Cathy kicked off her heels and plonked onto her cosy sofa. She sat and watched the sad-looking flowerpots on her false balcony outside the large window. The poor neglected plants waved in hope of some water, and she felt guilty. She had placed them there to cheer up her view, but she was not green-fingered, and it showed. And now she had co-inherited a country cottage, yet she could not keep a potted plant alive.

Help!

• • • •

Mark seemed a nice enough chap. When they met in Ballybawn for lunch, Cathy was happy to hear he was still willing to give it a chance. What had they to lose? Both seemed to be questioning where or what their destiny was, so moving into Lizzy's home seemed the place to find their answers. It looked like it would be happening shortly.

• • • •

In Roman O'Driscoll's office, they both agreed to all the conditions and, since they were going to be housemates, said it would be best to just get on with it. The solicitor seemed surprised with their decision and repeated that they could take extra time if needed. Far be it for him to push two strangers together, he'd said, his added laugh just bordering on being forced.

But Cathy felt Lizzy must have had reason for giving them the place, and it was one they intended to find out. Sharing her thoughts with the two men, her statement seemed to drain the colour from Roman's face, and he still looked anxious as they shook hands on the closing of all matters.

• • • •

'Gosh, Mark, there's a lot to do up here.' Cathy brushed the cobwebs from her new bedroom window. The frames were rotting in parts, and years of grime lay on the glass. Mark had insisted that as she was a blood relative, it was only fair that she got to pick which bedroom she wanted. A faded, rose-patterned paper hung on the walls. Some religious pictures hung on the far wall from the window, and family photos adorned the dressing table. There was one of her father and Great-Aunt Lizzy sharing a happy moment, where both had their heads thrown back in laughter. Cathy smiled. That would be a keeper.

Mark was across the small landing in the other bedroom. Blue striped paper, with heavy curtains draping the window, decorated his room. In fact, that was all that was upstairs – two bedrooms. Lizzy had converted the back sitting room downstairs into a bedroom as she got older. It was evident that she had not ventured upstairs as she had aged.

Neither of the new owners could afford to spend money on bringing in cleaners, and since it was April with long evenings, they decided to tackle it themselves.

'Look at the view from here, Cathy,' Mark called out to her.

In his room, a large timber wardrobe sat against a corner. It was dusty but ornate beneath the grunge. Cathy started to hum a song from *Beauty and the Beast*, the wardrobe reminding her of one of the characters in it.

Pushing the heavy drapes back, she gushed, 'Wow, look at those trees. They go on forever. Imagine the summer mornings listening to the birdsong. Oh, Mark, it's wonderful.'

'Yes, and the size of the window! For a small cottage, it's huge.' He grinned with delight. The window was an old sash-style one, still layered with years of dust, but its size was magnificent, from floor to ceiling.

Back downstairs, they made a cup of tea. They were both still nervous about living together but neither actually dreaded it.

'So, how's this going to work? I mean, are we going to have a giant money kitty, or split the bills in half?' Cathy leant against the kitchen counter.

The room was small but adequate. Along one side was the countertop, below which was a row of cupboards, and there was more storage above the counter. Beneath the window, looking out onto green fields, was the sink; to its right was the cooker, and to the left was a fridge and freezer. The battered oak table sat in the middle of the floor with mismatched chairs around it. Mark sat on one, his tea before him.

'We will split it in half, do you think? Or better still, once we work out the cost of running the cottage, we can deposit a sum into an account to cover it each month.'

'Perfect, Mark.' *He was kind*, she thought, *and easy going*. Cathy briefly wondered if anything more than friendship would happen between them. She shuddered suddenly.

'You okay? Are you cold?' Mark's eyes showed genuine concern.

'No, I'm fine.' She was mortified to have been almost caught thinking about the guy. If he knew, he would probably scarper out the door.

While clearing out and cleaning together, they ironed out most of the plans on how life would work for them while they lived in Cregane Court. For some reason, Lizzy had matched them up, and neither of them knew why. But with a new start in life, and no rent to pay, Cathy's savings would stretch further. She decided she would work on the house while keeping an eye out for a job; Mark would be at his office. They would be like a lot of couples – one working at home, one going out to work. Only, they weren't a couple; just two people thrown together by a will.

• • • •

Gemma had shown concern about her sister moving in with a complete stranger, but Cathy reassured her she was old enough to mind herself. Plus, she pointed out, he was taking *her* on, and she could be a mad woman for all he knew.

Snowflake and Luke promised to visit, and Cathy said she would be back regularly for her coffee and pastry. Ballybawn was only forty miles away, and a good bus service ran between both city and village, so there was no excuse.

• • • •

Snowflake's disappointment at her new friend leaving and starting anew made her feel restless. This job was scratching at her, and she felt moody and grumpy. Maybe she should take a leaf out of Cathy's life and start somewhere different.

• • • •

'Who would have thought that I would be sitting here on a glorious spring evening, sipping a beer, sharing a home with a man I never knew before, and loving it?' Cathy stretched out her legs and pushed her bare feet into the soft grass. The view before them was of fields upon fields, with a small forest – more a grove, really –to their left. *This is what Heaven must be.* Cathy's thoughts were in a relaxed, sweet mode.

'Yes, Elizabeth certainly pulled one on us. But why us, Cathy?' Mark opened a fresh beer and took a slug. It was gloriously cold from the icebox.

'Who are we to question the wisdom of Great-Aunt Lizzy?' she smiled, knowing he was right.

'Well, I agree, but still, there is something we are missing. Why us? Why put in the clause about us living here together? There has to be more to it.' Mark sat up straight and stared at Cathy.

She figured he was waiting for an answer, so she sat forward in her chair and faced him.

'Okay, so far we have not come across anything in Lizzy's belongings to give us a clue,' she replied, 'but maybe we are looking in the wrong place. Tell me about Lizzy, what you knew about her. I met her at the usual family occasions – funerals mostly – but I think it's because of my dad that she picked me.'

'Elizabeth and my grandmother were close,' Mark remembered. 'They laughed at all the wicked carry-ons they got up to, drank wine in the evenings, and sipped sherry in the afternoons. Both were a bit eccentric in their dress, wearing clashing colours, dressing for what they felt like that day rather than what the weather said. I just loved being in their company. You know,' he looked more closely at Cathy, 'I can see Elizabeth in you.'

This last statement startled Cathy. Her puzzled face must have revealed her surprise, because Mark laughed heartily.

'Don't look so shocked. You have the same friendly attitude, your inner-self; I don't believe the true you has been unleashed yet.'

Mark drank some more and sat back, seemingly pleased with his description of Cathy.

'Am I now? That's interesting.' She mulled over her new friend's words. *Was she like Lizzy? She hoped so.* The woman had always seemed to know how to live life, and Cathy wanted to make her own count. She wanted to experience more, learn more, and if that was Lizzy's intention for having her live here, then Cathy was happy to accept that.

The two new housemates sat on in the spring sunshine, supping their drinks and listening to the light rustling of the trees – large, strong oaks, tall ashes, and sturdy, wide horse-chestnuts. Cathy sneaked a look at her companion. It was nice how he gave her great-aunt her full name, Elizabeth. It was respectful.

Chapter Nine

The days passed with both Mark and Cathy sorting and going through boxes of Lizzy's possessions. What they deemed well enough for the charity shops, they placed in one of the many outhouses, and what was considered rubbish was put aside in a skip they had hired. Mark drove to the city with the charity boxes, as there were more shops there to deliver to than in the local village, Ballybawn.

Each time Cathy went to the village for some groceries, she was approached and asked many questions about her intentions towards Cregane Court. She thought people were friendly and welcoming, but Mark said it was probably more nosiness. She laughed at his comment. She took people at face value, not thinking everyone had ulterior motives. Naïve, maybe, but she was who she was.

'So, what did you tell them?' Mark enquired.

'Told them there was nothing to share, that really we were just cleaning out the house and fulfilling Lizzy's wishes for now.'

Mark nodded in agreement.

During the walks to and from Ballybawn, she found herself enjoying country life and admiring the beautiful scenery. The easy pace and the sound of nature appealed to her. She certainly didn't miss the fast racing to and from work in the city, shoving and pushing amongst the crowds, the wail of sirens and blasting of horns. The only time she had been aware of nature while living in the city was when there was a storm or a downpour. Birds didn't really inhabit her street, except for the fat pigeons that cooed outside on her window ledge or tripped you up when you crossed the plaza.

Ballybawn was a world away from all that, and Cathy noticed a change in herself, both physically and mentally. The walks toned up her muscles, and the regular, refreshing sleep cleared her thoughts.

Mark took off to work most mornings, heading for his office in the next town. This left Cathy on her own, and she rejoiced in sorting out the cottage. It wasn't difficult, as it had only two rooms upstairs, four downstairs, and an entrance porch with two small windows which welcomed any visitor.

Up against the far wall, opposite the front door, was a marble-topped console table, on which sat a vase belonging to her great-aunt. Leading off the porch was the sitting room, which was the main downstairs room. It was square, with stairs at the back wall. Two comfortable sofas ran parallel to each other, with a low walnut coffee table dividing them, and there was an armchair snuggled into a corner. A vintage, bevelled glass mirror graced one of the walls, and on both sides of it hung the family coat of arms of Lizzy and her husband, Archie. In the far corner to the right, a door led to the only bedroom on this floor.

Off to the other side of the sitting room was the kitchen, and beyond was a modest bathroom with old-style bath and faucets. Vintage, Cathy told Mark, was the correct term nowadays. The country charm that one saw in home decor magazines was what one found at Cregane Court. Whether Cathy and Mark would change the décor remained to be seen.

In the evenings, Cathy delighted in lighting the stove – a black matte one, which stood on a raised, red brick hearth. A real fire was something she had missed living in an apartment. Late each evening, after they'd eaten, she would light the fire and make herself comfy on one of the sofas to share her day with Mark.

'Look at us, like a married couple,' he laughed, as she handed him a cup of tea after dinner.

Cathy had impressed herself with her new culinary skills. She'd pulled out some of her cookbooks that had been stored away for years, and enjoyed flipping over the pages to see what took her interest.

'Do you think the locals think that? That we are a couple, I mean?' Cathy mused, while dipping her chocolate digestive into her hot tea.

'Maybe. I don't know.' He laughed some more at the idea, but he didn't elaborate either about his love life.

Did he have a girlfriend? A partner? Cathy doubted she would find out tonight. As she watched from beneath her lashes, twirling the half-eaten biscuit, she noticed a slight cloud pass over his eyes, making Cathy wonder what he was hiding. *Had she hit a nerve?*

'Are you saying you don't fancy me? Cheeky sod.' She attempted to lighten the atmosphere, keeping,the tone of her voice playful.

Mark blushed but said nothing. *Would it remain this way?* Cathy wondered. Since he didn't offer any information, she didn't feel it right to press him on the subject of a girlfriend.

After a brief pause, he coughed then replied in a teasing tone, 'Oh but, Cathy, I do. Every night I fight the urge to sneak into your bedroom and ravish you.' Now they were both laughing heartily, their silly antics releasing the tension.

'Seriously, though, will living with a woman harm your prospects of finding *The One*?'

'I could ask you that question, Cathy. Where are you on the relationship ladder?' Mark poured more tea for them both and topped up the fire.

'Oh, I'm still at the bottom rung,' she chuckled. 'Well, maybe three steps up, but nothing important. There was one guy, but well, it fizzled out. He wanted to share himself with too many others while he was with me.'

'Ouch. Nasty.' Mark's face held sympathy for his friend, but he gave nothing away about his own personal life.

• • • •

That April was a warm one, with just a chill in the evenings. Birds were busy nesting and the trees rustled in the spring breeze. Sitting out in the orchard to the right of the front door, Cathy soaked it all in. Hanging from some branches nearby was a swing, the rope well worn, and the seat smooth from children playing on it. She wondered who they had been. *Where were they now? Had her father played here amongst the apple trees?*

It would have been a wonderful playground, climbing and running through the orchard, eating the apples fresh from the branches. Her mind began to think of all scenarios, and she dashed inside for her notebook and pen and began to write. She could see them now, the characters for a book. She felt their presence, heard their childish laughter, and their gentle footfall around her. The place sang to her.

Cathy sat and wrote for hours, bubbling with excitement as her story unfolded. Inspiration hung from the apple trees like a spider's web. This is what she would do, she promised herself. She would write the book she had always felt lived inside her but had never surfaced until now. Pausing to look around her, she became more aware of what Cregane Court had to offer. There was a hidden beauty, a secret beneath the obvious orchard, fallen hen-houses, and a stream choked by brambles and overgrowth.

Bursting with ideas and plans, she could not wait to share her vision with Mark. Tonight called for a special meal with wine. She was celebrating what she could vision for the future, but she did not know how to bring it to fruition. She walked to the village and got some steaks from the butchers and a bottle of red, with some cheese, from the local shop.

'Very fancy, wine on a Tuesday night, must be a special occasion. Is it?' The shopkeeper asked, as she placed the cheese and bottle into some brown paper bags.

'Oh, it is. Very special, possibly the most important night yet,' Cathy replied, giving enough information to tease the woman but still not answering her. She was getting good at not revealing everything at once – something Mark told her she needed to master when living in the country.

• • • •

'What do you think?' her eyes blazed with excitement. Surely he could see the potential?

'Well, it's an idea. Never thought of it, but possible, I suppose.' His tone was measured.

Was that a good or a bad sign? She didn't know.

'Look, I know it will take money and work – lots of both. But it is possible!' She didn't want to even entertain the thought of it being nothing but a dream.

'What would you call it?' Mark noticed her enthusiasm dampen a little and tried to sound more upbeat.

'Cregane Retreat Centre? Cregane Court Creative? I don't know. But seriously, what do you think?' She moved over to sit beside him on the sofa.

'Look,' she babbled on, 'I drew up some plans. We could do up the large outhouse as bedrooms; we'd easily get four rooms and a small kitchen, plus bathroom, in there. The structure is in good condition, and it would be easy to design the interior. Plus, where the old hen-run was, well, we could put a chalet-type building there, with two more rooms, call it *The Hen House, Where Ideas Are Hatched.* Then further down from that, we could put another chalet of two rooms and call it *The Orchard, Where Plans Come to Fruition*. Then over by the—'

'Hey, slow down,' he said kindly. 'You really have been thinking about this. Only today?'

'Yes, today.' She sighed. 'It was while I was sitting beneath the few apple trees that I could see its beauty. I could feel the children, the laughter, love, and so much more that this place has endured through the years. It is filled with inspiration. Look at the views, the nature, and then there's the local village for any artists, writers, sculptors, whatever creative mind wants, to come here and go to for a quiet drink – think of it as a haven from the rat-race of everyday life.' She spread her hands in an arc, sweeping in the air to express her words.

The more Cathy spoke, the more alive she felt the whole possibility become. She could see it, but more importantly, she could feel it.

Mark admitted the location was perfect. Everyone had cars nowadays, and people were always looking for somewhere to go, to get away from it all. Without committing to anything, he promised to think about her ideas and work out some costings.

That night, Cathy slept the soundest she had in years. Her hours of planning and considering the possibilities for Cregane Court had tired her out and filled her dreams with happy thoughts. Her head floated on the soft pillow with dreams of the future.

• • • •

Across the landing, Mark lay awake, thinking of his housemate's proposal; it had merit, he couldn't deny that. *But could they make it work? Was it time for him to take a risk and leave the safety of a nine-to-five job to follow a whim from beneath an apple tree?*

Chapter Ten

The bus to the city left every two hours, starting at nine-thirty, with the last trip at five-thirty. Cathy wondered what happened if you wanted to go to the city for an evening out, but if she was honest, it was these out-dated, old ways that were so appealing about Ballybawn. No-one seemed to care or notice that the latest modern buzzword or gimmick didn't rule in the village.

Sitting on the eleven-thirty run, Cathy was looking forward to her trip to the city. She had so much to share with Snowflake, and even Gemma. There was only so much you could text to a person, and even during phone calls there was always one of her friends distracted, whether that was Sno with customers, or Gemma with the girls.

Tonight, she was staying with her sister, but first she was meeting Sno in the café, and hopefully Luke might pop in. The rush of the lunchtime crowd startled her as she walked along the streets. *Had she forgotten the push and pull of the crowds already?* Music was blaring out from shops and fighting with the noise of traffic, so it was a blessing to reach the café and step inside its doors.

Sno immediately came forward to hug her friend. She'd swapped her evening shift to be there when Cathy arrived.

'It's been ages, weeks,' she scolded, 'but I forgive you, as you are looking so well. It must be good for you out in the middle of nowhere.' Sno chuckled as she held her friend for a few more minutes.

'Hey, I've not left for the jungle,' Cathy said with a laugh. 'But yes, it feels longer than it has been. How are you?' Cathy sat at what had always been her favourite table while Sno fetched them coffee and some custard tarts. She told Cathy she'd been tempted to put the closed sign on the door so they could have some peace, but the last of the lunch-hour rush were straggling back to their jobs, so she and another waitress attended to those first.

'I want to hear it all. The juicy bits not to be left out, and more about your wonderful business idea.' Sno threw off her apron as the last of the people went out the door, and announced she was on her break.

Cathy began her tale of adjusting to 'living out in the wilderness', as Sno described it. Even speaking about it made Cathy feel a warmth for the place, and she was surprised how much she longed to return there tonight and not have to face Gemma instead.

The two women sipped their drinks and chatted back and forth until they were interrupted by a knock on the window. When they saw it was Luke, Sno jumped up, thrilled to welcome him in. After more hugs, Cathy shared her ideas with them both.

'It sounds idyllic, all this nature and tranquillity, but what will it be like in the depths of winter? Frost and snow and storms?' Luke shivered as he spoke. He was only too aware of the elements and how nasty the weather could be.

'Look, it's going to be hard work, but think... it is possible,' Cathy said confidently. 'We have to get planning permission to adapt the buildings that are there, but nothing ever came from clicking your fingers. Plus, I was hoping you might come out and help?' She looked at the man before her. He was thinner since she had last seen him; his green eyes seemed a bit duller, his blond hair longer. Surely he didn't want to stay on the streets forever?

'What? Me?' Luke was taken aback.

'Yes. You could have bed and board in exchange for manual work and things, you know, help me to get the place in shape. What do you think?' This was an on-the-spot decision, not something she had thought through. She just prayed Mark would agree.

But seeing Luke looking so pale and thin, she just wanted him to be safe. *Offering him a place to live could only be a good thing, couldn't it?*

'I don't know, to be honest. I mean... I... God, Cathy, I don't want to sound ungrateful, but well... I don't know.' Luke blushed as he struggled to take in her offer.

Cathy could have kicked herself. She hadn't stopped to think about how he would feel. He probably had hundreds of questions and doubts. *Could he leave the city? Was he the type to settle in one place?* After his time on the streets, with all the freedom to go where he wanted and when, maybe a regular style of life wouldn't suit him. More than likely, he had lots more questions than Cathy could think of.

'Luke,' she told him, 'it might be strange for you, but think of this. You will be able to draw again. You will have a warm, safe place to do it in, and maybe even offer some classes or sell your work to the locals. There are always craft fairs and fundraising events happening. Maybe you could give a picture as a prize to them, get your work out there. This might be the opening you have been looking for. Who knows? Just have a think and let me know, okay?' Cathy was surprising herself with each moment that passed.

What would Mark say about her latest thoughts? She didn't want to offend her housemate; they had a good relationship, and she didn't want to be the one to upset it. But she felt this offer to Luke was the right one. She felt more in tune with her feelings and gut instinct since moving out to Cregane Court, and was sure it would be alright.

She glanced at her watch. It was time to go and visit Gemma, and immediately her heart sank. Being with her two friends had been great. Catching up had done them all good, and Luke promised he would not delay in getting back to her. Sno encouraged him to take the offer now, but he declined to do so. Cathy understood, though.

He didn't want to be seen as a charity case, and she didn't want that either. She really needed help with the project, and having Luke with her and Mark would be a step forward, she just knew it.

Luke would get in touch when he was ready. It would totally be his decision. After all, he would be leaving what he knew, the streets he lived on, and friends he had made. There was always more than just the surface of one's life to be considered; the layers of circumstance beneath were important, too, and Cathy understood all this.

••••

'But where are you going to get the money to run a hippy commune?' Gemma poured the last of the wine, clearly convinced that her sister had gone nuts since moving. No doubt, she was wondering if Cathy was turning out to be just as eccentric as Great-Aunt Lizzy.

'It will not be a hippy commune, Gemma, will you listen?' Cathy tried to respond calmly. 'It will be a retreat for people who are involved in the arts, a place to get away to. There are grants and funding out there, which Mark is looking into. He is happy to handle the financial side of it.' Cathy felt drained. Her sister always did this, knocking back any ideas she came up with, finding fault wherever she could.

'So, our taxes are funding this mad notion? Typical.' Snorts of disgust were heard as she looked at her.

But Cathy returned her sister's stare. *How on earth were they related?* 'When it's more cleaned up and we are settled, you must call out with the girls. They would love the orchard. There's an old swing there and it's so peaceful. They could hunt for rabbits and hedgehogs; they really would have a ball of fun.' Cathy could picture her nieces running wild and happy in the gardens. Cregane Court had really got under her skin.

'And what about Mark? Any news there between ye?' Gemma asked.

'No, we're friends. In fact, we get on really well. He's a lovely bloke. You'd like him.'

'Cathy, I'm a happily married woman, thank you very much.' Gemma was offended by her sister's remark. She wasn't the loose type, chasing men.

'I never said you weren't. For God's sake, Gemma, you can be friends with a man without jumping into bed with him.'

The women finished their bottle of wine and headed to bed. The day had tired Cathy out. The rush of the city and the excitement of sharing her news with her friends, and with Gemma, meant Cathy was more than ready to slip between the sheets and snuggle beneath the duvet.

• • • •

Gemma looked in her bathroom mirror. Reflected back at her was a young woman old before her time. Wrinkles were teasing her eyes and the corners of her mouth. She didn't like what she saw. She wouldn't be without her family, yet life lacked something for her.

Since moving to Ballybawn, Cathy appeared different; she was happy, for sure, but there was something more to it than that. Her eyes sparkled; Gemma's didn't.

She tossed and turned in bed with frustration. *What was it Cathy had that she hadn't?* As she struggled with her inner thoughts, her eyes finally closed just as she realised what it was Cathy had. Fulfilment. Cathy had fulfilment in her life.

Chapter Eleven

There was a buzz about Cregane Court. Cathy had enquired at the local village about some handymen for labouring work, and she was delighted when her questions were met with a good response. Three men had arrived to help with the clearing of the double-floored outhouses, and Cathy told them of their plans for the place. The men agreed it was a fine idea, and for sure she had the space for it. Skips were hired, rubble was shifted, and new materials were ordered. In a few weeks, a new roof had been put in place, and the time came for drawing up some plans for the interior.

Word had spread around the village about the great ideas the young couple living in old Lizzy's place had. And the community appeared to approve of the idea, as people greeted Cathy with smiles and well wishes for her project, plus lots of questions.

Early morning, as May begun, Cathy heard some whistling. She knew none of the workmen were due at the house today, but she could hear the clatter of timber and some shovelling. Still in her PJs, she sneaked a look out the window but could not see who was there. Grabbing her dressing-gown, she went outside.

'Hello? Hello?' she called out.

'Well, it's about time you got up. This retreat won't build itself, although you've a good start made on it.'

'Luke, you came!' She rushed over and grabbed him in a tight squeeze. 'Oh my God, this is wonderful. Come on, let's get some breakfast.' She tugged him on the arm, and he threw down the shovel and followed her inside. Grabbing a pan, she filled it with sausages and bacon, while in another she had mushrooms and tomatoes. Luke boiled the kettle for coffee and tea.

'How did you find the place?'

'Got the bus to the village and asked a local where Cregane Court was, Simple.'

'So, tell me, are you here for good or just a visit?' she asked, hoping for the former, as they sat and munched on toast and the fry-up.

He didn't reply at first, casting looks around the kitchen, taking in the new surroundings. After a few minutes, he turned his gaze to Cathy and smiled.

'For good, if the offer still stands.' He raised his eyebrows in hope, and her nodding head gave him his answer. They raised their cups and toasted his decision.

• • • •

As the afternoon turned to evening, Cathy and Luke were sitting beneath the apple trees when a large car drove into the yard. She didn't recognise the car and stood up to greet the visitor. It was the day for surprises, Luke commented, as she left him sitting.

'Good afternoon, Miss Reed. I see you are doing some work to the old place.' It was Roman O'Driscoll, the solicitor.

'Hello, Mr. O'Driscoll, what brings you out here?' Cathy felt uneasy. There was something in his manner that unsettled her. She watched as he strode around the outside of the house as though he was inspecting the place, stepping over the mounds of dirt and cement, picking his way around the yard.

'What exactly are you doing to the place?' He paced over and back, then looked in on the large outhouse that Cathy planned to turn into rooms for rent. 'Have you got planning permission for whatever you are thinking of doing here?' He turned quickly towards her, his brow furrowed with earnest. His stance was almost confrontational, and Cathy stepped back from him.

'Mr. O'Driscoll, I—'

'Roman, please.'

'Mr. O'Driscoll, why are you here?' Cathy snapped at him.

'I was passing and had heard stories about your fancy ideas. I thought I'd take a look.'

His smile did nothing to endear him. If anything, she was waiting for a forked tongue to dart out at her. The stillness around her was loud in a weird way; there was not a sound. Even the flutter of a bird was missing.

'While I appreciate your interest, there's nothing really to tell you,' she replied. 'I'm sure you have heard all there is to hear. Now, if there's nothing else, I'd like to get on with my day, Mr. O'Driscoll.' Cathy turned to walk back to Luke, happy she was sending this horrible man on his way. She glanced back to check he was leaving.

'You could just sell it. This place.' His hand swept in an arc.

'Sell it? You of all people know that that is not possible.' Cathy's alarm at his words rang loud, her eyes wide with wonder.

'Ah sure, we all know there's ways around these things,' and he winked. That smile was back, more sinister than before. Cathy wanted shot of this man, to get him off her property.

'Think about it, Cathy.' His tongue lingered on her name; it sounded creepy.

'I want you to leave, Mr. O'Driscoll.' She turned once more and walked with purpose towards the apple trees.

Luke saw she was upset and waited for the visitor's car to pull away before he placed his arm around her.

'What happened?' he asked. 'Come on, let's go inside and have another cuppa.'

Cathy did not speak. She realised she was shaking, and right now a cup of tea with a friend felt good.

• • • •

'How dare he!' Mark was furious when he heard how underhand and nasty the solicitor had been. He paced the kitchen floor, tired after his day's work, yet Cathy's news had infuriated him. 'I'm glad you were here when he called,' Mark spoke to Luke. 'I wonder if he would have been more forward and pushy if Cathy had been alone.'

'She was well able to stand up for herself,' Luke replied, smiling at Cathy. He didn't want to tell Mark how shaken up she had been after the visit, if she wasn't mentioning it herself.

As Luke dropped off to sleep in Lizzy's downstairs room, he decided he liked Cathy's housemate, particularly as he showed such concern for her welfare. He was also easy on the eye, his curly hair inviting to be touched. He wondered if there was anyone in Mark's life, that special someone who Luke should watch out for.

• • • •

There was no argument from Mark about Luke staying. In fact, if that dodgy Roman O'Driscoll was snooping around, it would be good for Cathy to have company. Although they had only lived together for about a month or so, there was already a bond there, and he felt unexpectedly protective towards his new housemate.

Nevertheless, he was worried about the solicitor's motives. *What had Roman O'Driscoll meant about there being ways around selling the place? Had he an interest in Cregane Court?* He remembered how unhappy the solicitor had seemed when Mark had phoned to tell him of their agreement to Elizabeth's conditions. At the meeting, O'Driscoll had suggested they might want more time to see if they had made the right choice. *Yes,* he decided, *O'Driscoll and his intentions needed to be questioned more.* And Mark intended to ask those questions.

• • • •

Luke cooked dinner next evening. He was determined to do his share of chores if he was going to live there, but a tingle of nervousness rumbled inside him. He was leaving a life on the streets, friends he had made, a way of living and looking after himself, to help a woman who showed trust in him. Many would think he should be counting his blessings, but he had chosen to live that way, even though it did not suit everyone. He had learnt a lot from living on the streets, but Cathy was right, too. If he wanted to follow his dream with his art, this was his chance.

'So, what sort of art do you enjoy?'

Mark and Luke shared some beers out in the orchard. This spot beneath the apple trees had become the go-to place to unwind. The moss-covered trunks of the old trees, with their branches spread wide, held many stories and secrets that had been shared beneath their canopies. Ruts were worn into the bark where others had lain against it, bald spots in the moss, worn with age.

'I like to draw with different materials – sometimes pencil, others charcoal, oils or acrylics,' Luke explained. He was stretched out in the garden chair, while Mark leant against a tree.

'So, everything,' Mark remarked. Then they both laughed. A spark flew in the air, the energy charged with their laughter.

'Are you into anything other than numbers?' Luke enquired. He liked the way Mark's eyes were shaded as he stood in the tree's shadow.

'When I was at school, I loved woodwork. But my folks didn't see any future in carpentry and encouraged me to take business. So, I did. But now and then, I like to mess around with some wood. It's my escape from the humdrum world of finance.'

The heaviness in his voice revealed a longing that lived inside him, and Luke wondered if Mark was hiding some deep desire.

'Well, if this retreat centre takes off, you will have plenty of opportunity to practise your woodwork skills. There's a lot of work ahead of us,' Luke commented, hoping Mark would reveal more of what he was thinking. He found himself drawn to this man, stirrings that had not been aroused before.

'What do you mean, if it takes off? It's going to be the place where the world and her mother will be clamouring to stay, and do not doubt it for one minute,' Cathy scolded the two men as she approached them.

Mark handed her a beer, and all three raised a toast to the future of Cregane Court. As she claimed a spot beside Mark and nudged him playfully in the arm, Luke watched. *Was there one of them hiding feelings the other didn't know about?* He didn't think so, but he would tread carefully.

Chapter Twelve

Mark sat in his office, letting the phone ring. He was still bothered by Roman O'Driscoll's passing remark to Cathy. *What was behind it? Should he confront the solicitor or let it go?* Since he'd moved to Ballybawn to live, he had really enjoyed heading home there in the evenings. It wasn't all due to sharing with Cathy, but since she had come up with the retreat idea, life had a glow about it. Now this room, this office, seemed dull and bleak. The pathetic attempt to make it pleasant, with framed pictures of inspirational quotes, now just looked gaudy and unreal. *His desk, littered with files and his computer, showed a life of rigged living,* he thought. *Where was the fun?*

In contrast, his weekends digging out rubble and painting walls was proving to be a welcome change from figures and balance sheets. He had even asked Luke to sketch the idea he had for new stairs in the cottage. Mark liked Luke. *Really* liked Luke, but that was for a different day. The young lad had only recently arrived, but Mark could not forget the vision of Luke's strong, lean body when he took off his t-shirt while working on the site. Regular meals and home comforts had filled his original thin frame, and the physical work had shaped him nicely.

Mark was glad Cathy had invited Luke to join them. He trusted her to make the right decision, and so far, the young man was proving to be an asset to Cregane Court in lots of ways. A decision on their planning application for changing the outhouses was due at the end of the week. Mark knew what was required before they started any definite building changes, but the clearing out would have been needed at any rate. But there was one more thing bubbling inside Mark. A question that surfaced each night before he nodded off – yet, so far, he refused to entertain it. He was not one for rash decisions and he didn't feel he had the right mind space to tackle it at the moment. When he did, he would share his thoughts with his new house companions. He really had grown to see them as family – well, Cathy anyway. Luke... was Luke. Luke... was different.

• • • •

'Why not?' Cathy spoke.

The 'family' of three were gathered on the sofas, rewinding after their day.

'I think it's a great idea. We've not had anything to celebrate the occasion, and this weekend sounds like as good a time as any.'

Mark had suggested a housewarming party. Just his old housemates and some of Cathy's friends. They had been living in the cottage over two months now, in which time it had really taken shape. And with their planning permission for the large outhouse coming through, it felt like the right time to celebrate.

'Right, I'll ask my lads, and you sort out your friends. We can do some finger food and tell everyone to bring a bottle. What do you think?' He was delighted that Cathy had agreed to his suggestion. 'Want to invite anyone, Luke?' Mark asked.

'No, this is your home, not mine. But thanks.'

'Hey, none of that rubbish,' Mark scolded. 'Listen, if you want to ask anyone, then do. You're part of this family now, too.' He placed a hand gently on the young man's arm, in a caring way. Luke smiled in return.

• • • •

The following Saturday night, cars rolled into the drive – or the yard, as Cathy called it. At the entrance of the drive was an iron gate which was a bit battered, but well-loved, from children swinging on it in the past. Now rusted in parts, its paint flaking, it was a dirty mottled white, but still stood out against the shrubs and bushes it opened against. It was the silly things like this gate that Cathy did not want to replace; she felt they had a story to tell.

Mark was happy to leave her to her romantic notions. He was more interested in getting the main buildings in shape. The rest was just cosmetic, and he kept telling her she had a good feel for the project, so that she would not question herself.

'Hi, welcome to Cregane Court.' She repeated this a few times as the evening got underway. Cathy was delighted that Sno had made it out. The day she had phoned the waitress about Luke moving in, Sno had whooped with joy and immediately texted Luke that he had made the right decision. For the party tonight, Luke had gone into the city to meet their friend and show her the way to Ballybawn.

Gemma had come, too, but had left her husband at home to babysit. The poor man was an angel, Cathy reckoned, to put up with her sister's odd ways.

'You've not done a lot to it, have you? If I remember right, it was like this back in our young days when we visited,' Gemma commented as she handed over a basket of food and some wine.

'Well, it takes time and money, Gemma, but it will happen. Thanks a million for all this.' Cathy pointed at the food-laden table. Her sister was marvellous to bring so much. 'It's really appreciated, Gemma, especially when you've a family to look after. I'm sure time is precious.' Cathy was in top form and genuinely thrilled with her sister.

'Well, we all know you can't cook, so someone has to save the night from a disaster. I wanted the others to know that one of the Reed sisters is capable.' Gemma turned around and left the kitchen to step out to the evening air.

Tears sprung into Cathy's eyes. *Why had there to be a sting in the tail to everything Gemma said?* Just then, she felt a warm and comforting arm around her shoulders.

'She really is the wicked witch of the west,' Mark whispered into her ear, then handed her a glass of wine and winked.

Cathy had not seen him come up behind her. She smiled and took a deep breath. Gemma was not going to ruin the night. Her friends were here, and it was time to enjoy herself.

• • • •

A large campfire had been lit in the front green area that offered views of uninterrupted nature. Most of the people were gathered around it, sharing beers and stories. Music played from the house, not too loud, but enough to fill the background. A fun, happy atmosphere covered Cregane Court, and Mark was laughing off a slagging from his former housemates and some of the office crowd who'd come along. They all agreed that they were seeing a different side to him. Gone was the quiet, respectable man of the office; here, he was one of the lads, joking and drinking without a care in the world. His friends all seemed genuinely delighted for him, remarking many times over that he had made the right decision moving here. Plus, they teased him, Cathy was a bit of alright to look at – nudge, nudge, wink, wink.

The joking and teasing about Cathy stung him. *Did his mates not know him at all? Was he really that closed-off from the truth that no-one knew the real Mark Daniels?* He laughed with them, though. Feeling an imposter of sorts was not enough to ruin this good party. He took a mouthful of beer then looked over towards Gemma, who was seated next to Luke. He could see what appeared to be a look of horror on her face. Whatever Luke was saying did not seem to be going down well. Mark decided to wander over and see what was happening.

'All good here, are we?' He pulled up a chair and sat next to them. Both were seated close to the house, in a small patio outside the kitchen area, marked off by some pretty pots of red and white geraniums.

'Yeah, I was just telling Gemma what a saint of a sister she has. How she saved me from the streets and myself. You know, the horrors of drugs and, well, if desperate for food, one would do anything for a bite to eat.' Luke winked at Mark.

The older man tried to stifle a laugh. He knew Luke had laid it on thick for Gemma, and she had reacted exactly as the snob she was. Pushing her chair back, she stood and adjusted her top and skirt. Her eyes lowered as she dusted down her clothing, and Mark imagined she was worried about any contamination that might have occurred while sitting to Luke the delinquent.

'Another drink, Gemma?' he offered.

'I think I'll get it myself, thank you. Excuse me, boys.'

• • • •

Gemma twirled where she stood and made her getaway, mumbling that she needed to check where she had put her handbag. Cathy had never told her there was a street person living with her. Inside the house, she found her purse and brought it to her car for safe keeping, hiding it under the driver's seat. Now to hunt out Cathy and give her some much-needed advice about the company she was keeping.

'Excuse me, am I too late to join the party?'

Gemma turned in shock at the deep voice. The lighting where the cars were parked was dim and she could only see a tall figure.

'I… I… can't see you.' Fear rose in her throat.

'Sorry, forgive me,' the voice stepped from the shadows. 'Roman O'Driscoll, solicitor to the former Mrs. Elizabeth Sheldon.' A hand stretched out towards Gemma.

'How do you do. I'm Gemma, Cathy's sister.' She took in the slick suit and polished shoes, and could see that he was a handsome man, now that he stood under the yard light. At least Cathy had had the sense to invite this respectable man.

'Come on in, Mr. O'Driscoll. I'm sure Cathy and Mark will be thrilled to see you.' Gemma led the way to the campfire. A singsong could be heard as they moved closer to the gathered crowd, the sound of a guitar filling the night air with music.

'Cathy, look who I found out near the cars? Roman, take a seat and I shall get you a drink. Would you like a beer or a wine?'

'A beer would be just fine. Gemma, isn't it?' Roman's smile showed perfect teeth.

What a gentleman, Gemma sighed. *This night could be redeemed after all.*

Cathy stood up in surprise; shock prevented her from saying anything. *Where was Mark?* She looked around but could not see him. Roman was already chatting with a friend of Mark's, so she couldn't ask him to leave now. And, of course, here was her sister with two beers in her hand. *Where the hell was Mark? Or even Luke?* Her mind was racing. *What was O'Driscoll doing here anyway? And who invited him?*

Chapter Thirteen

Cathy rubbed the temples of her forehead. *What the hell happened last night?* Her head pounded and her tongue stuck to the roof of her mouth like sandpaper. With great effort, she got up and stood in front of the dressing table. The gilt-edged mirror reflected back a demon with wild bed-hair and a pale face. She heard voices down in the kitchen and thought a big mug of hot tea would be lovely. Cathy slipped on her dressing gown and yawned; it was going to be a long day. Passing Mark's bedroom door, which was closed, she reckoned he was also probably suffering from too many beers last night. She would let him sleep.

'What was she thinking?' a voice drifted up from downstairs.

Was that Mark talking? Was he not in his room? Cathy stopped halfway down the stairs and listened.

'Does it matter? He raised the class of the party instantly. I don't know what you're upset about.' It seemed Gemma was in the kitchen, too.

'After his visit, I didn't think she'd invite him. Are you sure it was her?' Her housemate's anger was evident, and Cathy remained still, her knuckles white as she gripped the bannister.

'Look here, Mark, she's a grown woman and can invite who she wants to her home. Who knows? Maybe she fancies him. You know, the strong, tall, confident type; any woman would.'

The clatter of dishes followed, and Cathy decided to go and find out the full story. As she reached the bottom of the stairs, Gemma brushed past her and headed up to her sister's bedroom, which they'd shared last night.

Mark stood by the sink, staring into space.

'Good morning,' Cathy croaked sleepily.

'Really? What's good about it?' Mark dropped his mug into the sink, pushed past Cathy, and out of the front door.

Through the window, Cathy saw Luke and Snowflake outside gathering up the empty bottles and cans from the party, the firepit now a pile of cold ash and cinders. She was obviously the last to get up. Rubbing her throbbing forehead once more, Cathy flipped the switch on the kettle, grabbed her favourite cup, and popped a teabag into it. It seemed as though she had been at the centre of the argument between her sister and Mark, but she couldn't fathom why. And right now, her head was screaming for paracetamol.

Cathy opened the window and called out to the others. 'Hey, anyone want some coffee or tea? The kettle is boiled.'

Luke waved and Sno gave a thumbs up. Minutes later, the three friends were gathered around the table chatting.

'This place has so much potential, Cathy, its fab.' Sno sat back and stretched her legs out. It was Sunday, so she was in no hurry back for work this evening.

'Do you know what's upset, Mark?' Cathy asked. 'I heard him arguing with Gemma earlier. I only caught part of the story, but I do know it involves me.'

Sno shrugged, she didn't know anything. They both looked towards the young man beside them, who was munching on hot buttered croissants with a big smile on his face. Seeing their glances, Luke stopped smiling and placed his pastry back down.

'May as well tell you,' he said. 'He's not happy with you inviting Roman O'Driscoll to the housewarming, and to be honest, I was surprised you did, too.'

'What? But I never!' Cathy stood up angrily, scraping her chair on the floor. 'Why would he think I'd invite that snake? Christ, I was shocked to see him here. Where's Mark now?'

'Don't know,' Luke shrugged and grabbed his croissant once more.

'Why is it so bad that this O'Driscoll guy showed up?' Sno moved to Cathy's side and placed her arm around her friend's shoulders. Her soothing voice, gentle hug, and soft touch were a welcome comfort.

Cathy leant into her friend's embrace and sighed. *How did she, Cathy, manage to always end up being the bad guy?*

••••

The day dragged on and a foreboding silence hung around Cregane Court. The merry, fun atmosphere of the party had swirled into the sky along with the smoke from the campfire, the grey-white ash that remained resembling the ambiance around everyone now. There was still no sign of Mark; his car had gone, and no-one had heard from him since breakfast.

Gemma had packed up by lunchtime and was getting ready to head home. 'Thanks for a lovely time, Cathy. I enjoyed myself more than I thought I would.' She hugged her sister briefly.

'Glad someone enjoyed themselves.' Cathy shrugged in an uncaring way.

'Oh, cheer up, why the dull face? I'll admit, it got off to a slow start, but when Roman arrived, he really made it swing. Don't let him slip through your fingers or he will be snapped up. Even I wouldn't mind a go at him.' Gemma giggled like she was sixteen again.

'You're a married woman!' Cathy screeched, shocked at her sister's words.

'All I'm saying is, he's free and single, and going places. You could do worse. Don't let Mark decide who you should date. Oh, listen,' her voice dropped to a whisper, 'be careful around your other two buddies, Luke and Raindrop. They seem right chancy to me. Let some charity take care of them.'

'It's Snowflake, not Raindrop!' Cathy snapped back. 'And you are so wrong about my friends. I really don't like what you are suggesting.'

'Oh, stop fussing, you're always too sensitive.' Gemma marched into the sitting room where Luke and Sno were watching some television. 'Bye, you two, it was interesting meeting you both.'

• • • •

'I think an early night is calling me. I'm shattered.' Luke rubbed his face and yawned. It was 9pm and he was tired. After tidying up with the two women, the house and gardens were back to pre-party condition, and he had also moved some rubble to fill in time. He thought Cathy and Sno might want to chat before Sno returned to the city in the morning.

'Well, if you are sleeping on the sofa, I guess we need to get out of the sitting room. You can have your bed back, Luke. I'm okay with camping down here, tonight honestly.' Snowflake tilted her head to the side to see him.

'No, not at all,' Luke protested. 'You forget, I've slept on all sorts and in all places, so a sofa is heaven. I'm happy to let you have the bed, Sno. You've always been good to me.'

'You can always share with me now Gemma's gone, Raindrop.' Cathy smiled innocently.

'Raindrop?!' Luke and Sno said at the same time.

'Yes, my sister, in her own snobbish way, called you Raindrop before she went. Snowflake is such a hard name to remember!'

The trio laughed out loud, and what started as a good belly-ache laughter eventually saw them doubled up and wiping tears from their eyes. Cathy crossed her legs; she was sure she had peed a little.

'Don't mind me. I'm glad that everyone is having a good time.' Mark's voice cut through the air. One by one they stopped laughing and looked at each other, as he marched past and went straight to the kitchen to fill up the kettle.

The three friends followed him, still sniggering at Gemma's poor attempt at trying to be superior.

'Had a nice day?' Cathy asked.

'Yes. Coffee anyone?' Mark swivelled around to look at the others, but they shook their heads in response.

'I'm off to bed. Maybe I'll take my room after all, Sno, if you don't mind.' Luke shot Mark a side glance then turned and headed to his room.

'Looks like you're doubling up with me then, Raindrop.' Cathy smiled, and Sno shrugged her shoulders.

'Raindrop?' A puzzled look crossed Mark's face.

'You had to be here,' Sno shot back and left to go upstairs.

'Want to talk?' Cathy leaned against the kitchen doorway. Its timber frame was splintered in places and the paintwork marked from years of people brushing against it.

'Not particularly. I'm tired myself and might get an early night, too. Work in the morning, after all.'

'I didn't invite him. Not that it should matter to you who I invite to my home.' She turned on her heels and went to step away.

'Our home,' he replied. 'And when it's a snake like Roman O'Driscoll, it certainly does matter.' Mark brushed by her, coffee cup in his hand, and headed up the stairs.

All Cathy's happy energy drained from her at Mark's words. She didn't answer him; now was not the time. But she felt weary. *Why did she always mess things up?* She sat on the sofa and lifted the woolly throw that Sno had crocheted for her as a housewarming present. Its colours were bright and vibrant, reds, oranges and yellows, the pattern a swirling intricate design, almost Celtic with its twists and cables. It was a beautiful piece of work, and huge – at least a double bed size. Cathy burrowed beneath it and rested against the plump cushions.

In the space of two days, her emotions had gone from top end to low depths. *Why? Why had Roman O'Driscoll turned up? What was he after?* She was convinced there was definitely something both she and Mark were missing about Cregane Court. Lizzy must have had her reasons for leaving them her home.

She understood why Mark was angry at the solicitor's appearance last night, but she *hadn't* invited him, and she needed to make that clear to Mark. Then again, she didn't know Mark much better than she knew Roman. Her head ached with questions.

For the first time since losing her dad and her job, fear once more crept into Cathy's mind. Doubt accompanied it, filling her inside. A coldness made her shiver and she snuggled deeper beneath the throw. *Had she made a mistake? Maybe Cregane Court was not for her. A retreat centre in the middle of nowhere? How ridiculous.* Everyone wanted Wi-Fi now, and out here in Ballybawn village, Wi-Fi was a hit and miss at the best of times. Tonight, fear and doubt lingered in Cathy, while her eyes closed with the weariness of the past two days.

• • • •

Mark gazed out of his bedroom window. The evening sky had changed to a navy blue as the night closed in around Cregane Court. *Why had he let Roman O'Driscoll get to him?* How he detested that man. He shouldn't be angry with Cathy, though. She had every right to befriend whomever she wished. *But O'Driscoll? Had she not been upset by his previous visit?* He got into bed, then got out again. He hadn't heard Cathy come upstairs; maybe he should go down and talk with her. He didn't want there to be any resentment between them, though she hadn't seemed angry. He was the one who was spitting fire today and staying away from their home like a sulky five-year-old.

He should go down and apologise for his behaviour and hear her side of the story. She said she didn't invite him, but...? Mark sighed. He needed to apologise to Luke, too. The side glance Luke had given him in the kitchen earlier had hurt. *Gosh, what was he like? Why couldn't his life be like before – easy and uncomplicated?*

But he knew why. Cregane Court was why.

Maybe a good night's sleep for all of them would be best. Clear heads and a new day. Yes, that sounded like a better plan. Mark got into bed, his thoughts a bit clearer, and sleep soon followed.

Chapter Fourteen

Luke helped Sno with her bags and went with her to the bus stop. He was going to meet some friends and stay overnight in town, while Sno would shower, change, and then head to work at the café.

There hadn't been much talk at the house this morning, with everyone determined to do their own thing. Mark had left without breakfast or a single word to anyone. An air of discomfort clouded the house, but that soon lifted once they'd all left and Cathy was on her own.

The summer day promised to be a good one. She washed up the few delph and cutlery that were there, and hung out a wash on the clothesline down near the empty hen-house. She was turning into quite the domestic goddess, but nowhere yet near Nigella's standard. Gathering her wicker basket and purse, Cathy decided to ramble into the village, have some lunch, and stroll home later.

The hedgerows were filled with flowers and brambles, and birdsong surrounded her as she walked, lifting her mood. The road was not particularly busy and the motorists that passed her all waved as they grew level. She loved that although you didn't know everyone, they still acknowledged you.

Ahead of her on the right were two giant pillars. A lodge stood near the gateway, and further in a long passageway stood a country house – a dirty grey building with shuttered windows. The walled-in fields suggested an old estate of sorts, and Cathy wondered whether the house was still lived in or not, and what its history was. Further on, another large house stood stately in the fields. With such rich bygone days, the area would be a magnet for writers and historians, maybe even photographers. Smaller cottages like Lizzy's were scattered, along with a few more modern bungalows and two-storeys dotted in-between. Did Lizzy's home have history? It tickled her to think there might be a family secret to discover, and Cathy's writer's imagination began working feverishly.

• • • •

'Good morning to you.'

'Good morning, it's a lovely day so far,' Cathy replied, stopping by a wall overflowing with shrubs.

'Yes, the best time of the day definitely is the morning. Are you visiting the area?'

'No, I just moved here, about a mile or so back the road there. I'm Cathy.' She extended her hand to the man leaning on the timber garden gate.

'William Sheehan.' He shook her hand in a firm grip, and stared directly at her as he held onto her hand. Cathy coloured slightly from his gaze, and she noticed he picked up on her embarrassment.

'Oh sorry, Cathy, you remind me of someone. Don't tell me, I'll get it.' He paused, taking in her features, the wavy hair, and the upturned nose. 'Are you walking to the village?'

'I am. Do you need something?' she offered.

'No, but thank you for asking. Mind if I join you? I usually stroll in for a few hours. Helps pass the time of day for me.'

'I'd be delighted with your company, William. I don't really know anyone here, so maybe you can answer some questions for me.'

'Hold on so, until I close the door and get my stick and cap. These old bones need all the help they can get nowadays, and a man never goes anywhere without his cap.' He disappeared inside a small house, its whitewashed walls and blue door fresh and clean. A small bed of flowers to the front of the house and inside the gate was filled with summer plants beginning to blossom. William returned a few minutes later, a soft green check flat-cap on his head and sturdy walking stick in his hand.

The two walked in silence, happy with each other's company.

'I've got it! Elizabeth Sheldon. That's who you remind me of.'

Cathy started to laugh, surprise lighting up her face. He was a clever old man, for sure. 'You're right. I'm a grand-niece of hers. A friend and I inherited her cottage. That is amazing you recognising me like that. Did you know Lizzy well?' Cathy was ready to soak up any information she could get about her great-aunt.

His eyes twinkled with mischief, but he said nothing about Elizabeth. Although old, maybe in his eighties, William walked at a steady pace. And as the duo ambled along, he pointed out the different homes of locals, still keeping any stories of her great-aunt to himself for now. Their chatting and falling silent every now and then was companionable. As they approached the village, three roads led into the centre, where a monument watched over village life. Up on a grey concrete plinth stood a man sitting astride a bronze horse. The rider was dressed in military garb – clearly a local who had become famous and was now celebrated by his own community. Beneath the monument was a bench, and both Cathy and William sat for a brief rest.

'I saw some really large country houses earlier. Was Cregane Court ever part of the estates that seem to be around the area?' Cathy asked. 'It seems funny saying Cregane Court.' She chuckled. 'It sounds so regal and stately when it's really just a small cottage.'

'No. Cregane is the townland; the postal area, I suppose they would say nowadays,' William explained. 'Elizabeth was always having some sort of gathering, be it card games or sing-song evenings. She always made everyone so welcome. Kind to the bone she was.'

William took off his cap and placed it over his knee, drew a deep breath, and continued to talk. 'There was so much always going on in Elizabeth and Archie's home that it was said they were holding court. So Cregane Court stuck, and she kept the name and put it up on the wall. Is that plaque still there?'

Cathy didn't recall any plaque, but then the entrance way was overgrown. She made a mental note to check when she got back. William was a wealth of knowledge about the local area and waved at everyone who went by.

'Would you like to go for some tea?' Cathy offered, feeling the heat from the midday sun.

'Ah, no thanks, girl, I shall leave you to get on with your tasks. I really enjoyed our chat, and if you're ever passing my door, do call in, won't you?'

'I sure will, and you must call up to see Cregane Court. Promise?' She smiled at William. Looking to see if it was safe to cross the road, Cathy stepped back quickly as a car she recognised pulled up beside them. The driver opened the window and leaned out.

'Well, hello there. You're out and about early. I thought you would be relaxing and living the good life.' Roman O'Driscoll's grin oozed sarcasm.

The Joker from Batman immediately entered Cathy's mind, and she turned away without offering a reply.

'How are you, William? Enjoying the nice day?' His deep voice followed her.

'It's Mr. Sheehan to you, I'll have you know,' William snapped at the solicitor. He stood up from the bench and called out to Cathy, 'I'll have that tea, after all.'

• • • •

Sno got to the café a little earlier than usual. The noise of the city seemed so loud after the peace of Ballybawn. She was thrilled for Cathy that living with Mark appeared to be working out. He was a nice guy. But that fellow who had arrived at the party late, seemed to stir up trouble. Sno didn't like him, and decided to ask Cathy more. She had met his kind before: all sweet talk and laughter, but unseen bullying was taking place underneath, so well hidden that the victim never realised it. Cathy's sister Gemma had lapped him up, though, Sno recalled. She couldn't laugh loud enough at his jokes or agree enough with his opinions on life. As far as Sno was concerned, Gemma was another bully, and immediately an old saying popped into her mind: *birds of a feather...*

Sno ended up having a busy evening, with more people lured out by the promise of summer. By closing time, she was glad to be locking up. Her feet ached and, rushing for the bus, she felt deflated. Cregane Court had got to her, and she longed for the peace and easy attitude of a country village life. A couple of nights was all it had taken, and she was hooked: the night sky, looking at the stars, with the whisper of wind in the trees, and the hush of a quiet country road.

Maybe she could rent a place in Ballybawn and open a café of her own, Sno thought. Money was tight, but she managed and had savings. And her crafts might be something she could sell from a corner in the café. Everyone had admired the throw she had given Cathy and raved about her talent.

If Cathy could up and leave, so could she, she decided. For now, she would keep her thoughts to herself and make some enquiries. Feeling brighter, Sno hummed as she stood in the long queue at the bus stop for home.

• • • •

Mark worked late; deadlines were looming for the end of month figures. It would be late evenings all this week, which suited him fine. He didn't know if he was rowing with Cathy or whether it had all blown over, but a coolness was definitely in the air when they were together. He blamed it all on that bloody solicitor. *If Cathy didn't invite him, then who did?* Gemma had definitely said it had been Cathy. *Why was he doubting Cathy? Could her sister have gotten it wrong?* Christ, Gemma had been all over Roman O'Driscoll like a bad rash. She really wasn't a nice person, and Mark found it difficult to believe that she and Cathy were sisters.

Maybe he should text Cathy and tell her his plans, in case she waited to have dinner. Before his colleagues arrived in his office for the next meeting, he grabbed his phone and brought up Cathy's number,

Not home until late all week.

He hit the send button then opened the files on his desk. His focus right now was work; everything else would have to wait.

Chapter Fifteen

The garden gloves Cathy wore protected her from the many thorns that stuck to her hands as she pulled at the overgrown brambles and the long, glossy ivy that crept everywhere. It was another warm day, bright and clear, and she was determined to find the plaque that William had mentioned.

As she tugged and dragged at the plants, some of the old wall crumbled and fell to her feet. She didn't want to damage the stone work too much, so she thought it better to get the shears and snip at the offending branches. As the greenery gave way, flecks of old paint spotted the mortar. Cathy worked in a steady rhythm, snipping, then clearing, and then brushing, with all the branches, leaves, and loose dirt piled high in a corner. With almost one side of the entrance wall cleared, there was still no sign of any name plate. Maybe William had gotten it wrong, or maybe it had long fallen off.

She stood back to admire her work; it really opened up the gateway. And once the other side was weeded, with some fresh paint maybe on the stone wall, it would look cheerful and welcoming. It was time to stop for a cuppa.

In the kitchen, she turned up the radio that had belonged to Lizzy. It was working perfectly, and Mark had tuned it into a popular music station. Waiting on the kettle boiling, Cathy danced around the kitchen, singing out loud while placing milk and sugar on the table.

'Hello! Hello, anyone at home?'

Stopping, Cathy went to the front doorway to see who had come calling and immediately her heart sank. Gemma. 'What are you doing here?' Cathy's good mood had quickly evaporated.

'Nice way to welcome your sister.' Gemma brushed past and placed her handbag and jacket on a nearby armchair.

'Seriously, Gemma, what brings you out here? Did you text me? Have I missed a call?' She looked around frantically for her phone to check. She couldn't believe she hadn't heard the car pull into the yard.

'The girls are on a playdate after school, so they won't be home until after seven. Thought I'd pop out and see the progress. Are you making tea? I'd love a coffee.'

Cathy grabbed an extra mug. She knew her sister didn't like instant, but that was what she was getting. Snatching a packet of chocolate digestives from the cupboard, she placed some on a plate and put it on the table as her mind whirred. *Why the hell was Gemma back here so soon?*

'So, what have you been up to since the party?' Gemma grimaced as she sipped the coffee. She lifted a biscuit, nibbling on it as if to kill the taste of the drink.

'Busy cleaning,' Cathy replied. 'I started on the entrance walls this morning. Did you notice on your way in? There's a plaque hidden beneath the overgrowth somewhere.' Excitement about discovering the name plate bubbled inside Cathy, and her eyes lit up at the thought of it. She gushed to Gemma about meeting William. 'He's such a dear. He remembers Lizzy, but nearly everyone around here calls her Elizabeth. She was very much loved, by all accounts,' Cathy explained. 'William said he will call to tell me other stories about her and Archie someday. You know I'd forgotten about Great-Uncle Archie. I barely recall him. Do you remember him, Gemma?'

'What? Who? William? Never heard of him.' The bored tone left Cathy in no doubt that her sister wasn't even listening to her.

'Well, I must be getting on with it. Are you going to help me?'

'In these clothes? Do I look like I'm dressed for pulling weeds?' The disgust in Gemma's voice dripped around the room.

Cathy placed her cup in the sink and cleared away the table, then she pulled on her gardening gloves and headed out from the kitchen. Gemma had no choice but to follow.

'Has Roman been in touch?' she asked innocently.

Hearing the solicitor's name, Cathy swivelled around to face her sister. 'Why do you ask?'

'Just wondering. Such a handsome man, a rare breed. Does he call often?'

'No. He gate-crashed the party, actually, and I don't want him snooping around here. Neither does Mark.' The furrowed brows on Cathy's face left Gemma in no doubt that her sister meant business. 'Now, are you going to help or not?'

Horrified, Gemma got into her car and called out to Cathy, 'Well, since it took an hour to get here, I might just wander around Ballybawn and see what it has to offer. You never know who I might bump into.' She winked and then started up the engine.

Cathy watched her sister's car disappear up the road. *What a bitch*, she thought. The greenery taking the brunt of her anger, Cathy pulled on branches with great force, tugging, dragging, and kicking... and then she saw it. The old lettering was faded, the wood splintered, but the scripted writing could still be made out: *Cregane Court*.

'Well, bless Gemma,' she said aloud, 'she has her uses after all.'

••••

Cathy placed the name plaque on the kitchen table. It had come off the wall easily; a gentle tug and a wobble of the screws, and it was soon in her hands. She felt a sudden surge of loneliness, and tears rolled down her face. This was part of her heritage – well, her dad's family, but hers, too. He would have played here with his siblings and cousins, no doubt, when younger. And his father, Lizzy's brother, would have been here sharing the happy times when Elizabeth and Archie had held court.

Little snippets of regret popped into her heart, wishing she had made more of her time with family in the past. Though family did not always mean harmony, she knew. That was where friends came in; the family we want for ourselves, she reckoned. Cathy felt a sudden determination to make up for it now. She would make Cregane Court sing again, and it would shine once more amid Ballybawn village. They had been trusted with this cottage and land, and neither she nor Mark would let Lizzy down.

Searching for some paper and a pencil, Cathy drew out an outline for a new plaque. She reckoned the old one was beyond repair, but she would leave it aside for Mark to see. His text about working late had been brief, and she hoped it was definitely work and not this silly argument that was keeping him away. They hadn't spoken properly since, but she was always shattered by the evening and was either in bed early or soaking in the bathtub when he got home, so time for conversation had been scarce. But the weekend was ahead, and hopefully they could sit down and clear the air.

Wrapping the nameplate in old newspaper, she placed it on the kitchen counter and returned to her scribbles. Art was not her forte, so she would be better to ask Luke for inspiration; he was the artist. Since he'd left on Monday with Sno, he had not made contact. She just hoped he hadn't changed his mind about being involved in the cottage or country life.

••••

The parcel on the counter caught Mark's eye as he made some coffee. The week at work had him wrecked. He hated this side of accounting; final figures were so stressful – every cent needed to be covered, and it was on his head to do so.

The old newspaper revealed a lump of wood wrapped inside, a short sort of plank. He turned it over and saw the ornate script. It was barely legible, but there nonetheless: *Cregane Court.* His fingers slid over the plaque. The rusty screws hung loosely in their holes, some missing; the timber was darkened with age, split, rotting, flaking in parts. He held it in his hands and turned it over once more. *Oak*, he thought. *The weight of it and the feel. Yes, oak. What a find!* He couldn't wait to hear where it had come from and how Cathy had found it.

Cathy. He sighed. They really needed to talk.

Chapter Sixteen

She heard the cups being rattled downstairs; someone was busy in the kitchen. As her bedroom door was ajar, she heard the kettle boiling, the hum of it singing up the stairs. *Did she smell bacon?* The clock on her nightstand blinked eight, and her curtains strained to keep the morning sunlight out. Cathy stretched and admired the touches she had made to her bedroom. The large reading lamp overlooking her mustard wing chair had given her a reading corner that was perfect to escape to; the low side table – well, a tripod stool that she had picked up at the local charity shop – held her *to be read* pile of books; and the vase of fresh greenery and some wild flowers on her dressing table popped with colour.

She wriggled deep beneath the duvet and groaned. Her muscles ached from all the clearing at the entrance gate, cutting back the bushes and shrubs that had gone wild and overgrown their spots. Although she had soaked in the tub to ease her aches, she was still tender, particularly her arms. The dragging of the cut brush to the compost corner over by the old hen-house had been time consuming and hard work, but necessary to keep the gateway from being blocked.

'Good morning, may I come in?' A tapping on her bedroom door distracted her from her thoughts and she sat up.

'Of course.'

'Some tea and toast with bacon. A peace offering?'

'Mark, it smells divine. Thank you.'

He placed the tray on the bed and disappeared out of the room, returning a minute later with a cup of coffee in his hand. 'May I join you?'

Nodding, she poured out her tea then smothered the hot toast with butter. The tray held everything she needed. What a treat. 'How was your week?' She munched on her toast. The hot melted butter tasted so delicious.

'Awful,' he replied. 'I hate this time every month at work. It's so bloody stressful, especially when other departments haven't balanced their books through sheer lack of effort.' He rubbed his tired eyes, and she heard the weariness in his tone. An awkwardness hung around and Cathy sipped her tea while he sipped his coffee.

'I'm sorry if my behaviour upset you.' He kept his eyes downward and his feet shuffled on the rug.

'Mark, I'm sorry, too, for whatever. But to be honest, I really don't know why we are apologising or what it is that we did wrong.' The atmosphere shifted.

'Why did you invite Roman to the housewarming?' he asked. 'It really bugged me seeing him here. I thought you didn't like him.'

This again! Cathy thought that had been dealt with, but obviously not. The frown on her forehead should have told him she was not impressed.

'I said I didn't invite him, he gate-crashed!' she huffed, pushing the tray further down her bed.

'But when I spoke with Gemma, she said—' Mark's voice was raised a little.

'Gemma?' she snapped. 'Then Gemma got it wrong. And I *do* dislike him. A lot. She's an interfering bully, that sister of my mine. It's not the first time she has spouted off rubbish without caring whether it's true or not.'

'Yeah, she is a handful.' A weak smile played on his lips. He had annoyed Cathy, and now he regretted his words. 'How are you two sisters?'

Cathy sighed, calming down. 'Look, let's forget it, okay? We both agree that Roman is a pig. A pig that I think Gemma has the hots for.' Cathy leaned back into her pillows. 'But... I do not have to justify myself. If I had invited him that would be my choice, okay?' She didn't want to continue the discussion, but she hoped he understood that she was serious. She didn't have to clear her visitors with him, and vice versa. Mark took the tray from the bed and smiled down at Cathy.

'You're right, of course. I hope you know that my reaction was out of concern for you. Now, get up, lazy bones. I want to hear all about that chunk of wood in the kitchen.' And off he went with the breakfast tray, leaving Cathy to get ready for the day ahead.

• • • •

'So that's it,' she finished her explanation. 'I had to go searching for it once I knew it was there. You'd love William, too.'

'Is he a man with a flat-cap?' Mark looked thoughtful.

'And a stick, in his eighties or so. Do you know him?'

'I vaguely remember him. He used to call here for the card games.'

'That's right. He said all that. What do you think of the plaque?' It sat on the kitchen table in front of them. It had been brushed down and cleaned up a little, and the letters were clearer now that Mark had worked on it.

'It's a wonderful find, and you did a brilliant job at the entrance gate. You've really worked hard, Cathy.'

'I was thinking of getting a new name plate made, you know, to put up where this one had been. What do you think?' She saw his eyes light up at the suggestion.

'What were you thinking of? Something similar, or totally different?'

She shrugged. 'Have you any thoughts?'

'Well, I do have some ideas. Would you mind if I had a go at making it? I'd love to get some nice timber and shape it, you know; show the true soul of the wood. Maybe Luke could do the script, or design a logo or something.'

'Speaking of Luke, where is he? I've not heard from him since he left with Sno.' Cathy watched her friend carefully. She vaguely remembered that on the night of the party, both Mark and Luke had been missing when Roman arrived.

'Not heard either.' Disappointment shadowed his face as he turned from Cathy.

• • • •

The weekend was spent on clearing and cleaning. The labourers from Ballybawn were back to continue with adapting the large outhouse into self-contained flats, and everything was taking shape. Next on the agenda was the old hen-house area, but they would need some machinery to level off the field and dig foundations. Mark had done his homework well and applied for every government and local council grant he thought they might be eligible for. Some had come through, but others were still pending.

The kitchen was a hive of activity as the workmen gathered for lunch. Most agreed that although it was ambitious, the idea of an artists' retreat could take off. Some commented that it was good to see old places being utilised and not abandoned, especially with the dreadful increase of homelessness on the streets. The workers told stories of homes falling into ruin and being left there. So many dotted the countryside now, with everything seeming to be geared for the cities.

While the men went back to work outside, Cathy decided to tackle some more of the house. There were still cupboards and some travelling trunks in the attic that needed to be gone through, along with some of Lizzy's boxes that would have to be checked before being discarded.

She sat down on the sitting room floor, along with three large cardboard boxes. Inside were official-looking forms, envelopes filled with receipts, leaflets with coupons that were out of date, and deep in the bottom of a box was a diary. Dusty and old, the diary had been filled in by Lizzy, although she seemed to have used it in a notebook fashion rather than recording her daily thoughts. Cathy flicked through the pages; there were diagrams on some of the pages, and lists on others.

Getting up from the floor, she took the book with her and went to her bedroom. Settling on the bed, she read through the book and tried to figure out the numbers and the notes attached to some of the initials. Red marks were ticked down one side, and other notes were scribbled out.

Some of the ink went through to the other page, and Cathy reckoned Lizzy must have been angry when she tried to make out those notes. Wait until Mark heard what she had to tell him.

Chapter Seventeen

The local pub, O'Flahaven's, filled up as the night went on. Every weekend night there was a music group to entertain the locals, and tonight's offering had set up in the corner – a Meatloaf tribute band, with four members – the lead vocal resembling the famous singer in weight but not in voice.

Mark and the labourers had persuaded Cathy to come out for a drink. She really wanted to read more in Lizzy's book that she'd found, but had been outnumbered by the lads who insisted it was a good way to meet others from the village. And as Mark promised he was paying for the drinks, how could she refuse?

The counter ran around two of the walls, and high stools were perched along the way, while there was ornate old chandelier-style lighting, which was dim but welcoming. Posters of the local sports club achievements were dotted around, including signed jerseys and even the boots that had scored the vital winning goal against the neighbouring rivals. All this was explained to Cathy, and she nodded politely.

A beer garden out the back tempted most of the customers to sit in the evening sunshine. With the doors open, there was no escaping the music, but at least it was easier to have a conversation there than sitting inside. Several people came up to say hello to her and Mark, admitting they had heard they were making changes to Elizabeth's cottage. Getting the locals involved in the building had been a plus, and both were aware that it was good for everyone to feel included in the developments.

Cathy kept an eye out for Roman O'Driscoll. She wondered if he mingled with the locals or if he was only interested in those with land or business. As she headed to the, Ladies Room, she spotted William inside and decided she would pop over to say hello on her way back.

'They have great ideas for the place, I hear. They seem nice enough. I'd say she's older than him, though. She looks it anyway.' Cathy smiled to herself as she remained in the cubicle. Obviously, the women washing their hands at the sinks were speaking about her and Mark. As she didn't want to walk out and embarrass them, she decided to stay put until she heard them leave. But the conversation showed no signs of coming to an end. 'I'm telling you, I heard it was a type of commune, you know, for drop-outs and hippy types. I'd not like that sort in the village.' Water flowed from the taps as the women chatted.

'Ah no, they look a good sort themselves. My neighbour is working on the buildings, and he said it's a retreat for the arty type of people. He thinks it's a great idea.'

'Sure, most of those types are into drugs for inspiration and to help their creativity flow. I'm telling you, Roman wouldn't have said it otherwise.'

What! The tight space that held Cathy closed in on her and she wanted to go out and set these people right, but she froze. How dare Roman say such a thing! The evil...

But the women hadn't finished. 'Maybe. But still, it could be sour grapes with him,' one said. 'That solicitor was hoping to get the place for himself, I was told.'

With that, the duo left, and Cathy finally slipped out. Their conversation had her worried. Did some of the people in Ballybawn believe they were opening some sort of a cult? And what was that about Roman O'Driscoll wanting to own Lizzy's? She was more confused by the minute. As she left the toilets, her thoughts were all over the place, until suddenly her friend caught her eye.

'Hey, William,' she smiled to shake off her confusion. 'I didn't think rock music was your thing?'

The elderly man smiled, cupped his hand around one ear, and shouted, 'What did you say?' He pointed at the group with the other hand.

Cathy leaned in and repeated her words and he laughed. The counter before him was shiny from wear, and his cap was placed on it. Sitting at the end of the bar with a good view of the main door, he tapped on the counter with his fingers and watched everything going on. A pint of dark stout with a small whiskey was in front of him, and he sipped from the pint now and then.

There was no point in trying to speak with so much noise around them, so Cathy leaned back in towards him and said she would call in to see him in a few days' time. In answer, he saluted her, then went back to supping his drink.

When she returned to the beer garden, Mark was dancing, his arms waving madly in the air. *Yeah, he definitely looks the part of a hippy*, she thought, and laughed out loud.

• • • •

What was it with people in this house and early mornings? Downstairs, there was noise coming from the kitchen, cupboard doors opening and closing, then footsteps that turned to silence as the front door closed. She turned in her bed and thought no more of it. If Mark wanted to get up early, then so be it. Her pillow was too soft and welcoming to follow his example. *Was that man serious?* She now heard a chainsaw. *How was she supposed to sleep with that racket?* There was nothing for it but to get up.

Dragging her dressing gown on, Cathy walked out of her bedroom to the small landing. Standing at the other bedroom door was Mark.

'Who the hell has a chainsaw going?' He yawned and stretched, then rubbed his forehead.

If Mark was up here, who was outside?

Luke. The lad was chopping up some of the timber that had been cleared, unaware of his two friends standing near a wall watching him, neither of them looking too happy. When he paused and stopped the saw, Mark roared over at him, 'Luke! What do you think you're doing?'

Luke turned and smiled. Placing the big saw down, he strolled over to them.

'Hey, sleepy heads, what's up?' A grin spread across his face.

'Do you realise how early it is, and it's a Sunday?' Mark's head was pounding. *Why had he agreed to go back to Sean's house after the pub?* Sean helped out at Cregane Court and had introduced Mark and Cathy to most of the village last night.

'How about we have some tea, and maybe you can explain why you've been missing for a week?' Cathy turned and led the way.

Inside, the trio sat around the table. Luke looked bothered, and Cathy prayed he hadn't changed his mind about staying at Cregane Court. She didn't want to push him, but if he was to be part of the house, then he had to show some responsibility.

'So, how were they in the city?' Mark asked. He appeared subdued and hadn't really said anything since they all came into the kitchen.

Cathy sensed tension between the two men and wondered if it was related in some way to the night of the housewarming party. She recalled being unable to find both of them when Roman O'Driscoll had made his entrance.

'All good. Sno really enjoyed being here. She misses you, Cathy.' Luke raised his head to look at his friend.

'She'll survive, I've no doubt,' she replied with a grin, though she, too, missed their evening chats.

'I met up with some old buddies,' he told them. 'It felt strange at first to be back in my old haunts, but to be honest, I took off with Sno because I felt closed in here. Sitting out at the campfire, seeing the stars, the air, it felt free. I know it probably sounds daft, but well… I guess I went back to the city to see if I was more suited to a life on the streets.'

Cathy had not thought of this, and by the shock on Mark's face, neither had he.

'And? Are you?' Mark held his breath.

'No.' He smiled, and both his friends nodded in approval.

'The house with just ourselves is grand, and I don't mind it. But with all your friends and family here, I felt out of place, a bit cramped, and I guess I panicked.' There was sadness in his voice.

'I understand. You did make a major decision in a short space of time. And anyway, do any of us really know each other?' Cathy spoke softly.

They all needed time to adjust, and for all his bravery on the streets, Luke might need longer to adjust most of all. She and Mark had made a joint decision, and they were both older than him. She reckoned the lad couldn't be more than twenty-four.

'Have you seen any more of that solicitor? He sure is some thug.' Luke eased in his chair more, now that the air had been cleared.

'No, thank God. Although my beloved sister,' Cathy pulled a face and the others laughed, 'turned up out of the blue, and got annoyed when I wouldn't drop all and entertain her. So, she went as fast as she came.' Cathy shrugged. She would never figure out who the real Gemma was.

'Oh, yeah, I saw her in the city one day. Having lunch. She's all false front, if you don't mind me saying. Acts the part, and that's about it.' Luke struggled to hide his irritation.

'Look, spending time talking about those two will not get our work done. So, how about we go outside and get stuck into some more clearing? Oh,' Mark looked at Luke, 'we must tell you about our find.' It was the most he had said this morning.

'What find?' Luke was curious.

'All shall be revealed.' Mark smiled. 'But first, Cathy, I think we both need to get dressed. No matter how comfortable your PJs are, they are really not work appropriate.'

'Yes, boss.' She scooted off the chair and went to her bedroom, leaving the two men at the kitchen table.

'Right, I'll go cut up some timber.' Luke stood and placed his cup down on the table.

'Luke, are we okay? I mean, is it the truth that you left because you were not comfortable living here? It wasn't me, was it?'

'No. No, it wasn't you.' With his head down, the young man headed out of the back door. There was something in the way he'd answered that niggled Mark. He wasn't convinced that the younger man had been totally honest.

Chapter Eighteen

Roman O'Driscoll was not a happy man. All the talk around Ballybawn was of how great the young people who lived in Cregane Court were. They had definitely created a buzz in the village. The sleepy community had needed something after the recession and the rural cutbacks of bank and post office closures. They didn't want their village to become a satellite town; they liked that the big city had not devoured their small corner of Ireland yet.

The solicitor though, had other plans, which had been unfortunately put aside by Elizabeth Sheldon dying. *Why had she outlived her husband?* Roman seethed. Archie had been easy to manipulate about parting with the surrounding land at the cottage. But not Elizabeth. She had taken an instant dislike to Roman, and had told him so on many occasions. But Roman had invested too much time and money not to see the project through.

Project Forest Green was his retirement fund, even though he was only thirty-eight years old. And he already had the financial and planning backing, even though he had not yet got the land – well, not all of it. Once Cregane Court was in his hands, building would commence almost immediately. The cottage and outbuildings would be flattened, and two sets of six-storey apartments would be born, with a tennis court, gym, and private gardens – a gated community, with a small security lodge at the entrance.

Roman's vision was to provide high-end living, with no scamps from the village strolling around. And, Forest Green would only be the start. Once people realised the standard of life it offered, the perfect place to live, he reckoned the demand would roll in for more developments. But getting the cottage was the issue. He was still angry with himself that Cathy and Mark's planning permission for the first outbuilding had slipped through unnoticed, so he would need to make a few phone calls to the local council and remind them of the favours owed to him. He didn't like sloppy work, nor those who forgot who looked after them.

If Cathy applied for any other planning permission, Roman wanted to be tipped off quickly so that he could ensure it would not get approval. But his top priority was to convince them to sell the cottage to him. Maybe that rude sister of hers could help without realising it. Roman would have to make a visit to the city.

• • • •

Sno couldn't shake off the restless feeling since returning from Ballybawn. She needed to speak with Cathy – and Luke – and talk over her thoughts and ideas. They had become quite the close little family, and having Luke accompany her on the bus back to the city had helped ease the loneliness that overwhelmed her when she left Cregane Court. She had scolded herself several times that it was daft to feel so unsettled after just one weekend, but she couldn't shake off the flustered feeling as she struggled to get through each working day. The bustle of the city, the dirt, and the uncaring way people behaved towards each other, had all started to come at her like a roaring train, ready to knock her off her feet.

Maybe she should contact Luke and see if he was coming into the city again soon, she thought. She wanted to talk more to him about how he had settled out in the village. *Was it as good as she wanted to believe it was, or was she fooling herself?* Cathy's turn of life had sparked Sno to take stock of her own. She had come to realise that our time on the planet was short, and each day made it shorter. And until she dealt with the issue, these deep thoughts would not go away.

• • • •

'Why, Cathy, how good to see you! Why didn't you tell me you were calling? I could have missed you.' Gemma ushered her sister into her sitting room. Compared to the small, cramped cottage, Gemma's home was huge.

'I had to bring in a few documents to the council so I took the chance you might be at home. How are the girls?' She sat on the deep sofa, the soft suede covering comforting and soothing.

'Wonderful. Their father is taking them to the cinema tonight. So why don't I go back with you to the cottage later, save you having to get a bus?'

'Would you not go with Paul and the girls? Have a family night out?'

'Listen, I'm at home with those girls day in day out, so it's good for them to spend time with Paul. That's settled so, I'll drive you back. Sure, why don't I go in with you altogether to the council offices and save you another trip out here after finishing with them?' Gemma didn't wait for an answer, but went straight upstairs to change.

Cathy sank back into the comfortable couch and groaned. *Why, oh why, did she always walk herself into stupid situations?*

• • • •

Sno shrieked with joy when Cathy pushed open the café door. She was thrilled at this unexpected visit and couldn't wait for her customer to finish her order so she could attend to Cathy. Gemma followed her sister and immediately sat with her back to Sno with no acknowledgement of the waitress. It was obvious that she didn't approve of her sister's friend and she wasn't willing to make an effort to make Cathy happy.

'Well, what brings you to this neck of the world?' Sno hugged Cathy and sat beside her, ignoring Gemma. *Two can play that game*, she decided. It was luck she had arrived early to start her shift. She could have missed this surprise pleasure.

'Just some cottage business. When will you be out to see us again?'

'I need to speak to you about that, Cathy, when you have some free time.' She gave a side glance at Gemma, then quickly asked the women for their order.

Cathy told her she would love some tea with one of her favourite muffins, while Gemma asked if she had any ground coffee or was it all instant. Sno said she could get her either, but Gemma opted for a glass of water. It was clear she didn't really trust the waitress to make a proper coffee.

• • • •

'You know, the drive to Ballybawn is not that long really, once you know the road. I could call out to you more often as the girls grow up; even stay a few weekends maybe.' Gemma liked the idea of telling people that her sister had a place in the country with land, but that it was really shared between them and she used it as a country house for weekends while Cathy chose to live there permanently. Of course, there was no need to tell Cathy of this little untruth.

'Yeah, why not? Once we have all the work done, of course,' Cathy insisted, her tone reflecting her seriousness.

'What are you actually doing to it?'

'Well, we're going to go with the artists' retreat idea. It really is ideal,' Cathy loved talking about the project, even with her sister. Not having to wait around for a bus was worth taking a life with Gemma. 'Once the large outbuilding is converted – you know, into four bedrooms, a kitchen and dining area, and two bathrooms – we will move along to the old hen-house area. We are going to call the big building, The Shed, and we have names for all the buildings.'

Gemma frowned, concentrating on the road. 'Where's the money coming from? I take it Lizzy didn't leave you a cash lump sum, did she?'

Cathy laughed. 'Oh no, we got a grant, as we qualified somehow. Mark took care of it, as he does all the finances. Plus, we both had some savings which we've used, and we are doing a lot of the work ourselves. Having local workmen helping out is great, too, and so much better than getting some big contractor in. We've noticed that since they have been included in the work and know what we are about, they seem really keen for us to succeed.' Cathy had come alive as she chatted about the plans for the future, and felt as though even her sister seemed impressed. Gemma seemed to soak up everything Cathy had to tell her.

When they arrived at Cregane Court, both women were laughing and in good form. Once inside, Cathy smelled something cooking from the kitchen. Mark had made a lasagne and there appeared to be plenty for everyone. After he'd had a quick shower, Luke joined them for the meal, then they all moved outside to sit beneath the apple trees, sipping wine, while Gemma had sparkling water.

The late evening was beautiful, with sunlight peeping through the leaves and the hungry buzz of bees as they popped from flower to flower. There was a lazy feel about; even the clouds, plump and curly, glided slowly above them. No-one and nothing appeared in a hurry.

'Had you a nice lunch last week, Gemma?' Luke asked.

Cathy knew he disliked her sister, but was grateful he was at least making an effort.

'Lunch? Erm, where was I?' She sounded unsure, stammering a little in answer.

'At the Coffee Bean, on Main Street. You were sitting near the window.'

'Was I alone? It's just that I go for lunch a lot, and I'm trying to think.' Her cheeks reddened and she sat forward in her chair.

'Well, you were when I saw you on, um, Wednesday afternoon, I think it was.'

Cathy realised her sister was uncomfortable with Luke knowing her whereabouts. When he winked at her, she realised he was enjoying having a little fun at Gemma's expense.

'Oh, I probably just popped in for a coffee. Nothing special.'

'Well, you sure dress up for something that isn't special. You looked wonderful. Are you sure you didn't have a secret date? Maybe next time I will have to pop in and join you. It's always nice to meet a friend.' He stood to leave. 'I'm calling it a night, I'm tired from all that dumping rubble today. See you in the morning. Night, Gemma, drive safely back to the city. And remember, next time I see you, we'll have a coffee.'

• • • •

Gemma put her glass down on the grass, coughed and gathered her bag. *That little shit had spotted her!* She didn't know how much he had seen, but from now on she would have to be careful. She and Roman would have to be careful.

Her mind was swirling with angry thoughts as she headed home. As a result, the drive back wasn't as pleasant as the journey out.

Chapter Nineteen

Luke knew he had rattled Gemma; it had been a long shot, but his remarks had definitely hit a raw nerve with her. She had been on her own when he saw her, but now he had doubts – sown by Gemma herself. He'd needed his week back in the city. Living away from the streets had become an ordeal, and not the smooth change he had expected it would be. Living at Cregane Court would work, though, as he loved being able to draw again, and to create. Cathy was right, this was a chance to be true to himself and there was so much for him to discover and learn. *And maybe, just maybe,* he thought, *Mark might be a part of that journey.*

• • • •

Cathy had put away the diary notebook she had found in amongst Lizzy's belongings, but she needed to go through it properly; something about it niggled her. The list upon list of figures intrigued her, along with the letters. Maybe reading it properly would reveal more. The day passed with her sorting out other boxes and trunks belonging to her great-aunt, and by the evening she was ready to take it easy. Luke was doing the cooking and had promised it would be simple but delicious. The aroma of garlic, mushrooms, and onions reached her in her bedroom, and teased her taste-buds.

Before heading downstairs, Cathy retrieved the notebook from her dressing table and quickly flicked through it. *It was a balance sheet,* she thought, *with outgoing and incoming amounts. But why was there so much writing, and lots of dates?* Lizzy's estate had not included any money. In fact, she and Mark had been forced to pay off a few small debts, because there hadn't been enough money in Lizzie's bank account to settle them. Yet this notebook listed figures in their thousands.

Maybe Mark would understand it; he was the finance expert. It was all so mysterious, and Cathy wondered again if there was more to her and Mark inheriting Cregane Court.

••••

'Wonderful, really good, Luke.' She smiled at her friend.

'Like I said, simple but good.' He was pleased that the meal had been appreciated. He didn't often get the chance to cook, but felt it should be approached in the same way as he would his art. Maybe he should think about cookery classes. Cregane Court was opening up so many possibilities for him, and it was all thanks to Cathy's kindness.

'Raise your glass, please. I would like to propose a toast,' he said, grinning at Cathy. They had just lifted their glasses when Mark walked in. 'Hey! You started without me!'

'Sshh, Luke wants to make a toast,' she admonished him. 'Go on.' Her smile was warm and encouraging.

'Nah, it's okay. Just being silly.' Luke's face darkened and he shifted his attention back to his dinner again.

Cathy looked at Mark, then at Luke. *Something was up between these two, she was sure. It wasn't the first time this awkwardness had raised its head.* 'Here, sit down, I'll fetch you a plate,' she said, breaking the weird atmosphere. 'This man knows how to cook. I think he's been holding out on us.' She laughed as Luke pretended to be hurt by her words, holding his chest as if a sword had pierced him.

'It's only a stew,' he mumbled.

'A stew with red wine, tender beef that is melt in the mouth, and tasty herbs and veg,' she insisted.

'Sounds good to me. Thanks, Luke, my turn to cook next, I think.' Mark stared at him, but Luke did not meet his eye.

••••

'Okay, there's definitely something to do with money going in and out. The letters beside each entry appear to be initials,' Mark explained. 'Look, AS and ES would be Archie and Elizabeth.' Mark was on the ball; finance was second nature to him. But there were other initials he didn't recognise, and the dates were strange – some were one after the other; others weeks apart.

'Of course, I could just be making a mountain from a molehill,' Cathy offered.

'Maybe, but it's interesting that all this money isn't accounted for, as in there are no notes about what the outgoing transactions are for, be it house maintenance, electricity, or other usual bills.' Mark flipped over the pages, frowning as he tried to make sense of them.

Luke sat over by the unlit stove. He was sketching. Charcoals placed beside him, he hummed quietly as he worked.

'Luke, did you see the plaque I found? William told me about it, and Mark and I are thinking of having a new one made,' Cathy spoke.

'Yes, I saw it wrapped in the newspaper.' He continued sketching while he spoke.

'Well, why don't you design one, and Mark can use his wood skills to carve it?'

Luke stopped and looked up at her, then at Mark. Both were looking back at him. 'Are you serious?' His eyes sparkled.

'Of course, you're the artist, Mark's the wood fellow, so it makes sense. Plus, I know this will be a hardship but...' Cathy paused for effect, 'you'll both have to work together.'

The two men shrugged.

'So, it's a deal then,' she said. 'Great stuff. Another job in Cregane Court taken care of. At this rate, all our work should be finished by the time I'm sixty.' She pulled a funny face and they all laughed. It had been a pleasant evening.

• • • •

Gemma was looking forward to her Friday meeting with Roman. *It was just a little harmless fun, nothing more*, she told herself. Pretending to being interested in buying a property was no crime. She and Paul were solid, but there was no spice any more. And Roman certainly paid her attention.

She gathered he was interested in her sister, but why was beyond her. Maybe he thought Cathy had money, since Cregane Court was undertaking so many transformations. But Gemma didn't mind. Having lunch with such a handsome man boosted her ego, and being seen with him gave credit to her story about their country residence which she liked to mention to the other school-gate mums.

Roman had many strings to his bow, it seemed. Solicitor, auctioneer, and investor, he had confided in Gemma. Most people knew him in his solicitor's role, which suited him, as he preferred to keep his business dealings private.

Gemma was so impressed with this intimate sharing that she felt like Roman O'Driscoll's trusted friend. If only Cathy showed some interest in the man, Gemma would be delighted to have him as a brother-in-law.

• • • •

'So, tell me. Cathy has great plans for Elizabeth's home. She certainly is a woman who knows what she wants.' Roman poured some wine for Gemma.

'You would think, but really her choices in the past have been very questionable.' Their table was in a secluded corner of an upmarket restaurant.

'Are you not being a bit harsh, Gemma?' There was genuine surprise in his voice.

'Well, Roman,' she replied, with a flirtatious look from under her lashes, 'it depends on what the choices are, wouldn't you agree?'

'The changes at Cregane Court may seem very ambitious, but they will definitely be a benefit to the wider community.' He moved his food around the plate, less interested in eating than gaining information about Gemma's sister.

'Yes, yes, of course, but it's not Cregane Court I'd be concerned with. More the type of people she keeps company with, if you understand me.' Gemma's quiet tone was almost conspiratorial.

'Ah now, now, Gemma. What naughty stories have you to share?' he chuckled, intrigued by whatever gossip she had to share. 'Mark is a lovely man: good job, reliable, what's there not to like?' He smirked, knowing he had made the right choice in winning Gemma's trust. It sounded like she had something worth knowing after all.

Chapter Twenty

Luke and Cathy continued tidying up the grounds at Cregane. The Shed was almost complete, and online shopping made life easier than travelling to and from the city for items to furnish it. By the time they had finished, the outhouse had been totally transformed. Luke had shown great flair when it came to choosing colours: calm greens, mellow tones of greys for the bedrooms, and a rich navy and white theme in the kitchen and dining area.

Cathy's phone bleeped.

Heading out tomorrow to Ballybawn. That okay? Need to talk over something with you, Sno x

'Hey, Luke! Sno's calling out tomorrow,' Cathy's voice showed her excitement at seeing her friend.

'She can be our first opinion on the place. I'm sure The Shed will meet with her approval. Any news on the planning permission for the hen-house and the orchard?' Luke walked over towards Cathy and moved a chair by a window to angle it, plumping up a cushion that was nearby and placing it on the chair.

'You really are into this, aren't you, Luke?' she chuckled.

'What do you mean?'

'Well, I know you see yourself as an artist, but what about interior design?'

'Yeah, sure!' He roared with laughter.

'Look, you've been the brains behind all this décor. It really is an extension of being an artist, pulling it all together, only on a different style of canvas.'

Luke shrugged. 'Maybe. Never thought of it like that before.'

'You never had a blank building to work with before either, I suspect.' Cathy placed a hand on the young man's shoulder to show she was serious.

'Well, it's thanks to you, Cathy. You've shown great trust and kindness to me that... well, I've not had before. I do appreciate it. It was... it was what I wanted to say to you the night of the toast.' Luke smiled shyly.

'So why didn't you? I love my ego being boosted.' Cathy bowed in a playful gesture.

'Guess, I'm the sensitive type. Anyway, I've said it now.' He reached out and hugged her. 'Thank you, Cathy, for giving me a chance.'

• • • •

Sleeping with her curtains open allowed Cathy to see the stars, and it was a beautiful sight when the skies were clear. A lot had happened since April: moving to the country; adapting the large outhouse; making new friends in the village. Even Gemma seemed bearable somehow. Cuddled beneath her duvet, she recalled Luke's words of gratitude. Yet all she had done was brought him something to eat way back when they went to the café where Sno worked.

A small fire of satisfaction glowed inside her. She liked helping people. She had an empathy towards others and got the sense of a person when speaking to them. Gut instinct – that was it. Maybe sensing what was good in a person was her thing. Her gift. *Could she use Cregane Court to her own benefit? What was the fancy term they used nowadays? Ah yes, life-coach, that was it.*

She could maybe source online classes and retrain; Luke wasn't the only one who would grow and blossom. *Yes,* she told herself, *Cathy Reed would, too. And Elizabeth's home would be where it all happened.* Her eyes closed to the words of a Bon Jovi song, '*It's my life, it's now or never...*' and slipping into her dream was William at his garden gate, mixed with the rock and roll song.

• • • •

Roman saw a way to stop Cathy's runaway celebrity status in Ballybawn. His lunch with Gemma had been more fruitful than he could have hoped for. But to put his plan into place, he needed to wait. His contact in the planning office had informed him of a new application for Cregane Court, and a quiet word – sweetened with a financial tip – had seen the application refused.

He would get Elizabeth's home yet. Patience, and a few more lunches with Gemma, and he would have enough information to discredit Cathy Reed and Mark Daniels.

••••

'Well, what do you think?' Sno sat cross-legged on the sofa, her face lit with excitement. She longed to hear what Cathy and Luke thought of her plans, but so far both had remained quiet. Doubtful, even.

'Have you found premises for this new venture of yours?' Luke asked.

'Well, no, not yet. There is a place over the corner shop in Ballybawn, which would be a start. What do you think, Cathy?' The excitement in her voice was starting to waver.

Cathy listened to Sno's reply to Luke and was pleased her friend had done her homework. 'It's good you've not got a place,' she told Sno.

'Pardon? How is that a good thing?' Sno repositioned herself on the sofa and stretched her legs before her.

'Because... why not use here?' Cathy shrieked and jumped up to hug Sno.

Luke burst out laughing, but Sno shook her head, looking confused.

'It makes sense,' Cathy explained. 'The more talent we can showcase and sell, hopefully it will draw others of like minds. We have Luke, artist/designer; Mark, a carpenter and financial wizard;

Sno, crochet/knitting, crafts in general; and me to pull it all together.'

'Excuse me, Luke a designer?' Sno twirled to face the young man.

He laughed again. 'Yep, I'm going to look into it. Her idea, mind you.' He pointed at Cathy.

'He has done a fantastic job on, The Shed. When you see it, you'll totally agree.' Cathy smiled, then continued 'Plus, I was thinking about something Luke said to me, and now with you saying I've inspired you to take a look at your life, Sno, I'm thinking of training as a life-coach.' She paused. 'Madness, or a good idea?'

'Good idea for definite.' Luke offered.

Sno nodded. 'Yes. But what about your own writing?'

'On the back burner for now, I guess.' Cathy was thrilled at her friends' reaction. 'How about we celebrate tonight when Mark gets home? We can tell him our plans and see what else we can come up with.'

Cathy's heart filled with happiness. She was loving the changes that Lizzy's cottage had made to her life. It oozed magic, and Ballybawn was essential to its success. Her family might be limited to Gemma, but it was her friends who made her life content.

• • • •

Mark strode in with a face like thunder. Without a nod or a greeting, he stalked past the trio in the sitting room, instantly deflating the mood in the house. The buzz and excitement of all their plans and hopes of earlier suddenly fell flat. Cathy anxiously followed him upstairs to ask what was wrong.

'Just give me a minute, okay?' He slammed the bedroom door.

Stunned at his behaviour, she turned on her heel and left him. 'It's probably work,' she told the others quietly. 'I know he gets stressed now and then.'

'If he's not happy at work, why not leave?' Sno shrugged her shoulders. 'Simple.'

'Not so simple, Sno. Mark's not like that,' Cathy told her. 'He takes his position seriously. There are people depending on him to get the company figures balanced each month so that they get paid. He can't just up and leave.' She poured a glass of wine. *Why was she defending him?* She wondered.

'Unlike me, you mean.'

'What? No! I don't mean that at all.' Cathy replied immediately.

'What you're saying is, I can afford to up and leave my job because, after all, I'm only a waitress, unlike the great King Mark up there.' Sno gestured to the ceiling, 'Sure, anyone can make a coffee or a tea, but then it's not a job you need brains for.'

'Hey, calm down, ladies,' Luke interrupted. 'No-one is saying anything of the sort, Snowflake. Cathy didn't mean it like that at all.' He poured a glass of wine and handed it to her.

'No thanks, I'm going home.' She searched for her bag and walked to the door in a strop. 'Of course you'd stick up for Cathy. After all, she saved you from the streets, you're her pet project.' The words were spat across the room.

'What? Snowflake!' Cathy shouted. 'That's nonsense.' The door was slammed closed, leaving Luke and Cathy together in the sitting room. He took a gulp of wine from the glass in his hand.

'What the hell was that about?' he asked, puzzlement etched on his face. Neither made an effort to go after her; they were both still shocked. Just five minutes earlier, they had been laughing and sharing a glass of wine.

'No idea. Luke. And you're not, you know. She's just angry about something and we obviously missed what it is.' Cathy sighed, troubled.

'I'm not what?'

'My pet project.'

'I know. Like you say, she's angry.' He lifted his glass. 'Cheers to friends; crazy ones included.' They clinked glasses and drank their wine. Sno wouldn't have gotten far; it was late, she would need to walk to the village, and there were no evening buses to the city. Cathy was certain she would walk back in the door soon enough.

• • • •

'Care to explain last night?' Cathy was in the kitchen frying some eggs and bacon, the fat from the meat hissing and spitting in the heat. She shook the pan gently and tossed a teacloth onto the worktop.

'Nope, nothing to explain.' Mark pushed bread into the toaster and then grabbed the orange juice from the fridge.

'Well, I think there is. You came home in a foul mood, upset the happy one we had here, and banged a door in my face.' Cathy flipped the eggs.

'Sorry about the door.'

'And?'

'And we're not married, so stay out of it.' He downed his orange juice.

'Mark, come on. What happened? It's not like you to be a jerk.'

'You don't want to know, Cathy, okay?' Hurriedly, he buttered the toast and plonked the empty glass into the sink.

'Try me.'

'Look, just leave it be. Where's Luke and Sno?' He took the buttered toast and went to leave.

'Outside, and gone, in that order,' she snapped in reply. Two could play this game. 'About Sno,' she said, 'I would like to offer her a place here to showcase her crafts. She's planning on leaving the café and I suggested she move here.'

'Fine by me. Go for it.' His attitude reflected his indifference.

She listened to his car leaving. Something was not right, and she was determined to find out tonight when he returned. *Had Luke something to do with Mark's dark mood? What had happened between those two? And where in the hell had Sno got to?* She had not returned, even though both Cathy and Luke had phoned her relentlessly.

• • • •

Luke had rented a ride-on lawnmower and was going to mow the front lawns. At present they were large squares of green, with no flower beds or shrubs. It was easy to keep them trimmed, but Cathy wanted to plant some small trees – something both men had found amusing when she mentioned it. *'More trees? Are you serious?' Luke's laughter had reached the clouds, filling the sky at such a suggestion. 'He's right, Cathy. Any more trees and it will have to be named Cregane Forest.' Mark had done his best not to laugh too much.* So, for now, the front lawns were green, trimmed, and as smooth as a billiard table.

Since there was nothing of importance for her to undertake today, she decided to visit William, leaving Luke to drive around the lawns with his headphones on, his body jerking to whatever music played in his ears.

Chapter Twenty-One

'Hello, anyone home?' Cathy stood by the open door and called out.

'Why, come in. Come in and welcome. I was having a shave.' William extended a hand in greeting and Cathy shook it warmly. He held his razor in his other hand, and had a towel thrown around his shoulders. A radio was on at a low level in the room. After greeting each other, the old man retreated to the bathroom and Cathy heard the slosh of water in the basin.

'If it's a bad time, I can call back,' she shouted.

'Not at all, girleen. Wait now 'till I put the kettle on.' William returned without the towel, and busied himself with filling the kettle and placing cups and side plates on the table. 'So, how's it all going up in Lizzy's old home, as you call her?' A warm smile lit the man's face.

'Good. Nothing to report really. The large outhouse is completed and looks great. We now call it, The Shed. And we've submitted the planning permission for the other outbuildings.' She allowed the old man to set the table. This was his home, and if he needed help, he would ask. William struck her as an independent and private man, and she was not going to push her help on him unless needed.

'Have you been into Ballybawn lately?' he asked.

'No, William, not for a couple of weeks now.' She noticed that he paused, as if he was going to say something but decided against it. The teapot was set before them, and he poured them each a cup. 'A great cup of tea, thanks, William.'

'Ah, the secret is the loose leaf, not that dust bag they throw boiling water on.' He winked.

'So, what have you been up to since I last saw you rocking it up to Meatloaf in the pub?'

'Who? Oh, you're talking about the music, I presume. A load of noise, but to each their own. Live and let live is my motto.'

'A good one to have, too.' Cathy sipped the remains of her tea.

'Ah, girleen, not everyone agrees with us. There's many in this town that like to think they know best above everyone else, and won't take no for an answer. They're right, and that's that.'

'Guess those people are everywhere,' Cathy agreed, a picture of her sister immediately springing to mind. 'Still, Ballybawn has given us a great welcome, so friendly.'

'Have they now? Good to know. But don't take it for granted.' William lit up his pipe and sat back on his fireside chair, his cap not far from his hand, placed nicely on a chair nearby.

A strange thing to say, thought Cathy, as she looked around her. The lace curtains were clean and in good condition. The fire was already lit, even though the day outside was pleasant. On the far wall was a picture of the Sacred Heart, with a red lamp lighting beneath it – a staple in older homes in Ireland. A dinner was bubbling on the cooker in the kitchen, its enticing smell making her stomach grumble. The television was hung on a wall, and dotted around the room were photos of old Irish Republicans of 1916 and the War of Independence, and a framed copy of the Irish anthem – the words in black print, clear and encased behind shining clean glass.

The old man noticed her looking at the photos on the wall.

'Ah, they don't make them like Pearse and Barry anymore.' William puffed on his pipe before removing it from his mouth and tapping it on the timber arm of his chair.

'We can and should learn from our past, I believe, yet time moves on, William.'

'Yerrah, yes and no, yes and no.' He coughed, and his armchair shook with the effort.

'Do you need some water?' Cathy stood up.

'No, but since you're standing, would you turn off the gas beneath my pot of bacon and cabbage, please? Wouldn't do to have it burn. '

'It smells lovely.'

'I'm of the old ways, girleen. I like my dinner at one o'clock in the day, not at sunset when it's time to be thinking of closing up for the evening.'

'Are you going into the village later?' Cathy sorted the cooker and returned to the sitting room.

'Might do. Don't you mind any stories you'll hear, okay? Some folk are just nasty.' William looked serious as he spoke.

'What stories?'

'Never mind. Just ignore them is my advice. People don't half want to spread gossip.'

'Such as?' But he wouldn't be drawn any further, and Cathy left his house wondering what he meant. Both William and Mark seemed to be holding back on her. It was all so strange.

• • • •

Mark was home by the time Cathy returned. She had continued into the village after leaving William's home, but didn't hear any stories. In fact, the bakery staff greeted her with warmth when she purchased chocolate cream doughnuts. While strolling home, she thought that maybe she hadn't heard any stories because the stories were about her, and who would be brave enough to ask her outright what they wanted to know? A slight thump of a headache hit her temples as she entered the cottage, and she placed the buns in the fridge and then opted to go and sit in the orchard. It really was a beautiful place to relax, with the rustle of the trees, the view of the fields, and so much beauty around.

The evening air was crisp. No breeze, just quiet, clean air, not even birdsong. Her headache seemed to sense the peace and slowly began to disappear. But she could not help thinking it might be the calm before the storm. William knew something and wasn't sharing, Mark's behaviour was decidedly odd, and Sno had not answered her calls. There was definitely something up, and she could feel a slight stirring of fear in the pit of her stomach.

She stretched her hands above her head and her legs out before her, forcing a good pull along her spine. *How could she think life would sail by without some hitch?* Cregane Court was blissful, but she was not foolish enough to think there weren't hidden thorns.

As she looked around her, the peaceful setting cheered her heart. She could see its potential and that was what she would focus on. Nothing else mattered but getting the retreat off the ground. She closed her eyes, imagining the whole place alive, buzzing, and all the joy and love and work that would be created here. The soft pad of footsteps drawing near made her sit up and check who was joining her. Mark. And he didn't look happy.

'We need to talk, Cathy.'

'Do we have to? You don't look too happy.'

'Well, it's not all bad, but look, there's no nice way to say this. But, Luke...' He left the name hanging in the air.

'Luke?' Cathy recalled the awkwardness between the two men. *Had they rowed?* She knew she had invited Luke to live at the cottage without discussing it with Mark, but she thought that had been cleared. *Had she overstepped their friendship by not including Mark?*

'I'm sorry. I know I should have asked you first, and the same with Sno. But both were spur of the moment thoughts and, well, I got worked up with excitement about getting him off the streets to live here.'

'It's not that, that was ages ago.' Mark shook his head. 'I like Luke. He has been an amazing help here and he sure earns his keep.'

'So, what is it then?' She waved her arms in frustration.

'The stories.' His face was taut, anger pulling down on his lips and his forehead wrinkled with displeasure.

Again with the stories; first William, now Mark. Cathy shook her head in disbelief.

"It's around the village that we are housing homeless people who have mental issues or addictions. That we are sneaking them into the community under pretence of a retreat centre. That it is more a halfway house we will be running. And that, that is the real reason we are doing up the place.'

Cathy was shocked. 'But the people know him. How did they even know Luke was homeless? Not that it should matter. Is this what has you upset? These stories?' She stood up, placing her hands on her hips and shaking her head.

'Yeah, look, maybe he told people himself. And Snowflake. Well, her appearance – shaved head, tattoos, and piercings – will add to the over-exaggerated gossip.'

'So, there's tales around the village. I'm sure it will die down as fast as it reared its ugly head.' She silently prayed she would be proven right. 'Are you regretting Sno being invited to join us?' She needed things to be clear between them.

'No, and it's not that simple. An objection to our planning permission for over there,' he gestured towards the hen-run, 'has been lodged with the council.' Mark shook his head. He really hated the small-mindedness of people, and disgust simmered inside him. He wished people would get on with their own lives and leave others be. His eyes clouded over as the annoyance bubbled up some more.

'So, we might not get any more planning permission? Which means we can't develop the cottage and land any further?' Cathy saw that Mark was struggling to keep his anger at the news under control. 'How did you hear about these stories?' she asked.

Mark sighed. 'At work. One of the lads lives in Ballybawn and asked me was it true we were going to rehome homeless people and nut-jobs. He blatantly told me that! And many others were not happy about that sort of people living near their village. Homeless, druggies, and mental nutters.'

'Nutters? Is that me?' She tried to make light of the issue, but the comment fell flat.

'This is no laughing matter, Cathy. I can't afford to be associated with gossip like this. I hold an important position, and if the company's clients got a hold of this nonsense, it wouldn't be good.'

'Look, you've just called it gossip and nonsense, so relax. It will die down.'

'I wish I had your confidence.' The two of them stood in silence, the seriousness of what was going on settling between them. Even the peace of the land around them could not soothe the disappointment that had raised its head.

'So, what should we do?' Cathy didn't think it was such a big deal, but she needed to keep her thoughts under wraps, as Mark seemed to think it was.

'Well, we can appeal the planning application, find out if there's a link between that and the talk about Luke and Sno.' Sighing, he turned on his heel and made to go inside.

'Mark, what if we don't get the planning, and there is a link? What then?' Cathy walked after him, catching his arm.

'I don't know, Cathy. Maybe cancel the retreat idea? Maybe sell the cottage? I don't know.'

'But we can't sell.' Her eyes widened with shock.

'Remember what Roman O'Driscoll said, there's always a way.'

Cathy stood still and watched Mark leave. Alone in the orchard, she felt tears spring to her eyes. Surely Mark was over-reacting? *A good night's sleep and it won't look so bad then*, she told herself. She looked up at the early night sky; dark navy clouds were gathering over the fields. The stillness she felt earlier was present, even though the storm had rolled into town for both her and Mark. She decided to call it a day and go to bed. Her mind was in turmoil, there was so much to think about and sort. Climbing the stairs, she heard Luke moving around in his room below. He must have come home while she and Mark were speaking in the orchard. Had he heard any of their conversation? She would know more in the morning.

Her sleep over the past few nights had been broken and troubled. Dreams of William, her father, even Gemma, had a sinister darkness in them. William – what did he know? Had he tried to tell her something today? She needed to call again, and this time ask him what it was he meant about stories. And selling Cregane Court? Wouldn't Roman O'Driscoll just love that? The old man had certainly been right this morning when he said people could be nasty.

• • • •

Mark lay on his bed. The large floor-to-ceiling window gave him a scenic view of the grove of trees. Tonight, not a branch moved. Here he was, thirty-two and co owner of a property. How quickly things happen in life. Back in April, he never knew Cathy Reed existed, let alone Luke or Sno! Now he mixed in a different circle, with lazy evenings, busy weekends, cleaning and gardening around the cottage. *Why did Elizabeth put him and Cathy together?*

The stupid stories about what they were up to didn't really bother him, nor the failure of planning permission. No, it was what was happening within himself that concerned him. He was changing. Different. A part of him that had lain low was now coming to the surface. Mark Daniels knew that from the moment he met Luke, he had fallen in love.

Work had changed, too. The stuffy, predictable daily routine was beginning to grind him down, while the cottage had shown him a different pace to life. In fact, life before Cregane Court had been black and white and safe. Now it was in glorious colour, with bright, strong, delightful tones and shades. Mark was feeling alive for the first time ever. But while it might be a changing and modern Ireland, he knew there were still some issues that scared people. Parts of the country needed to change, and stop treating those that brought these issues to their quiet village as the enemy.

He regretted snapping at Cathy. He hadn't meant it when he told her that they should sell the cottage. Coming home each evening was a pleasure. There was always some news about what had been added or painted, or who had dropped by. Sharing the house with his former housemates had been like existing; Cregane Court had him living! He heard Cathy walk across the carpeted landing in her bedroom and couldn't help smiling. He liked her. She was a good person, and such a contrast to her sister, Gemma. He certainly couldn't possibly imagine sharing a home with *her*!

And then there was Luke. *Did he have a future with the young man?* Mark wondered. *Or was he just a casual fling for the blond man with the piercing green eyes?* He had been unfair to Luke as well. On the night of the housewarming party, a few beers had given him the courage to flirt with Luke, and he'd been thrilled when Luke flirted back. When they had got the chance to sneak away into the darkness to share a kiss, it had been magical. But then Roman O'Driscoll had turned up.

Mark sighed. That man was trouble, for sure.

Chapter Twenty-Two

The next few days in Ballybawn and Cregane Court passed without much activity. Cathy deliberately went into the small village to see if she would meet any of the story-spreaders, but no-one approached her. The lady in the bakery was her usual happy self. One or two locals did look sideways at her, but nothing was said. Maybe she had been right; maybe the gossip had blown over, after all.

Back at the cottage, though, life was too quiet. Luke and Mark seemed to be avoiding each other's company, and when they were together with her, she sensed that unease of before. *Was she really imagining it, or was she just losing her marbles altogether?*

'I'm thinking of going in to see Sno tomorrow. Do you want to come with me, Luke?'

'No, I've started working on some designs for the new plaque, so I'll skip it,' he replied. 'But do say hello to her for me. Have you heard from her at all?'

'Not a word. She's not answering my texts or messages.' Cathy shrugged. 'I might stay at Gemma's overnight and kill two birds with the one stone, as they say.' She put down the book she was reading and stretched her body. She would go for a long soak in the bath and leave early in the morning on the first bus.

'Gemma? Gosh, you are brave.' Luke grinned. 'I hope Sno is okay, though. She's not been in touch with me either, but I guessed she wants some space, so I let it be. Maybe I *should* go with you.' Luke put down the TV remote he held; there was nothing on television worth his time.

'Well, as far as Gemma is concerned, it's better if I visit her, otherwise she will be out here visiting us,' Cathy told him. 'And Sno? Well, something must have upset her, and I want to see if I can help. Right,' she got up from her seat, 'I'm going for a long hot bath, so the bathroom is out of bounds for the next hour.' She started towards the bathroom when Mark walked into the sitting room. 'Hey there. How was your day?' She paused at the doorway.

'Not bad, how about you?'

'Just been telling Luke that I'm heading in to meet Sno tomorrow and staying overnight with Gemma.'

When Mark raised his eyebrows in surprise at Gemma's name, Luke laughed.

'Stop it you two. She's not all bad.' Cathy smiled despite herself. 'Anyway, while I'm away, please don't go fighting with each other, and do keep the place in order. No wild parties without me, okay?' Cathy wagged a finger at them both, as if she were scolding naughty children.

'Yes, Mammy, we promise,' Mark spoke in a baby voice.

'Hey, I'm not that much older than you, you cheeky monkey,' she chuckled.

'But you ARE older.' He laughed then ducked down as he saw a towel sail through the air towards him. Cathy missed with her shot, but their interaction had brought a light, happy feeling in the atmosphere.

As Luke and Mark looked at each other, something passed between them. Cathy was sure of it, but it was so fleeting she couldn't pin it.

• • • •

She pushed at the door of the café. It was busy with those on early morning breaks, buying the fresh sandwiches-to-go and women taking a well-earned coffee after doing their shopping. Cathy spotted an empty seat and sat down. She would wait for the rush to be over to speak with Sno. People came and went, and it was then she realised that her friend was not serving. *Must be on a break,* she thought. But time went by, and the waitress serving behind the counter came out to clear some tables.

'Excuse me, is Sno working today?' Cathy asked.

'Sno does the evening shift.' The girl looked at Cathy, waiting to see if she was going to order.

Cathy thanked the girl and left. *What had she been thinking?* She knew Sno worked evenings, so there was no reason why she would be here now. *Why was she so rattled and not thinking straight?* She pulled out her mobile and found her sister's number. 'Hey, Gemma. I was going to pop in for a chat, does it suit?' People swarmed around her as she huddled by a doorway to hear her sister speaking.

'Cathy, where are you? Are you in the city?' Gemma spoke in hushed tones.

Cathy held the phone tighter, trying to hear her sister. 'Yes, at Sno's café. Why? Are you near here? We can meet. Tell me where and I will come to you.'

'Erm, no, no, I'll come to you...' '*Here now... put her off*' 'Okay, I am on my way to you, bye.'

Gemma had hung up before Cathy got to answer, but she could swear she'd heard someone speaking in the background. She sighed. Probably one of her sister's school-gate friends, and Cathy would certainly not be good enough to join that brigade. She went back inside the café. When the young girl stared at her, Cathy smiled and gestured to the table and sat down.

'Are you ordering this time?' the girl asked.

'I'll have a tea, please, and a scone with cream and jam. No hurry, I'm waiting for someone to join me.'

The waitress shrugged and went about arranging menus in a folder. She certainly took Cathy's words to heart about being no hurry, as she then brushed the floor and put out extra napkins on the counter before she finally made a pot of tea for Cathy.

'Ah, there you are.' Gemma swept through the door in true diva fashion. She inspected the chair before she sat, and wiped some crumbs off. 'Why didn't you tell me you were going to be in the city?'

Gemma placed her bag on the free chair beside her, having glanced at the floor first.

'Good to see you, too.' Cathy replied.

'Well, I'm busy. You were lucky I could meet you now. So, what brings you in?'

'Do you want anything?'

'No, no, I've just eaten. Well, maybe a coffee, black.'

Cathy went up to collect her order and ordered Gemma's coffee. Once they had been served, the two sisters sat and chatted. It was small talk at first: how Ava and Lily were doing, how Paul was, and the weather.

'So, you still haven't told me why you are in the city,' Gemma persisted.

'I came in to see Sno and was hoping to stay with you to catch up, but now that I've met you, sure I can go home this evening.' Cathy munched on the scone, savouring the sweetness of the jam and cream on the crumbled bun.

'You can still stay,' Gemma replied haughtily. 'It's nice for the girls to see you. So, how is Sno? I don't see her here.'

'Sure, I clear forgot she works evenings. Honestly, I don't know what I was thinking.' Cathy paused. 'Who was with you when I phoned? Sounded like you were talking to someone.'

'Just a friend.' Gemma was staring out the café window, but she coloured slightly, like a naughty schoolchild caught copying.

Cathy followed her gaze and gasped. Roman O'Driscoll was striding by, briefcase in hand, swerving between the crowds.

'Oh, that's enough to put me off the rest of my bun,' Cathy groaned.

'Cathy, that's not nice!' Gemma snapped. 'He's not that bad. Handsome, actually.'

'He is a creep.' Cathy stuck out her tongue as if he made her sick. 'Well, I'm glad he didn't spot us,' she continued.

'Roman wouldn't come into a cheap place like this,' Gemma scoffed.

'Roman? Are you and him that friendly then?' Cathy enquired with a raised eyebrow.

'Stop it. Let's go home. I've the girls to pick up soon from school.'

'One question before we go. How did you know Luke was homeless before?'

'He told me. The night of the housewarming, why? Is he causing trouble?' Her eyes hardened and looked almost threatening – enough to send a shiver up Cathy's spine.

• • • •

The information Gemma had shared with Roman had been gold, and it didn't take him long to drop a few doubts around the village about Cregane. People privately didn't want the cheap or troubled sort of people in their neighbourhood, no matter what they said in public. Adding a bit here and there to Luke's story, and throwing doubt on Sno's background, had livened up Roman O'Driscoll's day for him. His morning coffee in the village café had provided him with the perfect opportunity to sow the seeds of all sorts of trouble if Cregane was to go ahead. And it was easy for the gossips to believe his words; after all, he'd handled the late Elizabeth's will, so he had inside knowledge.

Like the seeds of dandelions, his words had blown into Ballybawn's sky, landing on each and every doorstep and windowsill. Once planted in the minds of those looking for something to entertain them, he needed to do no more. Whisper after whisper flowed, and even he was surprised what he heard back after a few days of starting the rumours. *Oh, the joys of gossip and small-mindedness,* he couldn't help thinking with a smirk that evening. Even his chat this morning with Gemma had been productive, and it was just a pity her sister had phoned and disturbed them. Still, the way Ballybawn was stirring up questions against Cregane's plans, it wouldn't be long before the future would turn difficult for Cathy and Mark. Then he would flounce in and offer to take the troubled cottage and land off their hands.

It would be a win-win situation for them all. Mark and Cathy would get some money, and he would get what he wanted for his building investment. Roman was convinced Forest Green would see the light of day, after all.

Chapter Twenty-Three

After an office meeting, a guy from the village had approached Mark again, asking about the gossip. It brought on a headache, and Mark decided enough was enough for one day and headed home early. He decided he'd do something for himself, get out in the air and turn some wood. He spent a lot of his spare time now whittling or carving, and it always soothed him. He loved the feel of the timber in his hands, the different textures and colours as he changed a hunk of wood from a lump without shape into an admired piece of art.

'Hello!' he called out to an empty house. He knew Cathy had gone to the city, but he'd thought Luke might be around. It seemed as though Mark was on his own. Changing from his work suit, he put on some jeans and a soft knit jumper then headed out to an outhouse where he stored his tools and offcuts of timber. He turned on some music from his phone, picked some gorgeous oak that he had found, and set to work. Wearing gloves, one hand held the knob to the front of the smoothing plane, and his other rested on the raised back of the tool. With firm gentle strokes, he stripped it down until it was smooth. He was thinking about the new plaque for Cregane Court. This wood would be beautiful for it, rich and strong, but he'd first need to ask Luke about the design, size, etc. He set the oak aside and picked up another piece instead.

'Turn that off, it's awful!' Luke stood in the workshop doorway.

'Hey, where have you been?' Delight rose inside Mark at the sight of the young man.

'Been to the village for some milk and bread. Had an interesting conversation with a few locals. Not the nice kind of conversation, I mean.' Luke leant against the frame, his eyes dull.

'Oh, care to share? I'm about to take a break anyway, and I need to talk to you about the plaque.' Mark didn't like to see Luke look troubled, and had to fight the urge to go over and give the younger man a hug.

'Yeah, let's have a coffee. Why are you home early?'

'I'm guessing the same issue you spoke about at the village.' Mark pulled off his protective gloves and threw them on the workbench, then he followed Luke across the yard and into the cottage. The kitchen was quiet after the noisy music that had filled the outhouse.

'So, tell me what happened.' Mark placed two cups of coffee on the table while Luke reached into the cupboard and brought out some chocolate biscuits.

'I was standing outside the Post Office and this old fellow came up and said straight out, "We don't want your kind here." I looked around then asked him if he was speaking to me. He said he was, and that I should clear back to the streets where I came from.' Luke bit into a biscuit and then stared at Mark. 'Now, tell me how that has got anything to do with you being home early.'

Sighing, then taking a deep breath, Mark placed his hands around the hot cup of coffee. 'Where do I start? It seems there have been some stories in the village that we are starting up a place for the homeless and people with mental health issues, and some of the locals are not too happy.'

Luke jumped up angrily. 'You're not serious!'

'Sit down. It's only gossip. Somehow, though, you've been dragged into it because of your past. Snowflake, too. But it's all a storm in a teacup,' he soothed. 'It will blow over.'

Luke paced the kitchen, anger flashing in his green eyes, then he turned and hit out at the table with his fist.

Mark jumped. 'Stop it, Luke. It's gossip, nothing more.'

'What has this got to do with your work?' Luke was clearly struggling to calm down.

'A guy I work with is from Ballybawn, and he's been asking me questions. I just felt like a half day, so I came home.' He rubbed his forehead, the headache threatening to return.

'How will we tell Cathy?' Luke's flush of anger was receding, and he looked anxious, knowing his friend would be hurt by the stories.

'She knows, and she's okay about it. You know that woman, nothing gets to her. She's the glue to hold us together.' Mark gave a feeble laugh, but Luke did manage to smile.

'Why hasn't she said anything then?'

'Like I just said, you know her. She's the one who convinced me not to worry about it. It's just narrowmindedness, that's all.'

'So, you were concerned that it could be more?' Luke asked.

'Well, it's probably a coincidence, but the planning for the other chalets was refused the same week I heard about the stories, and, well...' Mark shrugged his shoulders, then grabbed his cup and headed to the sink. 'It appears someone or some people are out to derail our plans for the retreat.'

• • • •

Luke walked out to the sitting room and started preparing a fire. The autumn evenings were chilly, and the nights drew in earlier each evening. September was a month that started the turn of the year for many. He went outside and brought some coal and more timber, then built it up and lit the kindling, and soon the flames were dancing in bright orange and amber colours. Their shadows cast odd-shaped figures across the room, and Luke sat deep in thought.

Cathy had given him a chance to make something of himself, and here he was causing her trouble. Staring into the flames, he wondered if leaving would be best. Perhaps then the stories would stop, and she and Mark would not be burdened by his presence upsetting any further plans for Cregane. His heart thudded at the thought of Mark's name. There was a connection between them; something he...

they... needed to clear up. That shared kiss had meant more than just a kiss, and he'd felt at home in the other man's arms. If only that bloody solicitor hadn't turned up and ruined the party. Leaving here would mean not seeing Mark every day, and he would be back living on the streets. The door to his parents had been closed firmly to him some years before, especially when they realised their son was gay. It was the twenty-first century, but even with all the progression in Ireland, some still frowned on how the gay community were making their presence known.

Luke's mind was made up. Although he didn't want to, he would leave the day after next, when Cathy was back. He would explain that since he was at the heart of the hassle for Cregane Court moving forward, it was better for him to leave. Cathy's kindness did not deserve to suffer because of him. He at least had to see if all this grief for Cathy and Mark would stop if he was out of the picture. No matter how much they said it was only gossip, people clearly still felt strongly enough to confront him with their concerns in the village.

'You look troubled. Want to share?'

Luke had not noticed Mark standing close to the sofa.

'Here.' Mark offered him a beer, and the young man took it and smiled.

'I was just thinking. I was going to wait until Cathy returned, but I think it best if I leave.' Luke raised his hand in protest when he saw Mark was about to speak. 'Let me continue. It might be gossip and nothing more... it might be, but what if it doesn't stop there? What if it escalates and others agree, or as they say, it grows legs? I don't want to be the one to stop Cathy's dreams coming true, or yours. It has to be nipped in the bud, and if that means I leave, then that's what I'll do.' He took a long slug of the cool beer, feeling better for having his thoughts out in the open.

Mark remained quiet. He walked around the sofa and sat opposite Luke in an armchair by the window. The view out over the rolling fields was picturesque, nature at its best; the pink glow of the evening sky deepening as the day began to close down.

'So that's it. That's what you are going to do?' Mark finished his beer and placed the bottle on the side table. The room was bathed in firelight, and the silence of the house blanketed the two men as they each considered the idea of Luke leaving.

'I know you might think I'm being hasty, but Cathy's kindness to me does not deserve her to suffer over me being here.' Luke broke the comforting spell of the cottage.

'What about me?'

'You? I... I'd miss you.' His eyes reflected his shy nature when it came to Mark.

'I'd miss you, too,' Mark whispered, holding his breath.

'Mark... are... are you... I mean, are you involved with anyone?' Luke stuttered nervously.

'No. Why?'

'Well, it's just that since the party, well, you've not mentioned anything, and I thought that what happened had maybe been a mistake on your part after too many beers.'

'Luke... God, no. I thought I might... look, it wasn't because of a few beers. I wanted to kiss you that night and I...' He paused and ran his hand through his hair. 'Why does this feel so awkward?'

Luke laughed. 'We're like two schoolkids.' He paused, then added quietly, 'I like you, Mark.'

'Me, too. I mean, I like you, too. Can we start again? Please don't leave. You being here is great. Cathy won't let you leave anyway, and you can't say no to her.'

The smile playing on the older man's lips looked enticing to Luke. He liked the way Mark's mouth parted slightly when he smirked. His blue eyes were more lavender than real blue, and his fine knit jumper stretched over his strong forearms and firm chest. Luke knew he was drawn to Mark like never before.

'Hey, you're deep in thought. Care to share?' The older man moved close to him, the light scent of sweat from his earlier work mixing with the warmth of the fire.

'Just thinking how gorgeous you are... or is that bold of me to say?' Luke raised his head to take in Mark's reaction to his words.

'Well, instead of just thinking it, how about you show me?' He reached out his hand to Luke and the young man moved towards it. Their fingers touched, skin upon skin – not soft and smooth, more roughened like light sandpaper; hands that were not afraid to work.

Mark pulled Luke up and they stood facing each other. 'Let's see how much we like each other really. What do you think?' Mark leaned in, and their foreheads touched, his breath caressing Luke's face.

Smiling, Luke stepped back and allowed Mark to lead the way upstairs to his bedroom.

Chapter Twenty-Four

Gemma poured some wine for herself and Cathy. The children were in bed and her husband was out with his mates. Cathy had wanted to return to the café to meet with that awful waitress, but Gemma knew how to bend her sister to her way of thinking. She knew only too well that Cathy always felt guilty if she upset anyone.

When the girls asked Cathy to play some board games, as they didn't often see her now she was living further away, she couldn't refuse. She adored her nieces. So, she'd caved in and stayed at Gemma's, deciding that she would see Sno tomorrow instead.

'Isn't this nice?' Gemma curled her feet beneath her on the sofa, wine in hand.

'Yes, it is. The girls are growing up so fast. Since when were they able to beat me at board games?' Cathy joked.

'I think we are all feeling our age these days. Each morning I look at them, and there's something else they can do for themselves and I'm no longer needed.'

A look Cathy had not seen before draped Gemma's features; she seemed older, the wrinkles around her eyes more prominent, her voice wistful. In the pit of her stomach, Cathy could feel not quite guilt but regret for always being so harsh on Gemma. She knew she dismissed her quickly whenever the thought of spending time with her raised its head. *Why was she horrid to Gemma? It needed to stop.* She promised herself she would try harder with her sister.

'You have your friends, and you are always out for lunches. And now you will have Cregane Court to call to too.' Cathy's voice lowered at the mention of the cottage.

'Are you happy there? You seem sad when you mention it. You can always pull out, you know.' Gemma sipped on her drink, her face showing obvious concern.

'What? No, I'll never pull out! We've had a few problems over the last while with some of the locals spreading gossip, that's all.'

'Oh?'

'Yeah, stupid stuff. It upset Mark, but I think I've got through to him to ignore it, yet it still niggles me.'

'What's the gossip?' Gemma's face seemed to light up.

'Some people think we are setting up a shelter for the homeless and to house people who suffer with mental issues. That's the nice version. They actually called them nutters, if I recall correctly. Imagine!' Cathy snorted.

'Well, I can see why they would be upset,' Gemma responded quietly.

'I had a feeling you'd agree with the not-in-my-back-yard crowd.' Cathy drained her glass, the rich red warming her throat as it hit it. The previously pleasant atmosphere had dissolved as quickly as it had appeared.

'Don't be so judgemental,' Gemma snapped back. 'Paul and I work hard at raising our family and keeping our home. We pay enough taxes, and very often these people that you mentioned have it all handed to them, without so much as a please or thank you.'

'Look, Gemma, I'm not going to argue with you,' Cathy said with an exasperated sigh. 'You know as well as I do that's not what we are doing at the cottage. It couldn't be further from the truth, but even if we were, so what? Those people, as you say, deserve help and support. We have a crisis situation in this country with the homeless, and as for mental health, well, that has been whispered behind closed doors for far too long.'

Gemma shook her head, frowning. 'Still, Ballybawn people deserve to be respected. Roman said they would be slow to accept change, and it looks like he is right.'

Cathy's eyes flew open. 'Roman? Since when did you became such close pals? What else has he said?' She immediately sat upright, her curiosity aroused, as she waited for her sister to elaborate.

'Pour some wine will you, Cathy, and stop the silliness.'

Cathy could tell by the way the woman blushed that she regretted mentioning the solicitor, but she wasn't letting Gemma off the hook. 'I'm listening,' she said, refilling both glasses. 'Go on, tell me about Roman's words of wisdom.'

Gemma remained silent. It looked to Cathy as though she was wondering how to get herself out of an awkward situation and was unsure how to respond. This was new territory for them both; Cathy never normally called the shots.

'Gemma, has Roman said something to you about the cottage?' She remembered now how her sister had blushed when they had seen him pass the café window. Had Gemma been with him earlier when Cathy phoned her? Was he the voice in the background?

'Stop fishing for something that's not there,' Gemma said grumpily. 'Now, tell me more about the planning application being refused. What was it you had applied for?'

Cathy sighed, knowing her sister was changing the subject. She would play the game for tonight, but she was determined to ask Gemma again about Roman.

'The other two chalets that we hoped to build,' she replied. 'We have the large outhouse converted and it looks really great. Luke did a brilliant job with the interior; he has been a godsend to us.'

'Oh yeah, him. You let him decide on the interior? You really do stretch being the fairy godmother part, don't you?' Gemma scoffed. 'What would a homeless yobbo like him know about furnishings and paint? I could have helped you there, you know.' Gemma cast a loving eye around her lounge, with its tasteful, calm shades on the walls brightened with pops of colour in the cushions and throws.

'I never thought of you to be honest, and Luke is very gifted when it comes to art. His drawings are amazing, and when we get a chance, we are going to showcase his art in the studio. Why do you think because he was homeless it means he has no talent?'

'Oh, not this again. You really are like a dog with a bone. I don't mean he has no talent; I'm just saying don't forget you have family who can help, too.'

Cathy wished she had returned to the cottage. Being here was draining her, and everything they said seemed to irritate each other. It was so stressful. It reminded her of when they were young and Gemma would walk into her room without knocking then pass comment about what she was wearing or what she was reading, always bossing her around.

Cathy determined she would pop back into the city tomorrow even if it meant she would be late home to Ballybawn.

• • • •

Cathy had not slept well at Gemma's. She tried phoning Sno again, but still only got the voicemail. She headed back to the café, knowing that Sno wouldn't be there but hoping to find out more from the other waitress. The morning was always a busy time, with people out for their coffee breaks and parents grabbing a coffee on the go before the school runs started back up in the afternoon.

'Hi, when you have a minute, can I ask you something, please?' Cathy stood at the end of the counter. She had ordered her tea and scone, but lingered until the waitress was less occupied.

'Sure, what is it?'

'I'm friends with Sno and I've been trying to contact her. Is she okay?'

The girl shrugged. 'I don't know. When is her shift?'

Cathy thought that was strange. Surely they would know who was doing what shift.

'The evening one,' she replied.

'Oh, that girl. She's gone. She left over a week or more. I only started here, and they've rearranged the shifts, I think. Anything else?' The girl smiled at Cathy.

'No, thank you.' Cathy tried to take in the information. *If Sno no longer worked there, where was she, and why hadn't she made contact?* She pulled out her phone and once more tried phoning her friend. This time, she left a message telling Sno she knew about her quitting her job and that she was worried for her. Now she was unsure whether to phone the others with this news or wait until she got home. She decided to wait.

Walking around the shops, she wondered how to waste some time, as she really didn't want to return to Ballybawn without knowing more. In all the months of their friendship, Cathy had never visited Sno's home and didn't know exactly where she lived, only that she got the number sixty-two bus. She wondered if Luke would know, but she didn't want to phone and panic him. It might be best for her to return to Cregane, after all.

Sitting on the bus to Ballybawn, Cathy could not shake off her concerns about Sno. *What was going on?* Passing homes and farms on the country road home, she wondered how many of the inhabitants were truly happy and contented. Her friends were her family and meant more to her than others, including Gemma. That was what tore at her heart; Sno was family.

Chapter Twenty-Five

Walking home from the village an hour later, Cathy deliberated whether to call in and visit William. She could press him on the stories about Cregane Court and get his opinion on whether they would damage her hopes for the retreat centre going ahead. But as she neared his house, his front door was closed – a sign that he was not home.

By the time she reached Cregane, Cathy's mind was in turmoil. She couldn't stop thinking about everything that had gone wrong in the past few weeks. Sure, Mark's mood had improved a bit, but he was clearly still worried about his work colleagues' opinions of Cregane Court. Sno had gone off the grid, with no contact, and the news she had left the café really concerned Cathy. Gemma appeared to have an interest in Roman O'Driscoll, though Cathy didn't know why this bothered her so much. And the planning application had been refused. As for herself, she hadn't had a moment to pursue her wish to become a life-coach, and her time seemed to be slipping away with all her other concerns. Luke was the only one who was happy, but Cathy knew that would change once he heard about the stories in the village.

Mark's car was parked in the drive. *That's strange*, she thought, *he should be at work*. The workshop where he kept his carpentry tools was locked up, so he wasn't in there. And there was no sign of Luke either. He was usually about the place, fixing or recycling something, but the cottage and its grounds were quiet.

She let herself in and shouted hello to the sitting-room, but it was empty apart from a couple of beer bottles on the coffee table. She headed towards the kitchen, thinking a cup of tea would be welcome, then decided she'd have a quick shower first to clear her mind and perk her up. Cathy raced upstairs to change into her dressing gown and then go down for the shower, but as she approached the landing, she heard whispers. Maybe it was a radio, or Mark was sick in bed. Another step up and she heard light laughter. *Did he have someone in his room?*

She quickly went in to her bedroom and changed. She didn't want to be caught on the landing if some date came out from his room; it would look like she was snooping. Then she dashed back down and into the bathroom. Surely Mark would hear the shower, giving him fair warning that they were no longer alone in the house.

The water was refreshing, and she loved the coconut and lime bath gel she had bought while in the city. As she stood under the invigorating spray, she thought about Mark in his bedroom above. She hadn't realised he was dating and was surprised he had not mentioned it. Maybe it was time for her to get herself out there and start meeting people, too. She was only two years older than Mark – not exactly over the hill, but still way too old for clubs and such. Some of her former workmates had used online dating. *Would that be the way to go?*

Feeling energised, she dried herself and dragged on her dressing gown, then stepped quickly up the stairs to her room. More whispering. There definitely was someone in there with him. Cathy was in a dilemma: *should she cough and let them know she was here?* She sat on her bed. *Why hadn't Mark said anything about seeing someone?* She'd thought they were close friends. She'd occasionally wondered if anything would develop between them, and whether that was why Lizzy had thrown them together. *Enough*, she scolded herself now. *She could find a man on her own; no need to get dramatic about it.* Dressed, and with her hair tied in a towel wrap, she went to the kitchen to make her lunch.

• • • •

'Better go and finish designing the plaque. We've come up with some good ideas, though. It's been fun.' Laughter filled the stairway.

Cathy put down the bowl of salad she had been preparing. That was Luke. It was Luke who had been in Mark's bedroom!

'Hey, Cathy, how did it go in the city?' Luke glowed with happiness. He grabbed a cup and proceeded to make some coffee. 'Want any coffee, Mark?'

The other man leaned against the kitchen doorframe and grinned. He, too, was shining with delight.

'Want to tell me what's going on?' Her face burned with embarrassment. *How had she thought Mark and her would ever have been a couple?* The two men fell silent, then Mark moved to drape an arm around Luke's shoulder.

'What's there to tell?' he said dreamily.

'Oh God, spare me from the two of you and your lovey-dovey act,' she told them. 'So, when did this all happen? Am I that oblivious to what's going on around me?' She shook her head in wonder. *How had she missed all this?*

'Nothing was going on, Cathy. You're not being cut out, honestly. Well, I fancied this guy for ages.' Mark moved closer to Luke and placed his other arm around Luke's waist. 'I never told him, because I thought I might scare him. Especially as he had only arrived here.'

'And after he kissed me, I knew I felt the same.' Luke cuddled into Mark.

'Kissed you? See, I am blind!' Cathy shrieked.

'The night of the party.' The two men remained linked in a warm embrace.

'Ah, so while I was dealing with a flirting sister and a nasty solicitor, the two of you were canoodling behind the garden shed.' All three of them laughed.

'So, you don't mind?' Luke asked.

'Hey, why should I? My friend and my friend together, what's there not to like?' Cathy winked.

Luke broke away from Mark and came to hug her. 'Thank you so much for everything.'

Cathy couldn't help but feel happy; their joy was contagious. 'I think we should celebrate.' She needed to grab this happiness and store it inside her.

The worrying thoughts of earlier were pushed away, and she wanted it to stay like that for as long as she could. She just couldn't understand why Mark had not mentioned anything.

• • • •

That evening, the three friends sat around the table for dinner. Mark had driven to the village to buy wine, and Luke had even lit some candles. The dinner was comforting food – a simple chicken casserole with fresh garden vegetables from the local greengrocer; dessert was a mix of mint and chocolate ice-cream from the freezer.

'Okay, so are you ready to tell us what happened in the city?' Mark started to clear some of the plates from the table.

'Where do I start?' she groaned. Remembering Gemma's fondness for Roman, and Sno not being at the café, hurt. Her head dropped to her chest with weariness.

'That bad? Ouch, I don't think I want to hear.' Luke covered his face with his hands and shook his head.

Cathy didn't want to spoil the evening with the news of Sno's disappearance. 'I know. Do we have to talk about it? I mean, this day has turned into such a happy one, thanks to you two.' She sighed, eager to change the subject. 'Tell you what, let's raise a toast to Ballybawn's newest couple, and leave the city horrors until the morning.'

Chapter Twenty-Six

The new couple were still on cloud nine and filling the air around the cottage with bubbles of love and affection. As the next few days passed, it appeared they had forgotten about her trip to the city, but Cathy knew she would have to burst the happy atmosphere and tell Luke that Sno still had not made contact.

She had phoned the café at different times to check if her friend had popped back in, but each time the answer was no. Her concern was growing, and she worried if it was something she had said the night Mark had come home in a bad mood. *She and Luke had loved Sno's idea of a craft shop, so why was she cutting them out?*

Luke was busy outside. Even though their planning permission had been blocked by an objection, he could still continue to clear the site and have it prepared. It was chilly but crisp as he worked, cutting back the overgrown weeds and brambles and gathering them into a heap. Inch by inch, the area was looking better. Beneath the rubbish, he came across old stones of the former hen-house – a partly standing wall covered in ivy and moss. Collecting all the loose stones, he made a pile in one area, and soon a swell of stones was stocked high. He looked pleased with his morning's work, and Cathy could see he was gaining muscles from the physical lifting and clearing.

'Time for a break?' She joined him. Handling the rocks, she remembered that one of the locals was a stonemason. She would contact him about reusing the pile Luke had built up; most could be recycled.

'Yep, I reckon the coffee is calling.' Luke wiped the sweat from his forehead and rubbed his hands on the old jeans he wore for outside work.

'You really are getting through the acre bit by bit. Honestly, Luke, it was a lucky day I met you.' She grinned as she gazed over the old hen-house site, now looking clean and in order. The brown hens

– a few white, too – that she remembered Lizzy once owned had lived in comfort here. Cathy recalled the high wire fence around the run and the gate into it, and the cockerel that crowed and proudly stepped around the run watching over his girls. Few were lost to the foxes in the fields around, as Lizzy had dutifully checked for holes in the fencing every morning, and rounded the hens up each evening before sunset.

Luke grabbed her arm and she snapped back to the present. 'Penny for them,' he winked. Laughing, they went inside and sat down to enjoy ham sandwiches and steaming coffee at the kitchen table.

'Hey, you've gone from looking wistful in the hen-house to looking troubled.' He frowned. 'Cathy?'

'Luke, it's time you should know. I'm actually very worried but, well, since there's no good time to share worrying news, I may as well spit it out.' Her shoulders sagged in weariness and she slumped back in the chair. She hated delivering bad news. Without warning, tears rolled down her cheeks then great sobs escaped from her, and she bowed her head into her hands.

'Christ, Cathy, what is it? Are you sick? Tell me, for feck's sake, what is it?' Luke was up out of his seat and over by his friend in seconds. He had never seen her upset like this before and looked really scared. His stomach knotted with the fear of what he was about to hear. *Should he phone Mark?* He handed her some kitchen towel and she calmed and wiped her nose, then took a deep breath. Looking up at him with puffy red eyes and damp cheeks, she attempted a weak smile.

'Sorry about that. I didn't realise I was so stressed. Guess it's all the bad news over the past few weeks and then, well, Snowflake has gone missing.'

'Missing? How? What do you mean?' Luke's face visibly paled. With his blond hair, he appeared ghost-like. The kitchen clock ticked in the silence, and it seemed forever before Cathy could get her breath to talk.

'Since she stormed out of here, she's not been answering any of my calls or texts, and when I went to the city, I found out she's packed her job in, too. No-one seems to know anything about where she is. I don't even know where she lives, for God's sake, and I'm supposed to be her friend!' Cathy's voice choked on her last words, and the tears filled her eyes once more. 'I held off from saying anything these last few days, because you and Mark are so happy, and Cregane has been a nice place to be in again.'

'But why? I mean, why jack her job in?' Cathy saw how guilt clouded his eyes. 'I feel really bad now, as I'd forgotten all about Sno not contacting me. I've been caught up in my own joy of having Mark in my life.' He shook his head angrily. 'I'm a terrible friend, too.'

'It might not be as serious as I'm making it out to be,' Cathy tried to sound less pessimistic. 'Like I said, the mix of all that has been happening around here, with stories and applications being thrown out, I guess I'm just tired and emotional.' She attempted a gentle laugh as she swept the tears from her eyes.

'No, no, you're right to be concerned. I didn't think we had upset her that much. I mean, leaving her job is a bit extreme, don't you think?' Luke looked thoughtful, as though remembering the last time they'd all been together.

'I only ever met her at the café, or she would come to my apartment,' Cathy told him. 'I'm wondering if she had already quit the job then came out here all excited with her ideas, but we kind of poured cold water on it a bit.'

'But we didn't, though.' Luke was adamant. 'We were thrilled, and you asked her to open her craft café here.' He was pacing the kitchen now, one hand on his hip as he tried to clear his mind and focus on where Sno could be. 'Right,' he said, after a few moments.

'I'll head to the city tomorrow and ask around some of my mates to see if I can unearth something. It will be alright, Cathy. I bet she's won the lottery and pissed off to the Bahamas, and is lying on a white sandy beach sipping cocktails and giving us the two fingers.' He placed his arm around Cathy's shoulders, as he tried to reassure his housemate.

• • • •

'Of course, go for a few days, but not for too long,' Mark held his lover in his arms as Luke told him of his plans to travel to the city.

'I hope she's okay. I feel guilty that I'd forgotten she'd not been in touch for a while.' Luke twirled his fingers through Mark's dark curls, his hair soft and gentle.

'Me, too. I guess when you're in love, everything else falls into the background.' Mark nuzzled Luke's neck.

'So, you love me then?' the other whispered back, relaxing into the embrace.

'From the moment I saw you.'

The two men closed the bedroom door and shared themselves with each other in the darkness.

Chapter Twenty-Seven

After breakfast, Luke got the bus from Ballybawn, Mark went to work, and Cathy planned on getting some research done. She wanted to probe deeper into becoming a life-coach. Helping others appealed to her, and it was something she reckoned she could do using Cregane Court as her base.

Surfing the internet, she found all sorts of packages of varying lengths of time and, of course, prices. *How would she know which to choose? Was there another way of helping others? Counsellor? Carer in a retirement home? Home help?* When she Googled helping others, many different career paths opened up to her. She needed to start earning again soon. Having no rent to pay had certainly helped stretch her savings, and with Mark sharing the utility bills, it meant their outgoings were affordable. But their plans for the retreat cost money, and she knew she needed to start bringing in some money soon.

To her delight, she found that Ballybawn Community Centre ran night classes in some of the careers she was considering, and she settled down to make plenty of notes to follow up. Until now, all her time and effort had been soaked up by the cottage being cleared and the surrounding land being brought under control from all the overgrowth. She was enjoying the feeling of having a buzz again in her life. Pleased with her morning's work, she closed her laptop. *Had she heard a car pull into the drive?* She wasn't expecting anyone, and prayed it wasn't Gemma popping in for a chat.

'Hello, anyone at home?'

She heard the shout as the visitor came around to the front of the cottage. The front door was facing the fields that rolled out before it, while the drive to the house actually brought the visitor to the back of the property. It was a quirk that Cathy liked. She waited by the window to see who would pass by to the door.

Roman O'Driscoll.

What the hell brought him out here? Cathy thought about hiding, pretending there was no-one at home, but then realised that they never closed the front door. It was open from early morning until late evening, unless the weather dictated otherwise. Damn Mark and his welcoming open door; he was at work and didn't have to put up with the Roman O'Driscolls' of this world. With her best smile plastered on, she went to meet the solicitor. She pulled her jumper down a little and wiped imaginary fluff from her trousers.

'Mr. O'Driscoll, this is a surprise.'

'Hello, Cathy. If you don't mind, I must say that leaving your door open might not be a sensible thing to do. Especially when you are out in the country. Alone and vulnerable, may I add.' He shot her a disapproving look.

She recalled thinking about him being a judge behind the bench, and realised that with the look he held now, he would suit the part perfectly. She smiled at her own thoughts.

'Glad you are amused,' he said, frowning. 'I dare say you might regret it someday.'

How she despised him. His shiny shoes caught her eye and she had to admit to herself that he was always immaculately dressed. The grey suit with a fine pinstripe hung well on him, the pale pink tie perfectly matching a fleck in his crisp shirt. She could see why Gemma thought he was handsome.

'What can I do for you?' she asked coolly.

'I came by to say sorry about your recent bad news. You must be disappointed.' A grin shot across his face, in complete contrast to the disappointment he mentioned.

'What news is that exactly?' Handsome or not, this man was vile, and Cathy felt uncomfortable in his company. He had an ego so big that it could fill the village.

'Oh, I was under the impression you had received your answer on your latest planning application.' His narrowed eyes gave him a snake-like appearance.

'Oh, that's nothing. It's all been taken care of. A silly mistake.' The words tumbled from her with ease. *Lies, all lies, but was he to know that?* 'Where did you get your information from?' Cathy stared at the man.

'You should know by now that there are no secrets in Ballybawn. A tight community such as ours, people look out for each other, so it's not surprising that news travels.' The simmering smile on his lips did not reach his eyes.

'It travels whether it is true or not, it seems.'

'Are you suggesting there's something else being shared?' He stepped closer to the doorway. *His small attempt at pretending to be interested and offering sympathy*, she thought.

'Oh, Mr. O'Driscoll, I suggest you go back to wherever you heard about the planning and I'm sure you will be told all the stories about the orgies and initiation ceremonies that will happen once the cult is up and running.'

He looked her in the eye and his voice dropped in tone. 'Cathy, one bit of advice. Don't try to be smart with me; you won't succeed. Your Great-Aunt Elizabeth might have thought like you, but I assure you, her husband Archie knew better. Pity she didn't die first.'

Cathy was shocked. 'Get off this property now,' she snapped, 'and do not ever, ever, set foot here again. You are a disgrace to every position you hold. But I will agree with you on one thing, you are right when you say it's not safe to leave the door open. It can let vermin like you get too close.' She slammed the door and bolted it. Leaning back against it, her breath came in gasps and she felt faint. Her eyes watered and she clung to the shelf in the porch, shaking. A glance at her white knuckles made her realise how tightly she clung to the timber.

The rev of a car engine told her he was gone. *What had happened? Had she just been threatened by that creep?* She rushed to the kitchen, grabbed a glass, and filled it with cold water. The coolness of the liquid helped her to focus and calm down, but a sickness still clung to her stomach. *Why, oh why, did Luke go on the early bus?* She could have done with him here to face that monster.

Dragging herself upstairs, she lay down on her bed. Never before had she behaved in such a manner. *Where had the boldness come from? Had she really stood up to him?* Her armpits were damp, sweat clung to her. The phrase 'fight or flight' came to mind; well, she had chosen fight, and it felt good. At least, it did now; not at the time. He had looked so vicious that she had wondered briefly if he might attack her.

But, she told herself, she had handled the situation. She had remained calm and told the dirty mongrel where to go, with his false sympathy and pretend concern. And now that she was thinking more clearly, a glow of satisfaction seeped into her. The nausea was fading and, instead, a little pride in her brave actions was taking hold. Cathy propped herself up into a sitting position and played the scene over again in her mind. Keeping him at the door had been a good move – not that she would have invited him in, but it meant she had been in control from the start. When he spoke about their planning papers and dragging Lizzy into it... well, that had been totally out of order. Her tiny bit of pride now turned to anger. How dare he speak ill of Lizzy! Bloody hell, how dare he threaten her, too?

A flush of strong fury swelled within her and she rushed downstairs and unbolted the door. She then flung it open and stepped outside. She would not be made to feel afraid in her own home, and she would most definitely not let the village bully intimidate her. Their home was one of welcome, just as it had been in Lizzy's time, and Cathy would fight tooth and tiger to see that was the way it would remain. Let Roman O'Driscoll try his threatening behaviour again with her and he would be left in no doubt that he had a battle on his hands. And Cathy promised not just herself, but Lizzy too, that she would make sure of that.

Chapter Twenty-Eight

'So, tell me again how you sent him packing.' William was thrilled with Cathy's story. He did not like the solicitor, and hearing how she'd handled his visit made the old man happy.

'I wish I had seen it. Orgies and initiation and cults,' he chuckled. 'Oh Cathy, you have done my heart well today. That miserable man has most of this village bought up, I'm sure of it.'

'Do you think, William?'

'Sure, he's the auctioneer, too, so if he's not selling it, he's handling the private papers of sale and such.' The man puffed on his pipe, a smile lying on his lips as he blew some smoke into the air.

'Want some more ginger cake?' Cathy had made some tea for them. After her uncomfortable encounter that morning, she had been filled with energy. Unsettled at staying at home, she had gone for a walk and ended up at William's.

'Why do people give him business? Isn't it obvious he is nasty and horrible?' She placed some cake before William and sat back down.

'Look, girleen, his father was the solicitor before him, so he just moved into his father's shoes and continued on with it. His father, in fairness, and God be good to him now, was a decent man. No funny business with him. He was a respectable and honourable man, but not his son.' William shook his head. 'No, not his son.'

'Do you know what he said about Lizzy? It really made my blood boil in anger after.' Cathy flushed with rage as she thought of the solicitor's horrible words. 'He said it was a pity that she didn't die first, before Archie!'

The elderly man paused, sucking his pipe, and stared at her. His eyes darkened at hearing her words, and he leaned forward towards her, his old armchair creaking. 'Are you telling me he really said that?'

'Yes, he also said Archie knew better than Lizzy, whatever he meant.'

William appeared to gather his thoughts as he leant back again in his chair, but Cathy knew he was angry by the stern look on his face. The turf fire glowed in the grate, some coal shuffling into place as it burned.

'This village needs to wake up to the evil of that man. Leave it with me and I will see what I can find out. I've a hunch about something, but it's best I not say anything now until I'm surer.' He stood up and got his stick, then placed his cap on and shrugged his shoulders. 'Pull the door out after you, Cathy, when you leave.'

His back turned to her, he did not waste a moment longer and headed to the door.

'Where are you going?' she shouted.

'For a walk to the village, girleen.'

'Want me to go with you?' Cathy stood and stepped after him.

'No. Finish your tea and close up when you're done. I'll talk to you another day.'

She watched him pace down his path and off towards Ballybawn, leaving her wondering what he was up to. Once she had washed up and tidied, she closed the door to William's home and returned to her own.

She kept remembering the way William had looked when she'd mentioned Lizzy and Archie. Clearly, it had stirred up something for the elderly man. There was something missing in this puzzle, she was sure of it. Something that might make sense of all the recent mishaps. For a moment, Sno came into her mind. Cathy missed her friend. She just hoped Luke would learn something new about her disappearance.

••••

Luke walked around the city streets, asking some of his old friends if they had heard anything about Sno. She was known for her kindness of giving free coffees or leftover sandwiches to some of them in the evenings, and several were surprised to hear she was no longer at the café. He stood at the number 62 bus stop and enquired about her with the bus drivers as they pulled up for passengers. Finally, he struck the jackpot when one of them recalled her, so Luke jumped on board to chat with him. The man said Sno always thanked him when alighting from the bus and wished him safe driving, where many passengers would just grunt or ignore him. He told Luke the stop where she got off, and said he would pray that she would be found.

Luke wandered about near her stop, asking passers-by if they knew her. Eventually, he got the answer he needed, when someone pointed out where she lived. The narrow railing around her front garden was rusted, the grass overgrown, the flowerpots stuffed with weeds and rubbish the wind blew about her doorway. Neglect showed in the garden. Sno was a hard worker, so Luke was sure she would not allow it to be like this. It was a sad-looking house and Luke didn't like the idea of knocking on the front door. *What if she was furious at him for tracking her down?* After all, she hadn't returned their texts or calls, so maybe she just wanted to be left alone. *Should he respect that and go on his way?* If it was him that decided to disappear like this, he knew he would be angry at being sought out. *What should he do?* The night was drawing in and soon he would need to go back to the city centre. Unless Sno invited him in. Then he would be happy to stay with her and find out what happened.

With a deep breath, he made up his mind to knock on the door.

Marching up the path, he shivered a little hoping he was doing the right thing. There was no-one at home at Snowflake's house. It was empty. Now what was he to do?

Chapter Twenty-Nine

The emptiness at the cottage without Luke and with Mark not yet returned from work, unnerved Cathy. Since returning from William's she paced the floor. He was up to something, she was sure of it, and she really wanted to know what. Patience was not one of her best points lately. She'd not heard from Gemma recently either. Maybe her sister was busy lunching and gossiping, even though she claimed her social life was non-existent.

Standing still, enough was enough; Cathy needed to do something. All these silly thoughts about what was going on in Lizzy's home were spoiling the dreams she and Mark had for the future. This was her opportunity for a fresh start, a chance to stand up to the bullies of life and show she was not going to be pushed to the ground any longer. Flashes of her sister popped into her mind. Silly memories of how Gemma would take Cathy's favourite doll and hide it, or tell her she was Billy-no-mates and that's why she stood alone in the school playground. Gemma had always sewn seeds of self-doubt for Cathy. And when she'd tried to tell her mother and father, they'd just laughed it off, telling her she was mistaken, that Gemma was only teasing, and not to be a baby.

But Cathy knew it was not just Gemma who'd caused her problems.

At work, she had been the one who worked through her lunch hour to meet deadlines; good, reliable Cathy. The others would tell her how she was the best at this or that, how she knew the system better, then leave her alone in the office to pick up the slack. And of course, they all had lives to return to, families that needed them, hot dates to go on, gym, book-club meetings. So she would work alone in the evenings whenever a deadline loomed.

Why had she let it happen? Why was she so easy to push around? Her eyes watered with shame; self-shame at never getting her act together and telling them all to feck off.

Looking around Lizzy's home, she soaked in the love she had for this place. Each brick and each imperfection meant something to her, defining who she was and who she wanted to be – a new Cathy. A strong Cathy.

Making her way outside, she walked around the grounds, the rough path and drive, the soft grass, the uneven earth of the orchard, listening to the rustle of the trees that protected Cregane Court. If it could turn her life around, it would do the same for others. It needed to be shared with others. *Luke was a good example,* she thought. His art and talent for design was blossoming since living here. Even Mark was thinking differently. And Gemma sometimes called to see her, so they were included in each other's lives more.

Yes, this was a magical place, a special place, and she was adamant she would see her and Mark's vision for the future realised.

With her head clear and determination swimming in her bones, she made a bold decision, but she knew Mark would be okay with it. She was going to invite the village to a night in Cregane Court, to let them see the work that had been done and share their plans with them. Once they saw and heard the truth about what would happen in Lizzy's home, she was sure everything would change. They would have the trust of the locals, the same people who had helped to build and give life to The Shed – the first of the units for the artists of all talents who would come and live the magic of Cregane for a week, or a month, or whatever.

• • • •

'Hey, what are you up to?'

Cathy had not heard her housemate come in. Mark was standing behind her, and picked up a sheet that lay on the table. She had been busy printing off some flyers, and now she was stacking them up on the table, ready to be given out in Ballybawn in the morning.

'A mad idea I've had.' She watched his face as he studied the sheet in his hands. So far, she could not see any reaction. *Had she done the wrong thing yet again? Had she messed up?* She slumped back in the chair. She had been so fired up over this idea, and now Mark stood there without expression, silent. 'Say something,' she whispered.

'Well, you seem to be inviting the whole of Ballybawn to a night of information in a week's time,' he read from the flyer. Then he put it back down and walked away. 'Want a tea?' he shouted back to her.

That was it? Cathy was stunned. *Did she want tea?* She got up and followed him to the kitchen. 'Mark, tell me what you think.' She leaned against the table, arms folded across her chest.

'Look, you have your reasons for doing this. I have no reason to question why, because so far you have not given me any reason to ever doubt you. If you think an information evening is needed for the locals, then so be it.' He continued getting the cups, milk, and sugar ready for when the kettle boiled.

'Really?'

'Really. I don't know why you're so surprised, Miss Cathy Reed. You are good at reading situations, and I happen to have complete trust in you.' He stood before her and smiled. 'Now, get out of my way so I can make this pot of tea.'

She threw her arms around him, holding him tight, and he happily hugged her back. Still with her arms entwined around his neck, she pulled back and looked at him.

'If you weren't in love with Luke, I'd kiss you right now and then whisk you up the stairs to bed.'

He saw the tears in her eyes and the flushed colouring on her cheeks.

'Hey, I don't know what it was I did to get such a hug and make you cry all at the same time, but lucky will the man be who gets your heart, Cathy.'

She stepped back and wiped her cheeks with a nearby tea towel. Embarrassed a little at her sudden rush of emotion, she looked at the floor in awkwardness.

'How about we have our tea?' Mark handed her a packet of coconut creams and she managed a laugh, the clumsiness she felt had passed. She was right. Cregane Court was special; it was a good place which brought out the best in people, and that was what she wanted to share with others.

Chapter Thirty

Luke was still in the city. He phoned to tell them what he had discovered, which was not a lot in terms of finding Snowflake. She had not returned to her home, nor had she been spotted out and about. Being so worried, he had checked the hospitals.

His comment shocked Cathy. It had never occurred to her that Sno might be ill or hurt, and her anxiety for her friend deepened. Although the two women had become close, there was still so much they didn't know about each other.

Gemma's old childhood taunt jumped to Cathy's mind: *Billy-no-mates, you can't keep friends because you're boring and no fun, ha.* Cathy's self-confidence was once more crumbling. Deep down, she knew she was being hard on herself, but years of being told you were the reason behind everyone's problems, years of being a doormat for everyone, had taken its toll. She had thought she was managing to shake it off, bit by bit, yet every now and then the foundations of her self-belief shook. Sitting in front of her mirror, all she saw was a weary-looking woman.

'Hey, Cathy, come on. The first of the locals are arriving!' Mark shouted up the stairs, snapping her out of her misery.

She remembered his words to her in the kitchen earlier that week that she was a good person who made good things happen. She forced a smile and the woman in the mirror looked happy. She could do this. She would be okay.

• • • •

The people from Ballybawn had taken advantage of the open evening invitation and had come for a look around Cregane, keen to see what the changes were. Others had never been there before, but knew of Lizzy's great party evenings and wanted to see where they had taken place.

The late September weather was so far behaving itself. There was not a chill in the air, nor a breeze to shiver neither plant nor person. People mingled around the yard, in and around the converted outhouse, but not in the cottage. That was private; it was Cathy's, Mark's, and Luke's home.

People admired different parts of the estate, how well the front lawns looked, the beautiful view out over the rolling fields, and the secret spot in the old orchard where the garden chairs were placed for a quiet corner. Some commented on the workmanship in The Shed, how talented the local workmen who had built it were, how tastefully it had all been brought together. It gave others ideas about how to transform their own homes, and so generated work for the builders involved.

A happy relaxed atmosphere hung in the air. Teas and coffees and an assortment of pastries from the local bakery were laid out on a long trestle table in the kitchen of the outhouse. Chatting and laughter mixed, as over thirty or so people from the village had gathered. Now it was time to get their attention and ease their fears over the rumours that had circulated in the area recently.

Mark stood on a chair and asked for everyone's attention for a few moments while he and Cathy said a few words, and added that they'd be happy to answer any questions afterwards. 'So, first of all, welcome to Cregane Court,' he said. 'I'm Mark Daniels. Some of you know me, others will have known my grandmother, Diane.' This brought some murmuring as people recalled the woman, and some remembered him as a young fellow around Ballybawn. 'Anyhow, recently we, that is Cathy and I,' he pointed at Cathy who stood at his side and she smiled in acknowledgement, 'well, we have been hearing all sorts of weird stories about what we are doing here in Cregane. Let me say first off, tonight is about putting all your minds to rest. Without any doubt, there is not going to be any sort of cult community happening here.' Some people laughed lightly, others nodded, while some even looked relieved.

Mark continued, 'In fact, what we hope to do is build some more chalet-style buildings. Small ones – an ensuite bedroom and a small kitchen-cum-living room in each one. There will be four of these chalets in total. Two where Elizabeth and Archie's old hen run was, and two a bit closer to the river. We plan to develop the river area as a walkway and have benches along there, which will be accessible to the local community, too. No closed gates or special membership to enjoy the facilities.'

He smiled. 'The only part of the retreat that will be kept for paying guests will be the chalets. That's really what we envision happening. This outhouse that we are all gathered in was falling down, but with your help,' he indicated several men, 'Tommy over there, and Harry, along with Jack, Paddy, and others, we were able to transform it into the beautiful self-contained unit you see tonight. Now that I have given a bit of insight into the structural plans, etc., I will hand you over to Cathy.' He stepped down from the chair and smiled at his friend.

He took her hand in his and helped her to step onto the chair. She was shaking with nerves, but he gave her hand a soft squeeze of reassurance. Once up on the chair, she had a better view of the crowd before her. They all stared at her, waiting, some drinking their tea or coffee, but most looking at her with expectation. She glanced down at Mark and he smiled once more at her.

I can do this, she thought, and took a deep breath. The crowd appeared friendly and they had been polite and attentive during Mark's short speech.

'Hello and, like Mark said, welcome. I'm Cathy, and yes, some of you know me and others don't. Our plans for here are fairly simple and clear. There's no secrecy, and any ideas or thoughts that can enhance our own are very welcome. The idea for a retreat centre came to me one day while I was sitting in the orchard. You have seen the beauty of this spot as you walked around this evening. The views are to die for, the grove of trees and birdsong are heavenly.' Many nodding heads greeted her words, spurring her on. Cathy knew they could hear the passion she held for Lizzy's home in her voice, and it strengthened her further. 'So, I want to share this ideal home with others. I'm talking about writers, artists, and creative people of all types. Carpenters, glass blowers, metal workers, crafts of all sorts, and of course, music. This place, Cregane Court, is an inspirational place, and many artists or creative people don't always have a special place they can go to, to develop their craft or to complete a project. I want to offer that to them here, and surely that can only be a good thing.'

She looked around her audience before continuing, 'So, please put to bed any fears or daft stories about it being a cult haven or a shelter for those less off than ourselves in society. While there most definitely is a need for such shelters and support houses, this isn't going to be one.' *Had she said enough? Had she said the right thing?* The faces watching her were hard to read. Some had furrowed brows as though they were digesting her words one by one, others were whispering to each other. She got down from the chair and looked at Mark.

He shrugged his shoulders and murmured, 'That's it, that's all we can do.'

'Excuse me, I have a question. When are the other chalets going to be built? Will you continue to use local labour?' The woman smiled at Cathy, directing her question to her.

'Yes, yes, of course we will use local labour.'

'But,' Mark interjected, 'we won't be building just yet, as the planning application was refused. We have appealed it, but no decision has been made yet.'

The raised eyebrows from some of the audience on hearing of an objection showed Mark that not everyone knew about this. *So, who did?*

'You've got some homeless here at the moment. How do we know you'll stick to your word and not let more come here?' It was a different woman who spoke.

'We don't have any homeless here. If you are referring to our close friend, Luke, who there has been scandalous gossip about, then yes, Luke lives here. This is his home, the same as it is mine or Mark's.' Cathy stared at the woman who had spoken, a challenge in her eye. The woman huffed at Cathy's response. Clearly, not all were going to be won over.

'Ballybawn is a quiet village. We don't want any of the city rough stuff coming out here. Often you creative types are all for smoking weed and other drugs to get inspiration, and don't deny it, I saw a documentary on it,' a man shouted from the back.

'Look,' Mark stood on the chair again to see who had spoken, 'I'm a financial manager and a creative type, to use your own words, and I don't take drugs. There will not, under any circumstances, be drugs of any kind allowed on these premises. And the documentary you watched was certainly not one about a retreat centre like the one we intend to run. But please do not be so naïve as to think that the village does not already house drug pushers or users. This sad, horrid addiction is in every crevice of every village, town, and city, unfortunately.'

The man spoke again, this time shoving closer to the front of the group.

'You think we are stupid or naïve to believe you just because you don't take drugs. Grow up, man. Do you realise how silly you sound? This place can attract any sort of lout or layabout from anywhere in Ireland, and you and your girlfriend here,' he gestured towards Cathy, 'won't give a fiddler's elbow what type or who they are, once you get your money. Am I right?' Now he turned to face the crowd, directing his closing question to them.

He was obviously set against Cregane, and now that he had sown the seeds of more discontent, Cathy feared he was going to harvest that doubt and fear in one fell swoop.

A few were nodding, clearly rethinking their views, and the man was encouraged to continue. 'Shure, we've seen the likes of their so-called artists already. Tattoos – nothing wrong with that I say – but the biker gear, the shaved heads, and the past these people have. Shure, we know nothing about who will be walking around out village,' he addressed the audience. 'These two only want a quick buck. I call for a protest against any more development here.' With that, he turned and smiled triumphantly at Cathy, while the restless people grouped like sheep, each bleating and nodding at his words, not knowing how to think for themselves.

'If you will excuse me, I'd like to say a few words.' A deep voice came from over near the refreshment table, and silence fell as everyone turned to see who had spoken. It was William. He stood up from where he was seated and, stick in hand, walked slowly to the front of the group.

Cathy had not noticed him arrive but was thrilled to see him. At least there was one friendly face amongst the sharks.

'I have listened to you all so far, and I would like to add my penny's worth to it all. I'm eighty-six years old and have lived in this village all my life. While I agree with the concern about what this retreat centre could bring in a negative way, what about the positives? So far, the young people who own the late Elizabeth Sheldon's home, God be good to her,' some blessed themselves in her memory, 'have used local labour for the refurbishment, so giving work to our own. And looking around here tonight, I must say what a wonderful standard it is, so well done to the men and women involved. They have already said they will be still employing locals to continue the work. Now, if they bring people to the retreat centre, think about this: those people will spend money in your shops, cafés, and pubs, so *you* benefit, too. Already, I know that young Cathy here shops in the village, her pastries tonight came from the bakery we all love. So, before we get carried away with the '*we don't want*,' stop and think what we stand to gain.' When he paused for breath, a ripple of applause started up. The locals that had earlier felt fear and doubt, now agreed with the old man that there was more than one side to the story.

William raised his hand to continue, and a hush wrapped around the room. 'I've one more thing to say. Will you listen to the voice of one of your own – me, who has lived his life here, and who is happy to support the young people bring much needed life to our village,' and he raised his voice in rebellion, 'or to a blow-in who thinks they know it all about Ballybawn.' He pointed his stick at the man who had earlier challenged Mark.

With this, a cheer went up. Some were still unsure, but at least when the people began to scatter off home, the evening had ended on a more positive note.

Cathy rushed to William and hugged him, while Mark shook his hand and offered to drive him home.

Chapter Thirty-One

Luke stood with his mouth open after hearing all that happened while he was away. There was still no news of Sno, but at least they had tried to reach out to her. The next move was up to her, but Cathy decided she would keep phoning; it didn't seem right not to.

'So, old man William rode in on his white steed, did he?' Luke asked, while they were gathered around the table for breakfast. Mark was glowing to have his lover home.

'Yes, he was great. And at least the evening didn't end on a sour note. Who was the trouble-maker anyway, did William say?' Mark was stirring porridge while Cathy ate some fruit.

'I can ask him when I next visit if you like?' she offered.

Mark nodded in reply, then added, 'I'm going to check on the planning appeal this morning. There should be some answer today.' He looked serious as he glanced at his watch. 'I better get to work.'

'What was the objection, anyway, do you know?' Cathy got up from the table to fetch herself some fresh tea.

'Believe it or not, whoever lodged the observation said the buildings would ruin the beauty of the area, that the skyline would be blighted.' All three shook their heads. Whoever had objected had not properly checked the plans, but had just complained to halt their progress.

Cathy and her friends had been very aware of how the chalets would look, and were determined that they would not detract in any way from the gorgeous surroundings. She wondered how the planning committee could have come to their decision when it was obvious the objection was not based on truth.

'Do you ever think this was an inside job, as in someone got a backhander to say no to the planning?' Luke asked.

'Well, if it was, it wouldn't surprise me.' Cathy sat back down a fresh brew in her hand.

'Ah, Cathy, it can't have been. Sure, I mean that day and age is well gone, the brown envelope days.' Mark scolded his friend for her negative thoughts.

'I know, it's just I'm annoyed, that's all.' She really was fed up with the setback. With luck and good sense prevailing though, the appeal might swing their way.

• • • •

She set to work on some press releases and advertisements for magazines and social media, determined to promote the retreat centre anyway. She wanted to get The Shed earning some income and raising much needed funds to develop the rest of the centre. Mark had already looked after the legal side of things, but she had to publicise it.

A list of all that was to be done lay on the table next to her laptop, and she ticked them off one by one as she completed each task.

Luke was out in the workshop sketching logos and scripts to use on the plaque. The music blared loudly as he worked, but there was no-one to hear it except Cathy, and she didn't mind. It was good to think she was not alone. The last time Roman O'Driscoll turned up had unnerved her a bit, but she was still proud of the way she'd cleared him off the premises. With her head bent over documents and photos, she never heard the knock on the open door.

It was harsh coughing that stirred her, and she left her desk and went to the porch. There stood Snowflake, two suitcases in tow.

• • • •

The two women faced each other. A stillness had fallen, the music dissolving into the background. Neither seemed to know what to do. *Should they hug? Who should talk first?*

Sno's dark eyes looked at the floor, not meeting Cathy's stare.

'Hello, Sno.' Cathy's greeting was a whisper. She looked at the travel bags by her friend's feet, and a feeling of *déjà vu* swamped Cathy. *Was Sno going to run off again?* She had a sense of walking on not just eggshells but very thin glass waiting to shatter in an instant.

'Hi, Cathy. Can I come in?' The woman looked tiny, housed in the doorway, waiting for permission.

'Yes, do.' She stepped aside and Sno entered. Cathy couldn't help but see how much thinner she looked, ragged almost. *Was she ill?*

'How are things here in Cregane?' Sno offered a smile as she spoke.

'For goodness sake, Sno, where the hell have you been? We've been worried sick about you, and Luke and I even went searching for you. Don't you think you could have answered our calls or texts?' The rage inside Cathy burned hot, the worry and fear she'd held about Sno's welfare spilling out in a torrent.

'I'm sorry, I lost—'

'Sorry? That's it? That's all you can say after storming out of here like a sulky kid and then vanishing for weeks on end, and all you mutter is sorry? Really?'

'I'm trying to explain, if you can shut up for a minute. Okay?' Sno raised her voice.

'Oh, please do go on, I'm listening. Actually, no, I don't want to hear it. Luke needs to hear this, too, so wait. I'll go get him!' With that, she turned and rushed outside to call her friend.

• • • •

Sno sat into an armchair. She really hadn't the energy or desire for this, and she really didn't want an argument. She just wanted to lie down. A bath would be great, but it didn't look like she was going to be offered one. With Cathy's dramatic reaction, she didn't even know if she was welcome. Maybe she had gotten it wrong. *Should she have stayed in the city, or maybe called ahead before turning up at*

Cregane? She had been stupid to think they wouldn't be annoyed, but God, what could she have done? Nothing, that's what. Cathy could blow hot air all she wanted, but Sno didn't need this grief right now. Grief. No longer a word she spoke about in reference to others, but something she carried deep inside her now, and it scarred her soul and clutched her heart more than she could bear. Her mascara slid down her cheeks, two soot black trails streaking her cheeks and chin as they spilt on to her top.

• • • •

Luke rushed in the door and straight to Sno. Grabbing her in a tight hug, he rocked back and forth, holding her in his arms. It was when he released her that he saw her tears.

'Sno, what the hell? What's happened?' He reached out and held her arm.

Seeing his gentleness with their friend, Cathy blushed with some guilt. 'She was about to explain her disappearance.' Cathy was still annoyed. 'Go on, tell us what was so bloody important that replaced us so quickly? A fella, was it? Thrown you out, has he, and you've come here looking for sympathy? Is that why there's tears? Well?' Cathy couldn't help the venom in her words. She had been so wound up with worry about Sno that now she was here, actually in front of her, she wanted to shake her and scold her and make her feel some of that worry, too.

Luke asked Sno if she wanted a coffee, but she refused, though she did manage a watery smile for him. Cathy's impatience bubbled up once more and she sighed – a sound that filled the already tense room.

'You have a right to be angry, Cathy, and you, too, Luke. There's no fellow involved. I-I've been away. I had to go to...' her sobbing, big choking gulps, shook her frail body. Gasping for breath, she tried to speak, but her crying only grew stronger.

Luke knelt beside the chair and placed his arms around her, throwing a warning look at Cathy to cool her words, while Sno clung to him.

Cathy touched her shoulder gently. 'I'll go put the kettle on. We could all do with a coffee.' Whatever troubled Sno was serious. Cathy had not seen such an outpouring of tears with anyone before. No matter what she thought right now, she couldn't figure out what it was that caused her friend to weep in such depth.

She brought three coffees to the sitting room and found Luke still kneeling and holding Sno in his arms. Her head snuggled into his chest and her body no longer rocked from her crying. In fact, her breathing was almost peaceful in its pace. Placing the hot drinks down on a side table, Cathy remained standing.

'Sno, do you want to sip your coffee?' Luke asked, his words soft and calming. She did not answer.

'Sno, do you want some tissues?' Cathy took a box from a shelf and pulled out a few sheets. The girl still did not answer.

'Sno.' Luke pulled back a little from the silent woman, and when her head flopped forward a little, they realised she was asleep. Sno had cried herself weary. Keeping his arms around her, he scooped her up and stood up with Cathy's support.

He whispered, 'I'll put her into my old room.' Once Sno was tucked up beneath the duvet and her boots slipped off, he pulled the door closed and re-joined Cathy in the sitting room.

'Wow, that was something else,' he said.

'It sure was. Should we get a doctor for her?' Cathy handed him his cup of coffee.

'Maybe we should let her sleep. There's healing in rest, my mother always said.' The unease in his voice belied his words, though, and they both sat with their own thoughts as they sipped the lukewarm drinks.

Sno was clearly hurting. Her pain still clung to the air, and a heaviness and feeling of distress clawed at Cathy. But they wouldn't know what had caused it until she woke up. And even then, she might not be strong enough to share the reason with them.

Chapter Thirty-Two

Cathy slept downstairs on the sofa. She wanted to be nearby if Snowflake woke up. They were all concerned about her, and Mark was astonished when he heard how she had collapsed in a heap of sobbing, and fallen into a heavy sleep. They all agreed that if she did not appear any better in the morning, then it was off to a doctor with her.

First thing in the morning, they all peeped in on the sleeping figure. She was in a deep slumber, and even a gentle shake on the shoulder only raised a soft sigh from her. Luke and Cathy were going to be around Cregane for the day – Luke working on the plaque design, and Cathy searching courses on the internet – so they let her sleep on.

By twelve-thirty, Luke's stomach was rumbling and demanding food, and he brought the design in with him to show Cathy. He was quite proud of his efforts. The timber for the new plaque was lovely. The oak was cleaning up beautifully, and Mark had brought it back to life with an attractive edging and a slight rope effect on the oval timber piece. Luke had drawn some oak leaves, three on one side and two on the opposite side, with the words *Cregane Court Welcomes You* in the centre at a slight off angle.

'Right, has she woken at all?' the lad asked, as he washed up before he made some lunch.

'Not a sound. I'm thinking we need to wake her, Luke. She really needs to eat, or at least drink something. How about I make some soup – the green Thai vegetable one you and Mark like?'

'That would be great, Cathy. No-one can refuse that. We'll leave her alone until it's ready and then we should know more about what's going on.'

An hour later, the smell of the spicy soup ran around the kitchen and seeped towards the downstairs bedroom. Sno stirred as she inhaled the appetising aroma of food. She struggled to open her eyes, her lids heavy from sleep and her body full of emotion. *Where was she?* The room was unfamiliar. Pulling herself slowly up, she saw Luke's smiling face look at her from a photo on the wall, and remembered she was at Cathy's. She also remembered how angry her friend had been. Sno understood why, but there was no energy left in her for a row. Wrapping a blanket around her, she left the room and headed towards the kitchen. She was cold, and her slight body shivered beneath the large throw.

• • • •

'Hey, you're awake.' Luke jumped up from a kitchen chair and pulled Sno in for a hug.

'Yes, I smelt something nice coming from here.' A weak smile greeted Cathy as she turned on hearing Luke shout out.

'Well, get back to bed and we'll bring some into you, then we can talk after,' Cathy advised.

'No, I'll stay here, thanks.'

'You will not. You will do as you're told. Now back to bed.' Cathy issued the order in a no-nonsense tone, but added gently, 'Please, you need to be minded.'

• • • •

The soup warmed them all up, and they left Sno to eat in peace. The questions could wait. Luke and Cathy were shocked at her thin frame. She looked as though she had not eaten in months, her pale face small and sad.

'Okay, do you need a doctor, Sno?' Luke asked, as he and Cathy gathered in the bedroom.

Sno was tucked beneath the duvet, a little more colour in her cheeks since she'd eaten, and a glimpse of brightness in her eyes. Whatever had happened had totally knocked their friend to the ground.

Cathy sat in an armchair in the corner by the window and remained quiet. She felt bad at her outburst the previous night, but knew it had only been due to her concern for her friend. *How could she make her see that?* She really didn't want to fall out with Sno.

'No, no doctor,' Sno said immediately. 'I will be okay. I know I owe you all an apology, but I couldn't help what happened, it was—'

Cathy interrupted, 'No, I'm the one that's sorry. I should never have shot my mouth off like that at you. I could see you were suffering, but I was just so angry with you. We were really worried, particularly when you had left so suddenly before and—'

'My mum and brother are dead.'

The gasps of shock could be heard all over Ballybawn.

• • • •

Neither Luke nor Cathy moved. Sno pulled idly at a loose thread on her top. *What was there to say?* Silence pounded in the room, and all three remained sitting, trying to soak comfort and security from each other's presence.

Luke bit his fingernails – a habit whenever he felt uncomfortable. He couldn't speak. He looked at Sno, who now had quiet tears running down her face. Then he glanced at Cathy. She was numb, not moving, as if she was barely breathing.

It was dark when Mark came home and found the trio together in the bedroom, silent and weeping, the house cold, and an intense energy weighing upon them all.

Chapter Thirty-Three

Over the next few days, not much work was done on the landscape. No-one had the heart to do anything. Sno slept a lot, eating her meals in tiny nibbles, her appetite almost diminished. Cathy and Luke were around most days and encouraged her to take a few bites at every meal, but sometimes it appeared that Sno had given up on life.

In between sobbing and sleeping, the horrible truth about her mother's and brother's deaths spilled out. She told them she'd been at work, in a sulk after leaving Cregane in a strop, and a weak smile teased her lips at this memory. Cathy encouraged her to continue; the reason why she'd stomped off like a sullen five-year-old had lost its importance.

Sno explained that she had received a call, from California University Hospital, and had been bluntly informed that her mother and brother had died the day before. Even relating this to her friends sent her into a spin of grief. The girl was weary with pain and heartbreak. Two days later, she had been on her way to California – Huntington Beach, to be exact.

When she got there, she was told that her family had died in a car crash. A drunk driver had run a red light and ploughed straight into them. To make matters worse, while in the USA, Sno lost her phone. The story, and how she had been faced with making all the arrangements in America, slowly spilled out. Poor Sno's pain showed in every crease and fold of her slender body, each pore filled with hurt.

'But what about your job?' Luke asked.

'When I realised I had to go to California, I handed in my notice. I was leaving anyway,' she glanced up at Cathy, 'to come live in Ballybawn. So, I'd also handed in my notice to my landlord. But honestly, I never thought... I didn't even know that Bolt, my sweet brother, had gone to live with Mum. What a lousy sister I am; I didn't even know where my brother was.'

Between sobs, she continued, 'I'd get the odd text, just to touch base, from them both. Not that I'm angry or cross with them, because I could have made more effort, too. And now, now they're gone... and I'll never get the chance to...' Her thin body shook as she wept once more, distress and upset wrapping around her. Sno still refused to see a doctor. Having her friends was all she needed, she insisted. Everything had been taken care of, and her family's ashes would be sent on in a few months' time. She assured her friends she would slowly pick up the pieces of her life, but promised that if she found she was not coping, she would seek medical help.

• • • •

'Why, Cathy, it's good to see you, girleen. I thought you had moved away!' The glint in William's eye told Cathy he was teasing her.

'Oh, William, it's been one sad story after another. How are you, tell me?'

'Apart from the usual aches and pains, I'm still above ground, so for that I'm thankful.' He laughed – a soft kind laugh that was comforting for Cathy. There had not been laughter in Cregane Court since Sno showed up. The atmosphere was still one of disbelief and sadness, and nothing seemed to lift the mood.

'What? Shure, that's a terrible thing to have happen. How is she now? Silly question.' William's face registered shock at Cathy's news.

She told him how desperate the whole issue was and how none of them knew whether to carry on as normal – whatever that was – or to mourn with Sno.

'Well, being there and supporting her is all you can do for now. It's good she had the sense to come to you. Imagine if that happened and you had no-one to lean on; it doesn't bear thinking about.' William walked to a cupboard and opened the ornate carved door on its front. He grabbed two balloon glasses and a bottle of brandy. 'Here, let's have a sup of this. It's good for shock, and what I've heard this morning has been some shock.' He poured the drinks and handed Cathy a glass.

They toasted the lives of Sno's mother and her brother, Bolt. Then they sipped their drinks, both sighing with anguish.

'What an unusual name the lad had,' William commented, as they sipped a little of the brandy.

'Yes, a bolt out of the blue, Sno explained to me when I first met her. The pregnancy was apparently a surprise for her mother. I liked it, though. I love the originality of it, just like her own name, Snowflake.'

'What about your meeting? Any further developments after that night?' the old man looked at Cathy through squinting eyes.

'Some of the villagers said they were happy with our plans, but we've not thought any more about it, to be honest, with all that's happened.'

'Hmmm... that old Armstrong man is always a stirrer. He likes the sound of his own voice. Has he been in contact with you?' William's face had taken on a cross look.

'Is he the guy who made the complaints on the night? The guy who objected to everything?' The brandy warmed Cathy from the inside, and the glow from William's fire felt cosy and homely.

He nodded and drained the last of his drink. 'Do you want another?' He gestured at the bottle and Cathy shook her head in reply.

'Well, I'm allowed another to help with my aching bones in this cold weather,' he said, winking at her. 'Has Mark heard anything about the planning?' he asked, when he returned to his chair.

'Nope. Although, he could have, but might not have wanted to say because of Sno. It seems little to worry about when compared to her heartache.'

As they sat on either side of the fire, Cathy reflected on her own family. Gemma wasn't always the greatest, but she was there. Cathy was not alone. This felt reassuring as she watched William throw another log on the dancing flames. Sparks of gold and orange and yellow shot into the air, bringing light to an otherwise sombre mood.

• • • •

Walking the road home, Cathy was wrapped up against the cold, frosty air. Her scarf, a bright multi-coloured one that Sno had knitted for her, hung cheerfully around her neck. She kept her hands deep in her coat pockets, and her thoughts were far away as she strolled along. She enjoyed the walk to and from William's; it allowed her time on her own to gather herself and find focus.

The car caught her by surprise when it stopped alongside her, and the window slid down. 'Can I offer you a lift?' Roman O'Driscoll sat inside smiling, his gloved hands gripping the steering wheel, the radio on low.

'No thank you.'

'Are you sure? I heard you had quite the crowd at Cregane; a kind of explanation night, I was told.' The sneer on his face unsettled Cathy.

'Goodbye.' She started to walk away but he rolled along beside her, the soft purr of his car engine barely audible.

'My invite seemed to have been mislaid,' Roman spoke with a slight sarcastic tone.

'What a shame. Oh well, I'm sure you have heard all about it. Now, please leave me alone.' Cathy's eyes blazed in anger, the comforting brandy still tasted in her mouth.

'Why are you so against me? I told you, I could help you out if you are finding Cregane Court to be a handful. There are ways around Elizabeth's will, don't forget that.' Roman revved the engine and drove off.

She stood by the side of the road and watched him go. He had brought up Lizzy's will again. *Why? What was it she was missing?* The notebook immediately came to mind. She needed to check the diary again and see what else it offered. Roman O'Driscoll would get Cregane Court over her dead body, and she did not see that happening in the near future.

Chapter Thirty-Four

'Did you see this?' Mark threw the paper down on the table. His cheeks were flushed red and he grabbed a beer from the fridge with such speed and determination that Luke waited to see if he would sit down or stand before asking him any questions.

Once Mark sat, Luke picked up the paper and flicked through it. 'What am I looking for?'

'Page five, right-hand column,' Mark snapped.

Luke sought the said page and glanced down along it. The headline was neat but prominent, and the article a few inches long. 'So, someone has decided to write about Cregane Court. Do I need to read it, or can I guess from your frowning forehead that makes you look like a baby whose lost its rattle that it doesn't make happy reading?'

Mark shoved away the beer bottle on the table. 'It's one thing after another. First the planning objected to, the debacle of the village open night, then Sno's mum and brother. Yeah, I know that's not Ballybawn's fault, but you know what I mean.'

'Well, let me see.' Luke took a few minutes to read the article. 'Hmm, I see, so we are intending on running a retreat that will take in those who feel the need to express themselves in the so-called arts, and in layman's language that means those who experiment with drugs and drink and free sex. No mention of the fact that the people have to pay for their stay here. I don't think the type of artist they are expecting in this article would have two cents to rub together.' He threw the paper down onto the table. 'It's just a load of crap, Mark. You couldn't pay for this publicity!' Luke laughed loudly.

'You would never believe that people would actually think like that, or that someone would go to the bother of publishing it.' Mark rubbed his forehead in despair.

'Obviously a slow news day or week, or whatever,' Luke added, and placed a hand on Mark's arm to soothe him.

• • • •

'Are you having a laugh?' Cathy was seated in the village bakery café with Snowflake, both enjoying a chocolate éclair and coffee.

Sno waited as Cathy spoke to Mark on her mobile. From what she could make out, the conversation was connected to Lizzy's house, but what exactly she would have to wait to hear.

'Well, that's interesting,' Cathy said, as she placed her mobile back in her handbag. 'Mark says there's an article on Cregane Court in this week's local paper, condemning our plans.'

Sno shook her head. 'Unbelievable. Did it say who wrote the piece?'

Cathy shrugged her shoulders. She hadn't asked, nor had Mark said. While they'd been in the bakery enjoying their coffee, the customers who came in and left had mostly greeted the young women. One or two had thrown side glances at Sno, but Cathy guessed that was more out of curiosity at her shaved hairstyle and unusual style of clothes.

'Let's call to William and see if he can shed some news on the article,' Cathy suggested as she drained the last of her coffee.

• • • •

The old man was listening to the radio when the two women called. After hugs all round, William insisted on putting on the kettle, even though Cathy and Sno told him they had just had coffee at the bakery café. The man was having none of their protestations, especially as they'd brought him a beautiful lemon drizzle cake that had to be tasted.

'Why are people so against us running a retreat centre?' Cathy asked him once they were settled with their tea. 'I mean, it can bring work and money to the area.' She shook her head, unable to understand the problem. 'I've yet to meet with any hostility from the locals,' she told him. 'Even earlier, while Sno and I were having coffee, we didn't encounter anything negative. Yet there's a piece in the local paper condemning the place.' She was feeling more worked up than she'd realised.

No-one seemed to personally know anyone who was upset about Cregane, yet there had been the planning objection and now an article in the paper.

'Calm yourself, girleen, it'll blow over.' The old man puffed on his pipe, then he laughed gently to himself.

Both women looked at him, waiting for him to share the joke.

'I've not seen this much activity in the village in a long time,' he chuckled. 'You surely have put the cat among the pigeons for some, but like you say, why, is the mystery. My money is on that rat, Roman O'Driscoll. He is so slippery; a horrible man indeed.'

'But he wasn't at the meeting,' Cathy protested, 'and we can't prove he is behind the article. Yet he still tells me he can get around Lizzy's will. I wonder why he does that.'

'Well, there's only one way to find out.' William stood up and faced Cathy. 'Challenge him. Tell him you'd like to hear what he has to say.'

'Worth a try,' Sno added.

'Hmm, I need to check Lizzy's diary, too,' Cathy responded. 'I need to work out what all the numbers are for.'

'Do that, Cathy, and maybe more will be revealed that will help make sense of this nonsense?' William began tidying up, taking their cups to the sink for washing.

• • • •

'Gemma, hello. How are you?' Luke opened the door to Cathy's sister. She stepped inside and sat down on the sofa, not taking off her coat.

'Cathy is on the way home,' he explained. 'She and Sno are walking. I'm surprised you didn't pass them.' He placed some coal in the fire stove. The room was cosy, but the cold of outdoors had swept in when Gemma entered.

'I shall wait for ten minutes then I must be going. The girls will be due home from school.' She looked around the room, trying to decide whether she liked the décor or not. It certainly had a welcoming feel, but it was a little too cluttered for her taste.

'Surely you can wait more than ten minutes? I mean, it's a long drive to make for such a short visit.'

'Well, I met a friend while I was here, so that's eaten into my time.' She blushed as she spoke; this fellow was making her feel guilty with his questions. *She was entitled to call here and have other friends in the area*, she reminded herself. Twenty minutes passed before some shuffling on the gravel was heard.

'I think I hear her outside with Sno. I'm sure that's them laughing.' Luke left the room and went to tell Cathy of her sister's arrival.

'Good to see you, Gemma,' she said as she came into the room. 'How are the girls and Paul?' Cathy hugged her sister.

'I was just saying to her,' Luke chipped in, 'that she would have passed you both on the road.'

'Oh, we called to William,' Sno offered.

Gemma relaxed with this news. 'That's probably it,' she hastily agreed with the former waitress.

The two sisters went into the kitchen for a chat.

'So, you had a meeting, I believe. How did that go?' Gemma sat at the top of the table.

'A good few turned up,' Cathy replied, 'and most were very receptive to the idea of a retreat centre.'

'Really?' Gemma's eyebrows raised in surprise. If Cathy knew that she had been out with Roman, there might be cross words.

'Why so surprised with that?' Cathy enquired.

'No, that's good, that's good. So, it's going to go ahead then. What are you doing for money, though, Cathy? Surely it will cost a lot?' Gemma knew she needed to be careful about what she said. Roman had told her exactly what to ask and not to step on their toes too much; just enough to get the information he needed. She felt Cathy's eyes watching her. Gemma knew she sounded a bit jittery, but hoped Cathy might think she was just in a hurry to go off to pick up the girls.

'We are fine with money, thanks. Or are you offering to invest in here?' Cathy laughed.

'Are you mad? Indeed, I'm not. It will never work. Ro— I mean, it could eat cash to get the place looking right, and there's a lot to be built and converted. The landscaping alone will be thousands, you know, to get it looking appealing.' Gemma coughed.

'Well, I don't agree.'

'And there's that article in the paper. That doesn't seem very encouraging now, does it?' Gemma stood, ready to head off back to the city.

'You read the article?' Cathy couldn't help her surprise. 'How? It's in a local paper.'

'Luke must have mentioned it while I was waiting for you.'

'Are you okay, Gemma?'

'I'm fine. Why you ever agreed to taking on this place, I will not understand. And with a bunch of strangers. Down and outs and misfits.'

'They are my friends, so please don't speak of them like that,' Cathy snapped, shooting an angry look at her sister.

'I'll speak whatever way I want,' Gemma bit back. 'I'm your older sister and I know better than you, don't forget. You were always taking the wrong path or making some mistakes. Poor Mam and Dad had endless patience with your daftness, but I won't. You would do better if you sold this place and moved back to the city, back to civilisation, and get a proper job and life, instead of this up-in-the-air nonsense, all rainbows and unicorns.'

Cathy's mouth dropped open at her sister's words. Before she could reply, Gemma had flounced out of the cottage, the roar of her car engine sounding as she drove up the hill towards the village.

Chapter Thirty-Five

Lizzy's old notebook lay on the table before Cathy as she pored over it to see what else she could learn. There was some scribbling, but the writing was not very clear. Sno was lying down, and her snores could be heard from the downstairs bedroom, with the door slightly ajar. Cathy smiled. It was good that they were together, all four of them. They were of the one mind and cloth. She felt relaxed and happy living with her friends. It was such a pity she did not feel the same way with her sister.

When she told the others about Gemma's harsh words to her, they had been annoyed that her sister should leave her feeling low and unhappy. Gemma was just a bitch, Sno had remarked. And while Luke agreed, he questioned whether there had been something more behind her visit. He was sure Gemma hadn't been checking on Cathy's welfare, and was adamant he had not mentioned the newspaper article to her. So, he wondered aloud, was her friend Roman whispering in her ear?

Cathy turned page after page of the notebook, still having no luck. The numbers decreased as the pages went on, the total getting smaller and smaller. *And what were the initials all about?* She faced the same questions as before, but was still left with no answers.

Sno stirred and came through to join Cathy at the table, turning one of the pages towards her.

'Can I have a peep?' she asked.

'Sure, I'll make some coffee.' Cathy sighed.

'Was there any other notebook in the box of stuff you kept?' Sno shouted out.

'The box is under the shelf in the alcove if you want to check it.'

• • • •

'I agree.' Mark was home.

Everything that Sno said made sense. The numbers were definitely a balance of sorts, and the decreasing amounts were due to money spent or given away. The initials beside the instalments were either Lizzy's or her husband Archie's, but Sno reckoned the others were Cathy and Mark or else the reverse, Mark and Cathy. Yet neither had received money from Archie or Elizabeth, and were happy to provide their bank statements to reinforce what they said.

'Who handled her affairs?' Luke enquired. The four of them had finished dinner and were seated in the sitting room enjoying a glass of wine. Outside, it was a stormy night, the trees rustling and groaning as darkness dressed them.

'Roman O'Driscoll saw to it all, I think,' Mark answered.

'So, do we ask him? Show him the notebook?' Cathy asked.

'Look, this might be crazy, but did Lizzy put money into a bank account for you both? Like a joint one?' Sno suggested. 'Your names, or rather your initials, only appear after Archie's death, am I right?' She sipped her wine, looking more refreshed after her earlier nap.

'But would we not have heard from the bank?' Cathy got up and poured some more of the Sauvignon Blanc for them all. 'There's no bank in the village, but I could ask William which of the two nearest banks would be the most popular, if any.'

'Mark, when your gran died, was there anything said about Elizabeth?' Luke snuggled up beside him on the sofa.

'Not that I know of.' Mark looked thoughtful. 'What are you thinking?'

'Well, you said they were both great friends, and Elizabeth didn't die until after her, so can you remember anything being said at the funeral that was out of place?' Luke's eyes sparkled with love for

Mark. Every time he was in his presence, the young man glowed. Cathy thought it lovely to watch, and couldn't help hoping that one day she'd find someone who would look at her in the same way.

• • • •

Gemma lay in bed that night, thinking about how she had almost let Roman's name slip. She was pretty sure Cathy had not noticed, but she would need to be careful. And she knew she would need to go back to Cregane to see if this notebook that Roman kept referring to was around. When she had pressed him on its importance, he had said it was about numbers and nothing of any real significance. Yet, she mused, he always asked her if Cathy had mentioned it.

Her husband moved beside her. Paul was a good man, but the excitement and connection between them was dissolving fast. Roman paid her attention, made her feel an attractive woman, and complimented her on her clothes and how helpful she was to him with regards to Cregane. She wouldn't hurt Paul. After all, she didn't want an affair. She just wanted to be appreciated, and that is what Roman O'Driscoll did. He thanked her for her help with Cathy and Mark, and shared little confidences with her. He'd even told her that Elizabeth's husband Archie had been unhappy in their marriage, and that he'd planned – if he could manage it – that Cregane Court would be Roman's. Archie, it seemed, had wanted shot of it and of his wife. *Bet Cathy doesn't know that*, Gemma thought, smiling smugly. But she would let her know when the time was right. Oh yes. Gemma knew what was best for her sister, and she would tell her when she learnt more from Roman.

• • • •

Sno stayed up long after the others had retired to bed. She retrieved the box of Lizzy's bits and pieces that Cathy had kept, and went through it carefully, stopping to read any scribbling she came across.

There were loads of photos, mainly of Lizzy with Mark's grandmother, Diane. Many had been taken in the orchard, beneath the trees, others down by the river, and some at the garden parties that Lizzy held. Archie appeared in one or two, but always a step to the side of his wife. *Strange behaviour*, Sno thought.

There were receipts for work carried out in Cregane at various times, and the usual mementoes people kept of happy times, along with some copies of the local newspaper. Sno opened them out but couldn't see anything of interest at first glance. It all seemed to be who had died, what sports team had won the local cup, or some villager's birthday celebrations with photos to mark the event. Nothing shouted out to Sno.

As she placed everything back in the box, a slip of paper fell to the ground. When she turned it over, Sno's heart leapt with excitement. In what appeared to be Lizzy's handwriting were some numbers and an address. She was pretty sure this was the bank account that they needed to find.

Chapter Thirty-Six

'Are you sure she hasn't mentioned a notebook?' Roman's knuckles glowed white as he balled his fists by his sides.

'What does the bloody notebook have in it that's so important?' Gemma's irritation was bubbling.

He remained silent. He needed that notebook. Archie had told him he had recorded all the money transfers to Roman in that book, so he needed to get it out of Cregane.

Looking thoroughly fed up with his mood, Gemma got up from the park bench and faced him. 'Goodbye, Roman. I suggest you ask Cathy yourself, since I'm such a failure!'

'What? No, no, not at all, I'm being silly. Thank you, Gemma, for helping. I just hate to think that your sister and Mark could sink money into a non-starter. It would be such a shame for the young couple.' He turned on his most charming smile and was relieved to see her sit back down.

'I'm going to invite her to mine for dinner. Maybe after a few glasses of wine, she might be easier to handle,' Gemma purred, waiting to be told how clever she was.

Roman did not disappoint. 'Great thinking,' he winked. *God, this woman is so shallow,* he thought. *She screams for attention; it must be hard on her poor, suffering husband.* Still, she was useful to Roman.

• • • •

Mark knew the bank address on the paper that Sno had found. It was actually two villages away, which seemed strange, but he and Cathy decided to pay a visit and see if Elizabeth had dealings there. The manager was happy to make an appointment to see them at the end of the week. In the meantime, a sense of mystery swirled around Cregane, the bad luck of previous events slowly lifting.

Luke continued to work on the plaque and Sno busied herself with some knitting. She decided to design some jumpers – unisex ones in multicolours. She knew the logo she wanted to create, and Luke offered to help her draw the pattern out. She was thrilled when she saw the lightning strike he had drawn across the chest of a jumper sketch. It would be called The Bolt collection, in memory of her brother, and the lightning strike logo would always be in blue, just as her mother used to say: *a bolt out of the blue*.

Cathy felt calmer, too. She was starting to believe there was an end in sight for all this hassle with Cregane. Trusting her instincts, she went back to creating the website, and uploaded photos and outlined what was on offer in Ballybawn and the surrounding area.

The village further from the city had an old castle, where re-enactments of the local battles from the past centuries took place each summer. A festival was built around these re-enactments and drew large crowds. In Ballybawn itself, the local cemetery held graves of famous actors who had discovered the tranquillity and kindness of the locals. They had relished getting away from the bright lights of their celebrity status. These attractions made the area around Cregane Court the ideal place for a visit. There were fine restaurants, music in the pubs, history to offer, and walks for solitude and inspiration – all easily accessed from her new home.

When she'd finished, she looked at the website and read it over, realising it was the best thing she had ever done. Bless Great-Aunt Lizzy for remembering her. She would be forever thankful.

• • • •

The work meeting was dragging on. Two hours had already passed, and they were no closer to reaching an agreement about budgets. Mark sighed. Work was becoming harder to bear by the week. He looked around the table and saw a circle of bored faces, some flushed from high blood pressure, no doubt stressed from worry about meeting deadlines. He was one of the younger people there, but the circle of suits bothered him. He looked at the woman to his right, wearing a navy skirt suit and white blouse. She looked tense and starched. He thought of Sno and Cathy, the colours they wore, the loose hair, and the happiness that followed them. In contrast, his workmate looked drained and colourless. She was probably juggling young children as well as the job. Irritation gnawed at him and his fingers tapped on the table. He desperately wanted this meeting to end so he could return to Cregane Court.

Finally, an agreement was met, and new deadlines put in place, meaning they would all gather here in a month's time and do it all over again. Oh, the joy. As he looked at his colleague, she offered a weak smile, and it was then Mark realised that he felt as unhappy as she looked.

• • • •

'You what?' they cried in unison.

'I've quit. Gave a month's notice as required, and I'm out of there.' Mark did a Usain Bolt gesture and laughed as his hands pulled on an imaginary bow and arrow.

'But have you thought this through? I mean, really Mark, it's a major gamble.' Cathy's wide eyes stared at her friend, fear tapping her on the shoulder.

'Best thing I ever did. Should have done it a long time ago. And I've you three to thank for it.' A grinning Mark beamed with excitement and delight.

'What are we like?' Cathy whispered.

'What's wrong?' Sno asked. She did not like Cathy's worried expression.

'Nothing. Don't mind me.' Cathy slunk back in the chair, struggling to muster up the joy the others shared. *What was Cregane*

Court doing to them? Maybe she was over-reacting; being silly, that's all.

Wine was uncorked and celebrations were enjoyed into the early hours of the morning.

But when Cathy snuck off to bed, she carried with her a sense of foreboding, her troubles picking at her as she struggled to sleep. *Had she done the right thing taking on Lizzy's home?* She was happy living with Mark, but all this responsibility with turning the home into a retreat centre was scaring her. Shuddering, she realised how strong this fear was in her. So many people had changed their lives because of her dream. She was the cause of upheaval and uncertainty in her friends, she was sure of it. Although they acted or seemed contented with their choices, she was not so at ease.

It was true what Gemma said, their parents had always been willing to pick Cathy up whenever life overwhelmed her. *Gemma was right in a lot of things*, Cathy reluctantly admitted to herself. Maybe a chat with her would be a good idea. That's what big sisters were for after all. Her eyes stung with tears as she churned over her concerns. Thanks to her, Luke had been brought to live away from his beloved city; Snowflake had quit her job; and now Mark, the sensible one, the one that took charge of the finances and showed resilience and common sense when all the issues they were dealing with flared up, had quit his job.

Cathy Reed had created a monster. Her idea for a retreat centre had not only upset the local village, but it had lulled her housemates and herself into a false sense of security. She would not sleep tonight. The sooner the meeting with the bank manager happened the better. It was only two days away and it might bring good news. God knows, they needed it.

Chapter Thirty-Seven

The meeting with the bank manager turned out to be a real surprise. They discovered that Lizzy had opened up a joint account for Cathy and Mark several years ago, with monthly instalments of a couple of hundred, which meant there was a few thousand of savings now waiting for them. The manager admitted he had been surprised when they had contacted him to ask for the meeting, as he had not been informed of Lizzy's death, which was very unusual. Solicitors normally do searches and notify banks and other institutions of a death, he told them. Cathy suggested that as the great woman herself did not have an account, that might be the reason for the bank not being notified, but the manager had still seemed doubtful.

As they drove back to Cregane Court, Cathy and Mark agreed that the money in the account would be very useful for the building works, and certainly took the pressure off financially. But neither could understand why Roman O'Driscoll hadn't mentioned the money to them. Mark wondered if the solicitor even knew that Lizzy had opened this account.

They agreed they needed to have a meeting with him, and Mark suggested they organise it soon, rather than letting it linger on. He also refused Cathy's plea that he meet the man on his own.

'We need to show a united front, Cathy,' he said. 'We need to do this together.'

Misery folded over her knowing she had to face the shady solicitor. The thought had taken away the initial thrill of having money. She decided a break from the village and Cregane was called for, and sent a text to Gemma that she was planning to call over.

• • • •

'I could have gone into the city no problem, Gemma.' Cathy pulled out the seat in Ballybawn bakery and sat down. Gemma had arrived before her and was already seated with a huge mug of coffee on the table.

'Not at all, Cathy. I love driving out, and it saves you having to get the bus. You can't have much money with all the renovations you and Mark have made to Lizzy's old place. Which reminds me, this lunch is on me.' She leaned over and patted Cathy's hand.

It was like a '*there, there*' moment that left Cathy feeling like an upset five-year-old. Which she was. Upset.

'Gemma, that's kind of you,' she managed. 'How are the girls? You've not brought them out yet to see the place. They would love the orchard and the swing.'

'All in good time.'

'Did I tell you that Mark quit his job?' The toasted special in the bakery's café was tasty and filling, their sandwiches of bacon, lettuce, and tomato were hot and savoury, the side salad and crisps a thoughtful touch. The background music was low, a gentle comforting hum of melodies that lilted in the air. Over in the corner, a fire blazed, a supply of logs stacked nearby.

'What? Why?' Gemma's eyes widened with surprise.

'He wasn't happy,' Cathy explained, 'and he thought if he doesn't do it now then it will never happen.'

'But how did he come to that sense of belief? I mean you both move into the house under ridiculous circumstances, and now the one person I would have said that has any maturity has left his safe job! And for what? Has he a plan?' Gemma's cup shook in her hand as she spoke. Clearly, she didn't approve of Mark's move.

'No plan that I'm sure of. Are you really surprised with that news?' Cathy's foreboding feelings slipped into the pit of her stomach at Gemma's protestations. Everything seemed to dim – the music and the glow of the fire. Cathy didn't like this feeling.

'Of course I am. What sane person does that? I think ye have all been bewitched with this house, getting fancy ideas and not a penny between you all.' Gemma's head shook from side to side in annoyance.

Wanting to remove the nauseating sense that was wrapping around her, Cathy blurted out their latest news. 'It's not all gloom and doom,' she said brightly. 'We got a nice surprise on Friday last. Apparently, Lizzy had opened an account for us many years ago and lodged money into it each month. Not a lot, but enough to take the pressure off us. It means, though, we now have to meet that awful Roman O'Driscoll and find out why he never informed us about it. Strange, isn't it?'

Gemma immediately sat upright, her eyes widening. 'That was nice of her. Any other surprises happen since I saw you last?'

'No. All good.' Cathy's mood dipped again, surprised that her sister was taking this news of their windfall so calmly.

• • • •

Gemma glanced at her watch. She knew Roman was due back in his office in another half an hour; she'd checked with his secretary if he was around the locality. She might just text him for a quick catch-up once Cathy left. The women ate in silence for a while and Gemma ordered more coffee while she wondered whether or not to bring up the notebook. *Would it be too obvious? Oh hell, Cathy probably wouldn't cop it that she was being led down the garden path.* Her sister was too trusting for her own good, and the people she hung out with proved that. Gemma was sure that the two misfits Cathy allowed to live with her and Mark would rob them soon enough. They were just biding their time, she was sure of it, particularly after the type of lifestyles they had been living. *Take that young bloke, for instance*, she thought. *How could he adapt to normal living after prowling the streets for years?*

'So, have you finished with all of Lizzy's things now? I mean are you finished clearing out her stuff?' Gemma sipped on her cappuccino, trying to look nonchalant.

Cathy replied, 'yes, we have pretty much everything sorted. Did you want something from Cregane? There's still some bits and pieces I have in a box. Nothing fancy, mainly photo albums and some books and such.'

'Books? What kind? Was she a reader then?' Gemma hid a smirk; Cathy had provided her with an opening at last. Now she could nose a little!

'Well, more like diary stuff, notebooks of all sorts. I'm just going through them at my leisure, to get a sense of what Lizzy felt for Cregane, I suppose. If I'm going to make changes, I want them to be in the same spirit as Great-Aunt Lizzy.' Cathy smiled as she recalled the old woman with the fancy shoes.

'Notebooks? How interesting. Are they of any importance? I mean, you mentioned finding a bank account, maybe the notebooks will turn up something even more lucrative.' *Bingo*, thought Gemma, *she has notebooks. Gosh, Roman will be thrilled.* Gemma watched as Cathy bit down on a chocolate éclair, cream spilling out and sticking to her fingers.

'We should be so lucky. But she really was a comic of a character,' Cathy chuckled. 'The number of parties and card games she held, she certainly lived life. There was no saving for a rainy day with her. Did I tell you she had a stash of wine in the coal cellar? A whole two crates of red and white from different parts of France.'

Cathy's words stabbed at Gemma's heart. Gemma couldn't understand how anyone could live without savings. *How did Archie put up with his wife's silly antics?* It was not that Gemma was a spoilsport; she was cautious, that's all. She really could see Cathy loving Lizzy's lifestyle; they seemed like kindred spirits. Her aunt had obviously not thought she was worthy of inheriting Cregane.

Lizzy must have known that she would have immediately put the For Sale sign up and invested the money, not set up a stupid retreat. *Yes*, Gemma decided, *Cathy and Lizzy were peas of the one pod.*

Gemma mused whether she would ever have been friends with Cathy if they weren't sisters. *Probably not*, she admitted to herself. Cathy was weak and a pushover, and this helping others was draining. Charity, after all, began at home. Now that she knew about the existence of these notebooks, it was time to say goodbye to her sister and meet Roman.

• • • •

'Well, time to go. Great to have met up. Text again when you're free.' Gemma stood, signalling the end of their lunch.

'Oh right, okay.' Cathy was a bit put out by her sister's sudden dismissal. She had actually been enjoying chatting about the house, and surprised that Gemma was so interested. Licking the last of the éclair off her fork, Cathy wiped her mouth with the napkin before speaking again. 'Have you seen him lately that snake O'Driscoll?'

'What? Why would I see the man?' Gemma bit back, stopping in her tracks. 'And you should call him by his name. I thought you were all finished with him.'

'The business about the bank account like I said.' Cathy reached across Gemma and opened the café door.

Stepping out, she walked ahead and turned to say goodbye to her sister, but Gemma's head was stuck in her phone, busy texting. It was Cathy's signal that Gemma had already moved on from their chat, and Cathy was once again ignored.

Chapter Thirty-Eight

Mark was troubled, but not because he'd jacked in his safe, well paid job. No, that was the bright star that shone in his life right now. He was thrilled at the prospect of no more biting his tongue when stuffed-up bosses snapped orders. Those same overfed guys with their flushed faces and big bellies as a result of all the rich lunches marked up as expenses, appearing once a month in the office to spout about their own importance. Freedom was what came to mind now when he thought about those parasites.

But had he swapped his troubles of work for troubles of a different kind? Maybe yet it was time to face the fact that he had someone in his life who he cared for deeply. Life could finally be the way he always dreamed of.

Luke. The blond-haired, green-eyed lad whose very presence made Mark's insides turn to jelly. His touch lit sparks in Mark's heart, and his kiss melted him completely. But Mark had not gone public... not yet. He was shy by nature, and at work had remained quiet on his sexual preferences. He didn't reckon that his colleagues would have given a damn, but it was his own choice that kept him from sharing. Maybe it harked back to his parents' attitude and the fact that they had never shown acceptance of anything in his life.

But now his workmates were holding a going away party for him, and no doubt Luke would want to attend. From the young man's point of view, they were in a relationship, so why wouldn't Mark show him off? This was the worry that gnawed away at Mark. A worry that needed to be handled without hurting Luke's feelings.

• • • •

Roman O'Driscoll sat in his office. The soft leather chair, comfortable and expensive, swivelled as he read the texts from

Gemma. So, Elizabeth had squirreled away some money after Archie died. She was a clever old lady, after all.

Roman and Archie had struck a deal that Roman would own Cregane Court, and so would get to build his Towers. And as Elizabeth's name was not on the house deeds – as was common practice back in the old days – Archie was entitled to will it away. The elderly man did not love his wife, and had given Roman a payment each month to invest for his future, so that he would have money to separate from her and pay her off a bit.

But while Archie's plan to leave Elizabeth and give Cregane Court to the solicitor had been all nicely laid out verbally, the man had died suddenly without signing any official papers. Neither man had factored in that Lizzy might outlive her husband.

If Roman was one thing, however, it was persistent. He would get the bloody place yet, and so far, his backhand underhand tactics were working. The only troubled spot was that the two young people who now owned the place had discovered a secret bank account, but thankfully they had not yet discovered the thousands which Archie had given to him. Roman had not declared this money; in fact, he had most of it invested under his own name – something even Archie had not known. Roman needed to be on guard this afternoon when he met with Cathy Reed and her sidekick Mark Daniels.

• • • •

'It's just strange that you never mentioned it at all. The bank manager said he would be in touch, by the way. Has he?' Mark meant business. He did not care what Roman O'Driscoll said; Mark wanted answers.

'Well, like I said, Elizabeth complicated things when she bequeathed Cregane to you both, what with the clause and all.' Roman tried to smile and appear friendly, but from the tone of his voice, Cathy reckoned he wanted to rush them out of the office and forget about Elizabeth Sheldon altogether.

'It still doesn't explain how the account slipped your mind,' Mark persevered. 'Are you not supposed to do searches and such-like?'

'Well, now that you have brought it to my attention, I shall certainly look into it,' he responded calmly. 'Have you the details there with you, the account number and such? And is it in both your names, or in Elizabeth's?'

'Mr. O'Driscoll, why do you keep telling me that there are ways around this clause that Lizzy added? You seem very sure that you can do this.' Cathy decided to do what William had advised and ask him straight out. She noticed the man's brows knit in a frown, as though trying to judge her sincerity. 'I ask because... well, for me anyway, it has all become such a hassle. The planning permission, the locals – well, a handful being nasty – then the hidden bank account. It just seems I've fallen into a country mystery that only the bravest can handle... and I am weary of it.'

Mark looked at her in disbelief. He opened his mouth, but nothing came out.

Cathy knew he must be shocked. They had agreed to put on a united front today, yet here she was saying she wanted to be rid of Cregane. 'I'm sorry, Mark,' she turned to face him now. 'But ever since I mentioned the idea of this retreat centre, it has been nothing but one disaster after another.'

She turned to the solicitor again. 'Mr. O'Driscoll, you have no idea how stressful it's been, on a personal level. If you were still sure you could ease my way out of this mess...'

The silence that followed almost broke her heart. She knew Mark felt betrayed, as he wouldn't look at her. On the other hand, though, Roman was busy tapping his fingers on his desk, as if unsure whether to believe her or not.

'I'm surprised, to say the least, Cathy,' he said eventually. 'Anytime I spoke with you, I got the distinct impression you were determined to go ahead with your project. In fact, you came across as not liking my offers of help,' Roman challenged her.

'I agree with all you say, Mr. O'Driscoll. But despite the fact that I may not have liked your help, as you call it, I am entitled to change my mind. Like I said, so much has happened. Mark knows exactly what we've gone through, and well, I can't do it anymore. I am happy to move out straight away, maybe stay with my sister. I'm sorry.' Cathy cast her eyes downwards, choosing not to look at either man.

'Well, then, if you are sure. What have you to say, Mark?' The solicitor turned his attention to Cathy's friend.

'I'm not leaving,' he replied quickly. 'Elizabeth Sheldon trusted me to take care of her home. So, how do you propose to deal with this new development?' He kept facing Roman, refusing to look at Cathy.

'Well, when you inherited the house, you both had to agree to live there. Since Cathy wants to leave, then you will have to vacate it, too.' Roman O'Driscoll could not hide the smile pulling at his mouth, and Cathy watched the greed shine in his eyes.

'You will have to fight me for it.' Mark pushed back his chair and stood up. His hands splayed on the desk before him, he leant in towards the solicitor and added, 'I don't plan on losing.'

'And how do you propose on paying for any legal battle now that you have no job? Get real, Mark. Your friend here has seen sense. Be like her. Your other friends, the misfits that you house, will have to go back to the streets – and this time they'll stay there.' His voice dropped to a more sinister tone. 'I have my ways. I can take you and all you own with the snap of my fingers.' He clicked his fingers to prove his point.

'Mark, please listen to him,' Cathy urged. 'We tried, so we did. The locals have blocked our planning, they've even written to the papers. Yes, they were lies, but it's just not worth it. I don't think

Lizzy realised what she expected of us.' Cathy remained seated, but her pleading voice bounced around the office.

'I agree, Cathy,' the solicitor soothed. 'Lizzy hadn't the brains, but Archie did. Mark, there's so much you don't know. Archie wanted me to have it; he was even happy to leave his wife.'

'How dare you! How dare both of you!' Mark stomped angrily out of the office, the door slamming after him.

Cathy sighed. She had hurt her friend in a way he didn't deserve, and he would probably never speak to her again. She knew she would have to go to Cregane and face his anger, but hopefully it would be worth it. Gathering up her bag and jacket, she stood to go. Roman held out his hand to her, but she didn't take it and he just shrugged.

'I shall be in touch,' the solicitor said. 'And you are doing the right thing.'

Cathy paused when she reached the door, and turned back briefly. 'How did you know Mark had given in his notice at work?'

He smirked. 'Your sister and I have shared lunch. I thought she would have told you.'

'Do the locals really dislike what we wanted to do at Cregane? Was it really such a bad idea?' There was sadness in her question, and a look of weariness crossed her face.

'The locals?' he scoffed. 'They are asleep most of the time. All it takes is a bit of gossip and some scaremongering. It's easy to manipulate people to do your bidding, Cathy. A letter to the paper is easily sent, and a promise is easily made to someone who needs something. People are greedy – some more so than others – and money in the right hands sings.'

She frowned. 'Is that what you did to break us down? Manipulate people to fight against us? Pay them even? It's okay, Roman, you've won, you can say it.' She kept the deflated tone in her voice, her demeanour one of defeat.

'You could say that.' He smiled. 'Truth be told, yes.'

Cathy shook her head. 'Gemma was right; she said you were smart.' She sounded sad and defeated. 'I should have listened.'

'Gemma is a wise woman,' he replied. 'She knows how to play the game, but she has a lot to learn, too. You have better ambition. I have my own ideas for Cregane, maybe you and I could work together.' He smiled encouragingly. 'Think about it. Shove those layabouts in Cregane to the kerb and join the winning side, Cathy.'

Chapter Thirty-Nine

'Is it true? Is what Mark told us true?' Luke jumped up from his seat when Cathy returned to Cregane.

'Where's Mark?' she asked. The house was quiet, no radio or music playing.

'He's upstairs,' Luke snapped.

Cathy went to the kitchen and filled the kettle. 'Do you want some coffee?'

'How could you? How could you sell out like that? The work we've put in, the time and effort, and all our plans. Why Cathy, why?' He paced the kitchen, anger blazing in his eyes, his fists balled by his side.

'Yes, Cathy, why?' Mark stood at the foot of the stairs. His eyes were puffy and cheeks blotchy.

'Because I had to. I needed to. For this.' She put her hand into her jacket pocket and pulled out her mobile phone. She placed it on the table, pressed a button, and immediately Roman O'Driscoll's voice filled their kitchen.

Mark was the first to laugh. He swept her up in his arms and twirled her around. 'Why, Cathy Reed, I love you. Do you hear me? I love you.'

'Excuse me, but can someone tell me what has happened?' Sno looked from Luke to the others. Her arms were filled with groceries from the village.

'Sit down. Mark will tell you everything.' Cathy went about making the coffee while Mark explained how she had dropped the bombshell of giving up Cregane while they were in the solicitor's office.

'I really believed her,' he admitted. 'She was good. You were good,' he said again, as he looked at Cathy across the table.

'Well, now what do we do? He thinks you are abandoning here.' Luke sat back and twirled a spoon between his fingers.

'I'm going to move out for a little while,' Cathy explained. 'I'm sure he knows about the notebook and those figures. It seems Gemma has been spoon-feeding him everything I shared with her. That's how he knew about your job.'

Mark nodded. It made sense.

'I'm going to share this recording with you all, so if anything happens to my phone, ye will have it okay. And Mark, I'm genuinely sorry about not telling you about my plan. I really needed you to be shocked.'

He laughed. 'Well, you did a good job. I thought I'd have a heart attack when you said you wanted out.'

'Do you have to stay at Gemma's? Can you not stay somewhere else?' Sno asked Cathy.

'Why?' She was puzzled at Sno's question.

'She's toxic, that's why. Every time you have been in her company, you return a little bit broken. Imagine actually living with her!' The others nodded in agreement.

'But where can I stay if not with her?'

'The Shed!' Luke shouted out.

Cathy looked bewildered. 'But I'm supposed to be moving out?'

'Cathy, if you've done a good a job at convincing that snake O'Driscoll, as Mark said you did, you can think of something to tell him that covers you staying in the Shed.' Sno had cleared the kitchen table and was beginning to wash up.

'It's true. We will just have to think of a reason,' Luke added.

'I have one, but well, you and Sno are not going to like it.' Mark reached for Luke's hand and held it. 'Sno, you didn't hear the recording earlier and, Luke, you only know part of the story, but he really dislikes both of you very much. Could we use that in some way to explain why you're staying around, Cathy do you think?'

'Maybe. Let's call it a day on the subject. I'm in the mood for a long soak in the bath and then I'll hit bed. My soft pillow awaits me.'

• • • •

She lay in the warm bubbles, the meeting with Roman playing over in her mind. *What had she done? Could she pull it off?* She so wanted to expose the creep for the true rodent he was. Cathy didn't reckon she'd ever forget the hurt on Mark's face in the solicitor's office. It had shattered her, knowing he was devastated in the office by her actions. She would tell William too about it when she called to see him next. After all, he had planted the seed in her mind about challenging Roman. Now she just needed to get more evidence of his crooked ways then expose him for the fraud he was.

She stepped from the bath, wrapping a fluffy towel around her, and detangled her damp curls. She couldn't help but giggle with the boldness she had displayed today. The old Cathy would never have spoken up or lied like that. But her love for Cregane ran deep, and she pulled strength from it each day. Lizzy would have been proud of her for taking on O'Driscoll, Cathy was sure. She was doing this for her great-aunt who had entrusted her to look after this home, and she would not let Lizzy down.

Upstairs, she grabbed her book from the nightstand and settled down to read, then unwrapped a bar of milk chocolate. Her treat sprinkled a little glitter on her night-time routine, and it was her favourite way to unwind. Unexpectedly, her mobile rang and Gemma's name flashed on the screen. *Not now, Gemma*, she thought. It was late, but Gemma was not giving up. Her sister continued to let it ring until Cathy eventually picked up.

'Hello, Gemma.'

'Cathy, is it true?' Her sister spoke in gasps.

'Well, it depends on what you are referring to.' Cathy decided to toy with her sister. She had been pretty sure O'Driscoll would fill Gemma in on their meeting.

'Are you leaving that awful house? I bumped into Roman in town this afternoon, and he told me you had seen sense.' Gemma paused and waited for a response.

'Oh, do you bump into him often?' Cathy avoided answering the question. The sweet chocolate was melting fast in her mouth, and speaking with Gemma tainted the pleasure of it on her tongue.

'No, usually we plan to... Look, tell me, is it true?' Gemma had almost let slip their planned meetings, Cathy realised.

'Yes, I told him I was pulling out. I'm tired of everything going wrong since we got here. No matter which way we approach our plans, they get blown up in our face. I feel I've had enough.' Cathy sighed down the phone. She was tired. It had been a long day, and talking to her sister really didn't appeal to her at this late hour. She wanted to get back to her book and relax.

'So, when should I expect you?'

'What?' Cathy was caught off-guard.

'Well, where are you going to go?'

'Gemma, I might stay here, but not in the house. Maybe in The Shed – you know, the place we converted? It might be good to keep an eye on what's happening here now with me not in the picture so to speak.' Cathy hoped she sounded convincing.

'Yes, that makes sense,' Gemma replied thoughtfully. 'You should run it by Roman, though. Well, delighted with your good news. Chat tomorrow.' Gemma hung up.

Cathy turned her phone off. She didn't want Gemma or, worse still, Roman ringing again tonight. She popped another delicious square of the sweet treat into her mouth and went back to her book.

Chapter Forty

As Luke and Mark helped her move her stuff to the outhouse, she noticed a coolness from Mark towards Luke and wondered if they'd fallen out. She hoped whatever was wrong wasn't connected to her.

'Is everything okay?' She pulled Mark to one side after Luke had returned to the cottage and they were alone.

'Of course, why?'

'You seem cool with Luke. Please say I'm not the cause of it.'

Mark explained that he had over a week left in his job, and he still hadn't told Luke about the party.

'The party?' she asked with raised eyebrows.

Mark looked anxious and looked around to see if Luke was within earshot. Cathy instinctively did the same. *What on earth was he going to tell her*? She hoped it wasn't something else to add to their woes. He went on to explain that he loved Luke, of that there was no doubt, but he didn't want him at the party. He had never flaunted his private life in front of his colleagues before, and it didn't sit well to do so now.

'Christ, Mark, that's not good,' Cathy replied. 'Do you really care what they think? It's different times, for goodness sake.' She shook her head. 'Luke is not going to be happy, I can tell you now.'

Her friend looked desperate, no longer the self-confident financier who handled fistfuls of cash and decided on investments daily. It did not make sense to her that he was so afraid of being talked about, but when he didn't reply, she took it that he was a lot more worried than she realised. 'Mark, are you listening to me? You can't do this to Luke. Who cares what people think or who knows? For God's sake, grow a pair, and be honest and true to yourself. If anything, the one thing I've learnt from Cregane is to be and do what makes me feel right and happy. I can't believe this is even an issue for you. Sorry, but really? Talk to Luke.'

Mark agreed he was being stupid and would talk to Luke that night.

Once Cathy was settled into her new surroundings, her bedroom made up, and her clothes and shoes tidied away, she went for a walk to William's house. She was trying to decide whether to tell him the truth or to go along with the lie she had conceived. His front door was open, so she tapped on it as she stepped inside. William was singing in his kitchen, the radio on as accompaniment.

'Hello,' she called out, so as not to frighten him.

'Ah, Cathy, the very woman. Welcome. Sit down, sit down. I've news for you.' He busied himself with a frying pan and the kettle, and soon they both sat at the table with plates of scrambled eggs and toast, and strong hot tea. He insisted they eat first before sharing his news. A full stomach, he said, could take any type of news, good or bad.

'So, remember back I said I had some stuff to do?' he said eventually. 'Well, I went to visit Mrs. Summers. You won't know her, but she had a lot to tell me about our favourite solicitor.' He paused to look at her.

Cathy was wide-eyed with curiosity, wondering what William had found out. She would need to tell him the truth about her plan with Mark; it would be unfair to keep him in the dark.

'Mrs. Summers was the housekeeper and receptionist, an all-round Jill of all trades, for Roman's father, God be good to him. When the man died an early death, she was kept to housekeeping duties only. The son had fancy ideas of progressing the firm, and bluntly told her she could either retire or stay on in the kitchen. Nice fellow, isn't he? Anyway,' not wasting another second, William continued, 'she said your Great-Uncle Archie visited Roman a lot. They had plenty of meetings, and from what she could make out, he was offering investment advice of sorts to Archie. Now, there had been rumours that things weren't great between Archie and Elizabeth. She was the party girl and he... well, he didn't like all the fuss. In fact, some said, that...' He stopped and drew a breath. 'What you think of that?'

Cathy sat silent. She hadn't heard of this Mrs Summers before – maybe Mark knew of her – but it was interesting to hear that Archie had been so friendly with the solicitor.

'The rumours you talk about, Archie and Elizabeth not getting on, it must have been true because—' She saw William raise his hand to silence her.

'Don't be listening to rumours. I didn't know whether to tell you or not before now, but I had also heard the stories and ignored them. That's why I've not said a word before.'

'But, William, he told me... Roman told me that Archie had wanted to leave Lizzy.'

Now it was the old man's turn to look surprised. He scratched his head and picked up his pipe. Cathy watched while he lit it, and decided to fill him in on all the latest details.

'Are you serious?' he said when she'd finished. 'You have him believing you want out? And what is the proposal he wants you involved in?' The man had a million questions.

'He didn't say anything extra about hid proposal, but he is definite about getting around the clause in Lizzy's will. So, had Mrs. Summers anything else to say?' She smiled at her friend. 'It seems we've both been busy.'

'Cathy, be careful,' William warned. 'This man seems to know his way around all the loopholes. He could be involved in very dodgy dealings.'

'I will. You know, William, I would never have attempted anything like this before – deceiving people I mean. Yet I love Cregane Court so much, I can't help but want to fight for it.'

'Lizzy did well to leave it to you. She must have known you would treat it right.' William sounded tired, as though his years were tugging at him.

'And Mark. She obviously trusted him, too. Maybe she thought love would blossom between us.' Cathy laughed at her own words.

'It could yet,' William suggested between puffs on his pipe.

'No,' she shook her head, 'he and Luke are a couple. I will have to search elsewhere for love, William.'

'Well, girleen, if I was fifty years younger, I'd snap you up myself, so I would. Strange that about Mark...' the man's voice tailed off in a daydream.

'Why do you say that?' Cathy bristled. 'Sure, there's nothing strange about—'

'Oh no, no. I don't mean anything nasty,' William reassured her. 'I mean, it was one of the rumours about Lizzy and Daisy, that they were a couple, and that is why Archie was so upset.'

Cathy realised her jaw had dropped open in surprise at his words. Lizzy and Daisy? Surely not? Did Mark know about these old rumours? Cregane kept spitting up surprise after surprise. 'And what do you think?' she felt she had to ask William.

'No, not at all, although it were different times in Ireland back then. But no, I think they were the best of friends who needed each other to keep sane from dealing with awkward husbands,' he laughed heartily.

Cathy decided she would keep this latest bit of gossip to herself. She knew, too, that she could trust William to keep her secret.

Chapter Forty-One

Luke and Mark were out in the workshop, working on the plaque for the cottage. They were determined to put it up and roll on with the idea of the Retreat Centre. There had been a good deal of interest since Cathy had launched the website, so the sooner everything was in place, the more ready they would be to welcome guests.

'Hey, guys, how's the work coming along?' Cathy brought two cups of coffee to the working men.

'Sshh, Mark, don't tell her anything. She's the enemy, remember.' They all laughed.

Their workhouse was well used. They had divided it in two, with Mark claiming one half and Luke the other. Mark had put up shelving for his tools, and moved in an old table they had found in the outhouse to work on. Once he had sanded it down and oiled it, the timber shone like new, the little bit of care and attention transforming it to its former glory. Opposite him, Luke had set up an easel and another table. Mark had also put up shelving for him, and the two men worked in harmony.

Cathy sat in a corner where a kettle and some coffee and tea jars stood on a makeshift counter. She watched as the two lovers worked in silence, each with their heads bowed in concentration. They looked happy, and she felt contented. *This was what family was all about*, she told herself. *Being together wrapped in an air of security.*

'Hey, answer that will you? You're killing our flow of inspiration,' Mark shouted to Cathy as her phone rang in her jeans pocket.

'Hi, Gemma.' The two men made faces at her, and she stuck her tongue out at them as she got up and stepped outside. The air was biting, and the trees were rattling their naked branches.

'Yes, I'm free, why?'

Her sister was up to something, and Cathy was unsure how to answer her. Now that Gemma knew she was not busy, she was coming to collect her for a chat.

'But what about the girls and school runs?' she asked. 'It's a long drive here just for a chat. Why don't we arrange for me to call to you? Or we can chat now, if you want? Is there something you're bothered about?' Cathy hoped to put her off calling, but Gemma rattled on.

'Right, see you shortly,' Cathy sighed as she ended the call and stuck the phone back in her pocket. Popping her head around the workhouse door, she called out, 'See you later, guys. I'm meeting Gemma.' Her voice lacked excitement at the prospect of her sister's company, but the two men only waved as they continued with their projects.

• • • •

The café was quiet. The mums from the morning school runs were finished their gossip, and the lunchtime business would not start for another hour or more. It was a pretty spot, with round tables and soft plush chairs spaced apart at a nice distance. One didn't feel they were sitting on top of each other or that the table next to you was part of your conversation. On the walls, abstract paintings filled with colour hung in rows, and the background music was almost a whisper. Cathy was well impressed.

'How did you find this place?' Cathy looked at her sister, who was studying the menu.

'Um, oh this place? Roman recommended it once.' She continued to read the leaflet in her hand, unaware of the look of surprise on her sister's face.

Cathy decided to let it slip by. Her sister and the solicitor were still as cosy as ever, it would appear. The waitress came over, notebook and pencil in hand.

'Oh, we are waiting for one other to join us. Can you give us five minutes, please?' Gemma's smile beamed at the young lady, who nodded and wandered off again.

Cathy didn't have to ask who was joining them. Her stomach flipped at the thought of the creep Roman sitting across from her. Still, she needed to play her part, so kept her thoughts to herself. 'How are Lily and Ava? I've not seen them lately. You must bring them out to Cregane.'

'What's the point? Sure, you will be leaving shortly,' Gemma replied, 'and why bring them out to a place they won't see again?'

Cathy bit her tongue. She recalled her sister saying something similar before, when she had told her that she had inherited Lizzy's home. Discomfort and anxiety fought to raise their ugly heads, and Cathy felt ill. Lying and deception did not sit well with her, and her stomach churned.

'Excuse me,' she said, quickly standing up. 'Bathroom needed.' In the ladies, she placed her wrists beneath the steady flow of the cold tap to ease the feeling of nausea, and concentrated on the coolness of the water. It chilled her blood flow and brought her breathing under control. *Why, why, why, did she get upset so easily with Gemma?*

Cathy stared at her reflection. The mirror above the sink was surrounded with a pewter frame, which blended in seamlessly with the duck-egg blue walls. It was helping to think of something that made her smile. Luke would love the colours here; the décor was pleasing and unobtrusive, ideal for encouraging calmness. She must get him to call here. Maybe the four of them could come here for lunch before Christmas.

She smiled, and the woman in the mirror smiled back. *Positive, think positive. You are doing this for your friends, for Cregane, for your family*, she told herself. Yes, they were her family; people she loved and cared for. Pushing the door open, she returned to find that

Roman had joined them. Cathy quickly pasted a smile on her face and grabbed the chair back for support.

'Hello, Roman, this is a surprise. I didn't know you were joining us. Some would say I was being ambushed.' She laughed as he stood to kiss her on the cheek. *Slime-ball,* she thought. It was the first time he had greeted her like that.

'Oh Gemma, that was naughty.' He wagged a finger at her sister, who blushed like a schoolgirl. *Oh God*, Cathy thought, *this one has fallen for him hard.*

'Gemma tells me you haven't moved out.' Straight to the chase.

Cathy nodded in reply. She would need to play this carefully. 'Should we order?' Cathy turned to call the waitress.

'It's okay, I've ordered for us,' Gemma said without looking at her.

'But you don't know what I want,' Cathy stammered in surprise.

'Silly, of course I do. I've not been your sister forever and not know what you like.' She glared at Cathy then smiled at Roman.

'Of course, I keep forgetting, you know me too well.' Cathy's anxiety did not appear this time. Instead, anger ruffled her insides. *How dare Gemma behave like that?* She did not know anything about her, because she'd never taken the time to find out.

'So, Cathy, what are the latest developments at Cregane?' Roman stirred his coffee, uninterested in the politics of the two siblings.

Cathy forced her anger down, determined she would see this through.

'What do you mean exactly? As you can understand, Mark is avoiding me and the others are not saying much, because they feel betrayed by me. After all, they may well have to move out.' She looked him in the eye as she spoke.

'I've the ball rolling on my side with the papers you will need to sign when you move out. After all, it was in the clause that Mark can't have the place without you. So, it won't be just the two misfits moving out, will it?' His grin showed perfect teeth, white and even.

He must pay a fortune to look so greedy, she thought. In another life she probably would find him attractive, even fancy him a little bit, but all she saw before her now was a selfish materialistic man. She glanced at Gemma, who had a silly grin on her face as she soaked up his very presence. *How were they sisters?*

When the waitress brought their food, the eggs benedict looked delicious. Gemma had chosen well for her. A fresh pot of tea and coffee were placed on the table, too.

'Yes. I'm sleeping better since I made my mind up,' Cathy told them. 'What was it you were saying about Archie when I was in your office, about him wanting to leave our great-aunt, wasn't it?'

Gemma gasped. This was her news to share. She had wanted to be the one to burst Cathy's bubble about their relative's perfect life. She had been saving it for a special moment, a time when she could knock Cathy off her pedestal of being Lizzy's favourite.

Cathy could see by her sister's face that the statement had obviously upset Gemma somehow, but she couldn't think why. She was convinced this man had been using her sister for Cregane, nothing more. There was no affair happening there. Cathy was thrilled at knowing her sister was not cheating on Paul, but she did not feel sorry for her. Gemma used people, too, so she and the solicitor made a good team.

'He came to me for advice, but since he was a client, I really can't say too much. Only to those who I know can keep a confidence.' He threw an understanding glance at Gemma, who smiled sweetly.

Cathy noticed the looks between the other two and nausea bubbled low in her stomach.

'But you told me he was leaving her, why? They're both dead now, and we are their family, so it's not like you are breaking any oath.' Cathy looked at Gemma who was nodding in agreement.

Playing to Gemma's love of gossip had her sister wanting to know more. The two Reed sisters watched him, waiting for his reply. He looked uncomfortable.

'No, it wouldn't be right to speak of the dead and their wishes. I would be compromising my role as their advisor. I know you both understand,' he replied, and lowered his head.

Christ, Cathy thought, *he'll offer to say a prayer in their memory next*. She looked at Gemma. Her sister had bowed her head, too. What a ridiculous farce this meeting was turning into.

• • • •

Mark watched Luke working. If they lost Cregane, how would the future look for them both? He went over to Luke's work bench and hugged him.

'What's that for?' His lover grinned.

'Nothing. I wanted to hug you, so I did. You make me happy, I guess.' He stared into Luke's eyes, the green sparkling from the overhead light, and flecks of brown he hadn't noticed before. He ran his fingers gently through the blond hair and twirled it.

Luke stood still, a smile showing his happiness at Mark's touch. 'Right,' he said, 'let's get back to work. I want this plaque finished and up for Christmas Day.' Luke winked.

'Then we had better get to it, although in fairness, there's not a lot left to do to finish it. The wood has come up beautifully. I love the little oak leaves.' Mark ran his hand over the piece of timber then stepped back from the table and placed his hands in his pockets.

'It's not just the plaque, Mark. We have to clean up the wall and entrance where it's going to be sited. No point having a beautiful sign and a grubby entrance.'

'Okay, I'll continue here, and you start outside. I guess I can finish this up by tomorrow and then I'll be free after the weekend to help with the outside. Sound like a plan?'

'Are you looking forward to giving up the office?' Luke asked.

'Yes and no.'

'Being in a suit doesn't suit you,' Luke told him. 'You're a different person when out here working with the timber. I believe you're doing the right thing.' With that, Luke kissed Mark tenderly and turned and left.

Mark was left with his thoughts. *Why was he hesitating about bringing Luke to the party? Why did it matter if Luke didn't go?* He knew he had to talk to him. He followed the young lad outside. 'Luke, I need to talk to you. I've to be honest and tell you that there's a going away party for me on Friday, and if you'd like to go, you are welcome. But I don't know if I want you to go.' He had said it. It was finally off his chest and it felt good. Mark hated secrets, and he needed Luke to know he would always be honest with him in their relationship.

'I see,' Luke replied calmly. 'Why would you not want me to go?'

'I don't know. Honestly. I think part of it is that I'm a private person, as you know, and I don't like others knowing my personal life. I've never brought anyone to a work do before, and I've always liked that there was a part of my life mine, not out there for everyone to talk about.'

'Do your work colleagues know you're gay?'

Mark shrugged. 'Probably. I've never actually announced it, because I don't see the need. It's a part of me; it's who I am. But I'm also a carpenter and I'd like to think I'm kind and caring, yet I don't introduce myself to new people as I'm Mark and I'm kind, like carpentry, gay, and hate sci-fi books, do I?'

Luke smiled and Mark stepped closer to the blond man who had captured his heart.

'Look, if you'd like to come, then do so. I'd be happy to introduce you. I needed to be honest, as I've not had this option of bringing my boyfriend to a work do many times before.'

Luke laughed. 'I think I'll give it a skip. I thought they would be giving you some sort of send-off, but I couldn't bear the thought of making small talk with a bunch of number-crunching suits for a couple of hours. You go and enjoy it. But remember, no flirting with the other office boys. I'll be warming your bed, remember.' Luke pulled him in for a quick hard kiss and then grinned.

'Thanks, Luke.' Mark breathed a deep sigh of relief. 'I fall more in love with you each day.'

• • • •

The trio had finished eating. They were having their coffees and Cathy thought they would surely go their separate ways. *What more was there to talk about?* But suddenly she felt brave. She had some questions, fuelled by curiosity she decided to ask.

'Roman, going back to our chat in your office. Why did you put so many obstacles in our way for developing Cregane? It's almost as if you want it yourself, but I can't see what for.' She pushed the cup and saucer away from her and waited.

The solicitor sat back and crossed his legs, while Gemma placed her cup down and, like Cathy, pushed it from her.

'Tell her about The Towers, Roman,' Gemma gushed. 'It's a fabulous idea.' Her face was filled with a smug look of satisfaction, delighting in being seen as Roman's confidante.

'Towers? Sounds intriguing. I'm dying to know.' Cathy sat forward, elbows resting on the crisp white tablecloth.

'Really, Gemma, that was an idea, nothing more.' His eyebrows lowered to a frown that chilled Cathy. He did not look pleased about Gemma's comment.

Cathy decided now would be a good time to go. She could quiz her sister in the car for more information about these towers. She stood up.

'Well, I guess I shall see you another time,' Cathy pulled on her jacket.

The days were colder now that they were in the start of November. She wrapped one of Sno's creations around her, the scarf soft and cosy.

'That's pretty,' Gemma complimented her.

'Thank you. Sno made it. She has made some great jumpers and other scarves, hats, cushions. She's aiming for the Christmas craft fairs. Poor thing, still struggling through her grief.' Cathy's eyes teared up thinking of her friend's loss.

Concentrating on her designs was helping Sno to keep focussed, and all Cathy and the two men could do for now was to reassure her that she had their support.

'Well, she should be looking for somewhere else to stay, instead of wasting time knitting. Silly woman,' Gemma puffed as she hauled on her own coat.

'I'll get this brunch, ladies,' Roman cut in, 'it was lovely to see you again, Cathy.'

'No doubt you'll text me, Roman.' Gemma pouted like a put-out toddler as he nodded and then went to the till area.

Outside, Cathy breathed in the fresh air. Another thirty minutes and she would be home. How she longed to see the gates of Cregane Court. This lunch had not been particularly exciting, but she had a nibble of news and Cathy was relieved it was over.

Chapter Forty-Two

Cathy took in the empty fields as they drove along the country roads. Trees, bare of their leaves, stood tall while others bent from the strong winds that gusted at this time of year. Even in November there was a beauty to the countryside – something she had forgotten when living in the city. There, street lights blocked the stars in the sky, buildings cast shadows, and people crowded each other on the streets. Unless you made a point to talk with people, like she had with Sno and Luke, a person could be very lonely.

She supposed that could be true in the countryside, too. But in general, there was a better community spirit in Ballybawn than when she'd lived in the city. Driving by the houses, scattered like a winding ribbon, she said a small prayer of thanks to Lizzy for giving her the opportunity of turning her life around.

'Would you ever consider living in the country, Gemma?' she asked, curiously.

'What, me? Gosh, no.' Gemma's tone matched the shocked look she shot at Cathy. They drove in silence once more.

William was standing by his garden gate as they passed, and he raised his stick in salute. Cathy waved to the man, and a smile spread across her face in delight at seeing him. She was fond of him, and loved the time they spent chatting together.

'What age is that old fellow? He must be a right bore.' Gemma gestured to the air with one hand as they passed his house.

Jumping to her friend's defence, Cathy snapped back, 'Far from a bore, he is one of the nicest people I've met. Very interesting, actually. He knew Lizzy and Archie. I love his stories.'

'Oh, and what had he to say about you and the other misfits turning the place into a commune?' Gemma snorted.

'Don't call them misfits, and I am not one either, thank you. I like William,' Cathy was defensive. 'Like I said, he is full of wisdom and kindness. Great judge of character, too.'

'Oh, is he? And who are you hinting at when you say that?' Gemma kept her eyes on the road, the country roads windier than she was used to.

'No-one. Why would I hint at anyone?' Cathy was tired of her sister's smart comments. She just wanted to get home and chat with the misfits. She chuckled at the thought.

'What's funny?' Gemma interrupted her thoughts.

'Nothing. Just thinking it will be good to be home.'

'Yes, I'm glad you've seen sense. Being back in the city will be better for you. How you ever thought you'd live out here in the wilderness is beyond comprehension. And with Roman's plans for the place, it will all be better in the end.' Gemma had obviously mistaken Cathy's meaning for home as the city.

Cathy straightened up at the mention of Roman. How he made her blood boil. He was so dismissive of her and others; a really nasty person. 'Tell me more about these plans, are they of benefit to Ballybawn?' she asked in what she hoped was an interested pitch.

'Oh, he has great ideas. It's not everyone he shares his ideas with,' Gemma added in a conspiratorial tone. 'Only close friends, you understand.'

Her sister really believed that the greedy solicitor actually had time for her. *Poor Gemma*, Cathy thought, *she must be desperate for attention*. 'Well, are you going to tell me then?' she asked.

'Ah, too much to go into, and we are nearly in Cregane Court now. I can tell you next time you're at mine.'

Cathy saw the familiar grove of trees to her left ahead, the turn at the end of the hill, and the small bridge, almost flattened with age, that jumped across the river bordering Lizzy's acre.

Gemma wasn't going to spill on her friend, so Cathy had only one choice if she wanted to know more about Mr. O'Driscoll's great plans for her home in Cregane. If she didn't grasp this chance now, while it was still in conversation, she might find it more difficult to raise the subject again.

'Why don't I go stay with you tonight? Would you mind? I'd like to see the girls, and it gets me away from Cregane for a bit.'

'Of course, Cathy. You know, if nothing else comes of your silly adventure in the countryside, it's brought us closer, I believe. Go grab an overnight bag and we can hit the road again.' Gemma was beaming.

Gosh, Cathy thought, *she really believes in what she says*. Whether they would ever be close was another question. If anything, Cathy found it harder to be in her sister's company as each day passed. But for now, she would play the game.

• • • •

Settled in Gemma's, the evening had drawn in and the house was cosy. Cathy enjoyed spending time with her nieces, and read them stories from their favourite book. They were growing up fast, and she knew they would love Cregane Court. The freedom to run and play in the grounds and the swing in the orchard, even the planned river walk, would be exciting for their adventures.

Sitting with them, she felt more determined than ever to make Cregane a success. Whatever it took, she would do her best – along with Mark and the others – to show the locals Roman's true colours. She would be the one to stop him, with William's help and a little bit of research.

But first she had to know what the solicitor was up to, and beat him at his own game. For that to happen, though, she needed her sister to spill the beans. Gemma didn't care about her sister's feelings or happiness, but it went against Cathy's good nature to hurt anyone.

She felt uncomfortable deceiving Gemma, but she didn't know any other way to get the information she needed.

'Right, the girls are settled. They really are full of fun.' Cathy joined Gemma in the kitchen. Her brother-in-law was out at yet another golf event, but that meant the two women could chat together in peace.

Grabbing a bottle of wine, Gemma led her sister into the sitting room, and they sat near the fire. Its warmth was inviting, the flames flashing oranges and reds in the centre of a beautiful marble surround.

Settled in their chairs with soft cushions and fleece throws over their knees, the women relaxed. Gemma poured the wine and Cathy accepted the glass she was offered. They sat for a while, the flames reflected in their eyes, their breathing even, almost sleepy.

'This is nice.' Gemma sipped her drink. 'When you're back in the city, we can do this more often. Have you thought about where you'll live? I doubt your old apartment is free. Places to rent are very difficult to get now – well, decent places anyway.'

'I've not thought about it.' Cathy stared at her sister, stung by Gemma's words.

'Well, I'm sure you could stay here until you get sorted. The spare room is there and, well, we are blood, after all.'

The thought of living with Gemma for any length of time did not appeal to Cathy, but reminded her of her real reason for staying overnight. She needed to find out about Roman's plans.

• • • •

Waking up, Cathy yawned and, oh God, her mouth was like sandpaper – dry and uncomfortable. She should not have had the whiskey last night.

The pillow was soft and comforting and the duvet warm and soothing. *Did she have to move?* She refused to open her eyes as she knew it would hurt; by lying here she could pretend she wasn't hungover. Last night, Gemma had been in full flow about the girls while the sisters sat and shared the wine, and no matter how often Cathy directed the conversation to Roman, the older woman changed it away.

Then Cathy's brother-in-law had come home and insisted the women join him in a nightcap, which turned into two drinks. *Never again*, Cathy thought. *Mixing the grape and the grain was never a good idea.*

The house was still. No-one appeared to be up yet, and Cathy rolled over to go back to sleep. She really didn't look forward to the headache that was beginning to thump across her forehead. She had to admit she had enjoyed sharing and reminiscing with Gemma. If only it could be like that all the time, but Cathy knew it was the wine that had mellowed her sister. No doubt the sarcastic and bullying ways would make their appearance later.

• • • •

It was after 10am when Cathy woke again, and this time she dragged herself out of the bed, her head pounding. She prayed that the help of some pain relief would make her feel human, and went to the bathroom in search of the pills. Her nieces were up and downstairs, as she could hear the TV turned on. It was the weekend, so there was no mad school rush or chaos in the house.

Grabbing some paracetamol from the medicine cabinet, Cathy made her way downstairs for a glass of water. She tried to walk with her eyes half closed, hoping it would ease her pain, but all it did was make her stumble down two steps and almost lose balance. She stopped to steady herself and heard Gemma talking in the kitchen. Her sister was giggling like a teenager. Who was in there with her?

Cathy was not in the form for idle talk with a neighbour or one of her sister's friends from the golf club; she really couldn't cope with being polite and chatty while dealing with a horrible hangover. She decided she would return to the bedroom and text Gemma that she was awake then come back down when her visitor was gone. She knew it was silly, but the nauseous feeling that rumbled in her tummy threatened to erupt at any time.

But Gemma's next words stopped Cathy in her tracks.

'Oh, stop it, Roman, that's a terrible thing to say. What? Okay, see you for lunch then. Bye.'

Roman? Was he here? In her sister's house? Cathy's heart dropped into her stomach. No, he couldn't be, surely not. She heard footsteps and Gemma appeared in the hallway.

'Morning, sleepyhead, I've the kettle on. I was going to bring you up some tea.'

How could Gemma bubble with good humour? Cathy wondered. *Did she not have the same mix of wine and whiskey as her?*

'Not too loud, I'm dying. How come you're not?' Cathy whispered. Her voice was croaky, and if she didn't drink some water to quench her thirst, her throat would be on fire.

'Come into the kitchen, you look terrible.'

'I feel terrible,' Cathy moaned. She went straight to the sink and filled a glass of water then swallowed the pills grasped in her fist. The cool water was lifesaving, washing the rough dryness from her mouth and throat.

'I thought there was someone here with you. I was about to go back up to bed.' Cathy dragged herself onto a high stool near the kitchen island. The cool grey marble beneath her palms felt pleasant.

'Oh no, I was on the phone. Just organising a lunch with a friend.' Gemma busied herself with making tea and putting on some toast.

'Why are you not hungover?' Cathy was still perplexed.

Gemma laughed. 'Well, I have a confession to make. I don't touch whiskey.'

'But I saw you drinking it last night.'

'Did you?' She laughed again and winked at her sister.

Going to a wall cupboard, she took out a bottle of ginger ale and waved it in the air. Cathy still looked confused.

'I learnt the hard way, dear sister. When Paul comes in from the club, he usually likes to have a nightcap, only it never stops at one. It can be two or three. So, I do the good wife thing and get the drinks for us. But I pour ginger ale into my glass and no whiskey. It looks the same but is alcohol-free.'

Cathy held her head in her hands; right now, she could choke the woman. No wonder she bounced around the house full of sunshine while Cathy suffered with a brass band marching inside her head and a rollercoaster running in her stomach. 'Clever, aren't you? So why didn't you do me the favour of saving me from myself and whiskey?' Her words were low and pained.

'Well now, who am I to tell a grown woman what to do? You were happy to have another drink, and I do have two young daughters to look after in the mornings.' Gemma buttered the toast and placed some in front of Cathy. The hot mug of tea was next on the island counter.

It was going to be a long day, Cathy realised, as the tea and toast battled to settle her sick feeling.

'When are you going to move out permanently, tell me? The offer still stands.' Gemma sat across from her.

Cathy tried to recall the offer her sister spoke about, but she really couldn't focus right now. Everything was so bright, but at least the tea was comforting. She could not remember when she'd last had a hangover from hell like this. Her idea of staying to get information from her sister had totally misfired, and instead she was suffering. But she knew she only had herself to blame.

'Cathy?'

'Sorry, Gemma, I'm really struggling at the moment. Remind me again, what offer?'

'Staying here until you get a place to live.'

'But I live in Cregane.' Cathy rubbed her temples with a gentle circular motion.

'Not for much longer, unless you buy one of Roman's apartments, which I doubt you can afford.' Gemma hopped off the high stool and put her plate and mug into the dishwasher.

'I didn't know he owned property. Maybe he could show me some.' Cathy straightened a little on the seat, her reason for staying overnight rushing to mind.

'Well, I don't know if he has anything for sale, but when The Towers are built, well then, maybe.' Gemma busied herself wiping down the worktops.

'Yes, that's true. But like you said, I guess I couldn't afford a top market place like he'll have.' Cathy needed to keep her sister talking.

'He might give you a discount, seeing as where they will be sited and all, but I thought you wanted to move back to the city?' Gemma stopped her work and looked at Cathy.

'Yes, I do, but he did say he wanted me to work with him that day in the office, so maybe, who knows?' Cathy smiled.

'Work with him? On The Towers? I thought that was top secret.' Gemma looked crestfallen.

'Well, it is, and it isn't,' Cathy cleared her throat. She needed to know more about these damn towers her sister kept mentioning. 'Shure, he knows we talk, aren't sisters always sharing stuff? I'm sure he didn't mean for us to have secrets from each other, being family.' Cathy got off the stool and casually put the mug and plate into the dishwasher, just as her sister had done earlier. She needed to keep her cool. If she upset Gemma, the woman would close up like a clam, due to her obsession to Roman.

'Of course. It's an exciting project, isn't it? Imagine the views from the penthouse across those fields. Cregane is a beautiful spot, so he shouldn't have any problem in selling the apartments.'

Cathy resisted the scream that was building inside her. *He was going to use Cregane for an apartment block?* 'How many apartments would he manage on the land, I wonder?' Her throat almost closed over as she spoke, but she desperately needed to continue this charade. She placed her hands behind her back and took some deep breaths.

'Well, there's room for two blocks, isn't that what he said?' Gemma studied her sister.

'Yes, he did. He sure knows his job.' Cathy nodded enthusiastically and leaned against the kitchen units.' You know, Gemma, you should offer to do the interior design for the buildings. You have great taste, and I bet the showrooms would look magnificent.'

Gemma smiled at her sister's suggestion. She prided herself on having a nice home, and often boasted about the compliments she received whenever she had guests visit.

'Would it be too much, though? How many in total would you have to do?' Cathy continued, seeing her sister warming to the idea of being Roman's interior designer. She hoped she could feed Gemma's ego enough to reveal more details.

'Well, two blocks each of six two-bedroomed apartments, plus the penthouse top floors, then there would be the lodge at the gate entrance. Oh, it would be a major job, but I could easily do it.' Gemma's eyes were alive at the prospect.

Cathy had a brief stab of guilt at seeing her sister's delight, knowing that if Roman's behaviour of late was typical, he would drop her sister the minute he got his hands on Cregane.

'Would Cregane be able to take all that construction? Is it not too small for such a big project?' Cathy looked out the window to the garden. Evergreen laurel hedging trimmed the garden, flowerbeds with small trees, their branches naked of leaves, and shrubs covered in red berries, were dotted around in the corners. On the lawn, a slide and swing set took centre place. A wooden chalet-style shed, painted in a rich green with lanterns hanging near the door, faced up to the house.

Gemma could easily do the job of interior designing, Cathy knew; her home and garden were wonderful examples of her taste and style. It saddened her to think that a man like Roman could get away with using her sister.

'What are you looking at?' Gemma joined her over by the kitchen window.

'I'm just admiring your garden; all the different greens. Each rich and varied like a forest even in this dreary November.'

'Ha, that's strange. That's what Roman is calling The Towers – Forest Green Complex. But thank you,' she preened, 'I do my best.'

The two women stood in silence beside each other. One dreaming of a new chance to bring something exciting to her life, to focus on while her daughters were in school. The other lost in thought as to how to stop the greedy solicitor from getting his hands on Cregane Court – such a wonderful, welcoming home for her, Mark, and the two misfits.

Chapter Forty-Three

It took ages to persuade Gemma to let her get the bus back to the village, by which time Cathy had picked up enough information from her sister about the solicitor's plans to build two apartment blocks on the site of Cregane Court. *How dare he!* He had the cheek to dismiss their efforts to create a place for people to improve their art and flourish in their creativity, yet he wanted to tear down the house, flatten the acre or more, and have people shoved into tiny spaces and call it progress.

Cathy's blood boiled with anger as she sat by the window on the twelve-thirty to Ballybawn. She had so much to think about, to talk about with the others. How could her sister be okay with all that Roman was doing, especially when she knew Cathy's future was at stake?

Gemma had also let slip that the solicitor had connections in the planning department and didn't foresee any problems with getting permission for his development. Although Gemma hadn't expanded on this topic, Cathy had felt her legs go wobbly when she realised that the bastard was the one behind their planning application being refused; she would put a bet on it. This guy needed to be put back under the rock that he crawled out from, and she intended to be the one to do it. *There has to be a way to sort this fellow*, she mused, as she stared out of the bus window. Perhaps there was an ombudsman or society she could complain to. She would do a little research and see what she could find. One of the guys at her old workplace had studied to become a solicitor, so she might just look him up and see what he could tell her.

As the familiar horse statue in the centre of Ballybawn came into view, Cathy gathered up her jacket and overnight bag to alight. Now that she had given some thought to the problem of Roman, she felt lighter, more confident, and determined to fight him and win.

On the walk home from the village, she decided to call in to William. She could do with a cuppa and a chat, and her friendship with the elderly gentleman was a comfort to her. She liked his manner and his wise words. It would also give her time to cool down about all she'd learned from Gemma.

'Hello, anyone home?' Cathy opened the door and shouted into William's home.

Within two minutes, she was seated at the kitchen table sharing her news with the elderly man.

'So, he has been after Elizabeth's house himself all this time?'

'Yes, he is as slippery as anything,' Cathy stormed. 'How he has stayed in practice is beyond me. Have you ever heard anything against him through the years?' Cathy tucked into a custard cream biscuit, dipping it into the hot tea and then sucking the filling. Delicious.

'Ah, girleen, sure there's often been the odd rumour about his behaviour, but no-one has ever taken any action against him. His father was a different man. Honest as the days are long, as they say. He often waived his fees for those that could not afford them, accepting a bottle or two of whiskey or a trailer load of timber for the winter, instead of payment. A different man to his son, for sure. That Roman fellow never had any friends in the village as a youngster; always a bit of a loner. It still shows in him.' William frowned. 'There's something off about him, if you ask me, and I think, Cathy girl, you're on to something with him.'

She sat back and considered her friend's words. *Could she really be the one to stop Roman? If he was as corrupt as she thought, had she it in her to follow it through? How would the solicitor react if Cathy investigated further?* She knew he had a temper. And her sister was involved. *Could Gemma get hurt?* They might not be particularly close, but they were still sisters. So many thoughts swirled in her head, and Cathy longed to be at home in her own bed. Bidding

William farewell, she got up to head off to Cregane Court. Her friend told her he would ask around the village about Roman, in a quiet way. She trusted William; she had no worries of him revealing her news to anyone.

• • • •

The four adults were gathered in the sitting room. It had been a dry day but icily cold, so the fire burned brightly in the stove, its heat comforting as they all shared their thoughts.

'He wants to knock all this and build two towers, and we are the ones accused of ruining the area? Gee, even a hippy commune would be better than that.' Sno sat cross-legged, her knitting in her hands. Her fingers worked feverishly with the yarn as she spoke. Orders for her designs had been flowing in since she'd put her knitwear on her online shop.

'How do we stop him? Or prove he is behind our problems?' Luke added to Sno's words. They all agreed that the solicitor's underhand efforts must be revealed, but how?

Mark remained quiet. Although he'd thought those days were over, he knew now that there were backhand payments, or *brown envelopes,* still exchanged within companies and government departments. One had only to Google it, and pages of corrupt, slick, greedy people popped up. The types who took more bribes than Santa gave out presents.

'Cathy, if we are going to follow up these allegations and— hold it,' he put his hand up when he saw Luke ready to jump in on hearing the word *allegation*, 'we need to know exactly how to go about this. Any ideas on that anyone?'

'Yes, actually,' Cathy responded. 'A guy, Gerard, that worked with me years ago, left the company to train as a solicitor and has been practising for some time now. I was thinking the same as you just said, Mark. We need to do this properly. If we go in with all guns blazing, we could really mess it up and Roman will have the last laugh. He might even win this place if he sued us for slander or whatever.'

The look of horror on Sno's face made Cathy add quickly, 'I'm only thinking out loud. I don't know the ins and outs of it all, but that's why I think I should contact Gerard.'

The three others nodded in agreement, then decided to call it a night and head off to bed.

••••

Cathy lay in her room, staring up at the ceiling. She had to be the one to stop Roman. She knew she loved this place. There was potential here for others to enjoy its peace and beauty, and she wanted to bring laughter and fun back to her great-aunt's home.

Settling beneath her duvet, her mind drifted to Gemma, and her heart ached for the little regard she seemed to have for Cathy. *Why would her sister back Roman?* She knew of his plans yet had never told Cathy. *Was she that jealous of her? Did she feel so little for her?* Cathy felt the sting of tears, but she would not let them fall.

She did not like lying to her sister, nor the way she had used her to get information about Roman, but she had been left with little choice. Gemma had known of his desire to flatten Cregane and destroy Cathy's home and future, yet seemed to be okay with it. Not for the first time, Cathy wondered how they could ever be sisters. She heard a fox cry in the grove, its eerie scream like that of a banshee. November was such a dreary month, with early dark evenings and wet cold nights. She shivered with the weight of her troubles as she slipped into a restless sleep.

Chapter Forty-Four

Inside the workshop was cold the following morning when Luke and Mark went out to work on their projects. They were determined to have the plaque finished and fitted as their Christmas present for Cathy. The entrance to their home had been cleared of all the overgrown brambles and the walls freshly plastered and painted, leaving it bright and cheerful. Once the new plaque was put up, it would be complete.

Sno cooked breakfast and laid out the cutlery and delph. She was planning to go into the village on Monday morning to post off some of her knitwear to customers, and wanted to ask the postmistress about the community hall. She was thinking about giving classes in the spring for anyone who might be interested. Her heart was heavy with flashes of her mother and brother burning her mind, but she used her knitting to keep busy and thought it might be something others would want to learn. She didn't want to fail Cathy, either. After all, her friend had given her a new home and a chance to follow her dreams. Sno shuddered as she remembered the bleak evenings working in the café, then going home to an empty house, which had only layered more loneliness upon her. She wanted to be a success, not only for herself but for Cathy; she wanted to help her friend's dream of Cregane Court be a success, too.

'Mark, can I have a word with you once you're finished here.' Cathy placed her dishes into the sink.

The breakfast of a full Irish fry had been delicious. Hot bagels with real creamy butter and a pot of tea, and another of coffee, had set them up for the day. Luke had a huge appetite, yet he was still slim and looked like he was starving. The women scolded him how they only had to look at a sausage and the pounds stuck to their hips.

'Sure, I'm finished,' Mark said as he joined her. 'What's up?'

She motioned for them to leave the kitchen, so he followed her out to the porch.

'Look, I need to apologise to you,' she said.

'You do?'

'Yes, I've been behaving as if I own this place, and I don't. It's your home, too. I thought about this last night. I acted without asking you, and well, I kinda took over regarding our friendly solicitor.' She looked up to gauge his reaction.

'Listen, no apologies needed. I know what you're saying, but you've always included me, and I know it's because you feel an obligation to Elizabeth to make this place a success that you are ploughing on with it all. Cathy, I don't think you are taking over or forgetting me. You're not like that. We are in this together, all four of us, okay? If you want me to accompany you to anywhere during this hassle, or to face Roman, then tell me.'

He reached out and hugged her, and she welcomed the comfort it gave her. She was not alone, and the support and love of her friends would spur her on.

'Thanks,' she murmured into his chest. 'I would never hurt you or take you for—'

'Sshh, all's good,' he interrupted. 'Now, go fight the big bad wolf,' he laughed and released her from his arms.

'I do need you with me.'

'I am with you,' he reminded her. 'When you meet your old work colleague, I will be with you. And when you want to face Roman, I can be with you. Although right now he thinks you and I are sworn enemies,' he chuckled.

'I never thought he would be so easy to get to talk, nor Gemma for that matter.' She pulled a silly face.

Mark pulled her in for another hug. 'See, it's going to be alright—'

'Ahem, should I be worried?' Luke stood nearby, grinning.

'Hey, he was mine before you got your paws on him.' Cathy smirked towards her friend.

'Yes, and I was your friend before you met him.' Luke raised an eyebrow in mock surprise.

'Oh, come here, you silly goose. It's wonderful to have people fighting over me.' Mark pulled Luke into the embrace and all three laughed. 'One last thing,' Mark spoke. 'Move back in here. We should all be together, under one roof.'

Cathy smiled. It was as though he had read her thoughts.

••••

The meeting with Gerard was arranged for three-thirty in the Amber Hotel. He was a senior partner in his company now, and Cathy was taken back when he sounded so delighted that she had phoned him. They had worked together and been friends for some years, but had inevitably drifted apart once he left to study law.

As Mark and Cathy drove to the hotel, she was nervous. *What if she was wrong about Roman?* She didn't want to ruin someone's career. But if he was up to no good, then he needed to be stopped. They spoke little on the journey and Cathy wondered what was on Mark's mind. He seemed happy with life. Since leaving his office job, she had seen a real change in him – one for the better. And having Luke in his life had helped a lot.

'Hello, Cathy, it's great to see you again,' Gerard stood to greet them. 'How are they all in the office? I know some were let go.' He was dressed in a smart suit, navy tie, and soft blue shirt, looking handsome. His warm smile reached his eyes, and Cathy remembered how she'd always found him genuine and sincere, unlike many of their two-faced colleagues.

'Oh Gerard, I was laid off ages ago. Most of us were,' Cathy replied. 'To be honest, I've not had any contact with the office crowd. I've kinda moved on in a different direction.'

'Well, I consider that a blessing. An awful gang to be stuck with, if I'm to be honest. So glad I left.' He laughed a deep hearty laugh.

'Sorry, you must be Cathy's husband? Partner? Other half?' Gerard extended his hand to Mark.

'Best friend,' Cathy answered quickly. 'Sorry, Gerard, this is Mark. We live together in Cregane Court, which is why I wanted to meet you.'

Once the introductions were over, Gerard ordered coffee for everyone, and they sat in a secluded corner of the hotel foyer where they could comfortably fill the solicitor in on their problem.

'Wow, from what you tell me, there's plenty to be concerned about.' Gerard was scribbling notes. 'This Roman guy, he handled the will, yes?'

Cathy and Mark nodded in answer.

'So, did you bring a copy of the will?' Gerard raised his head to look at the duo.

The friends looked at each other, shock registering on their faces.

'What?' Gerard picked up on the surprised looks of the two friends.

'We don't have a copy,' Cathy said.

'What? But who was the executor? Surely you were given a copy from whoever that was?' He sat back in disbelief.

'Ah, no. Roman, I reckon, was the executor, as it was he who summoned us to his office,' Mark added.

'Not necessarily,' Gerard told them. 'But look, first things first. Ask Roman who the executor was, and get a copy of the will from him or her. Once we have a copy, we can see the exact wording.'

• • • •

On the drive back, Cathy and Mark could not believe they had never actually seen the will. In all the excitement and shock of inheriting

Cregane Court, and meeting each other for the first time, it had never crossed their minds to ask to see the document.

'So, you think there's a case to bring against Roman O'Driscoll then?' Sno asked, when the two got back to the cottage and filled her in on the meeting.

'Look, I need to meet with Roman,' Mark stood up decisively. 'I'll be the one to go ask him about the will, and you can pump Gemma for more information. We need to act quickly on this.' Mark grabbed his car keys, then stopped at the door. 'Gerard is a nice fellow, by the way, Cathy,' he added, his smile hinting at more than he said.

'Are you going to Roman's now?' Cathy felt tired. She had not slept well last night and was hoping to catch a nap.

'Yes. Strike while the iron's hot.' With that, he was out the door and gone.

Sno and Cathy sat in the kitchen together. 'How are you feeling?' Cathy looked at her friend and noticed the dark circles beneath her eyes.

'Okay. Up and down.'

'Look, if you need to talk or feel some counselling can help, we can organise it. I don't mean to let Roman take over stuff happening here. I've not forgotten you.' She placed her hand on Sno's arm.

'Cathy, you and the two lads have been my saving grace. I'm good right now. Orders are coming in for my knitting, and I went and had a chat with the postmistress.'

'Oh, what about?'

'Renting the community hall for teaching knitting classes.' Sno shrugged. 'It's just another way of getting some income, small but welcome.'

'Sno, what about here? Why go to the village?'

'But, Cathy, there's nowhere here at the moment. You are in The Shed, and the workshop is full of Mark and Luke's materials. I thought I'd get the ball rolling until we have a dedicated room here for group meetings.' She paused briefly. 'Look, I don't want to say, but if you and Mark do lose the house, or the Retreat Centre never takes off, well, we will need income to live.' Her face clouded over with sadness at her last words.

'Mark and I, and you and Luke, are going to make this a success,' Cathy replied firmly. 'Over my dead body will Roman get to build apartments on Lizzie's land. But I do understand. We have guests booked in for the end of January, so it's a start.'

Cathy was now more determined than ever to see Roman O'Driscoll's greed stopped.

Chapter Forty-Five

'We need to talk.' Roman was livid as he snapped down the phone at Gemma. They arranged a meeting in Ballybawn, and he barked at her to bring Cathy. *What was her sister up to now?*

• • • •

Cathy waited for her sister to collect her for this 'important meeting' with Roman. Excitement ran through her veins. It seemed the request from Mark for a copy of the will had rattled the solicitor, and she wondered what today would bring.

Gemma's car pulled up outside Cregane and Cathy got in. The tension in the car was heavy and Cathy saw her sister appeared stressed.

'Are you alright, Gemma?'

'What do you think?' she snapped. 'I've had Roman shouting my ear off over something those misfits have been up to. Honestly, Cathy, you need to move out now and let me get on with my life. It's been nothing but hassle since you lived out here.'

Cathy's voice was calm. 'Gemma, I wish you wouldn't call my friends that.'

'Friends? I thought you'd cut ties with them. If you've been playing me, Cathy Reed, I swear to God I'll never forgive you.'

Cathy remained quiet. They had reached Ballybawn in minutes and pulled up outside the solicitor's office. Once inside, Roman didn't waste any time.

'Mark Daniels was here asking for a copy of the will, but you probably know that already.' He glared at Cathy. The thunder in his eyes scared her, and an ugly snarl stretched across his face.

'What's so wrong about that?' Gemma quipped, her eyes taking in the décor in his office.

'Shut up, stupid woman!' Roman shot her a stern look.

'How dare you. Who do you think you are to speak to me like that?' Gemma stood up in protest.

'Listen, and stay quiet for once. Well, Cathy, what have you to say?' He ignored Gemma's stance and concentrated on her sister.

'I agree with Gemma. Why are you so worked up about Mark asking for what he is entitled to? Why don't you show me it now – the will, I mean? I never saw it either. Tell me, are you the executor of Elizabeth's will?'

'Yes, he is. He told me,' Gemma replied.

Roman stood up and banged on the intercom on his desk. He asked for coffee to be brought in. 'Yes, I'm the executor. No secret,' he growled, glancing at Gemma.

'So, what's the problem?' Cathy pushed. She saw a shadow cross his face, and the atmosphere in the office rose. He looked pretty agitated.

'Elizabeth's will was, um, complicated,' he bit back. 'Look, why are you still in Cregane? I thought you were with us?'

Cathy knew he was cracking, and asking for the will was the start of it. From Gemma's actions, she reckoned her sister was changing her mind on the word *us* that Roman used. Enough was enough. Cathy wasn't, and wouldn't be considered an ally of theirs.

'I know about your plans, Roman,' she announced calmly. 'I also know about your buddy and the brown envelopes. I know that you are a corrupt, crooked, horrible man who, for some unknown reason, my sister has allowed to use her. But then, she's easily won over. You know, you two are welcome to each other; you're both as horrible and bullying as each other. I was never on your side. I needed to know more, and you gave it to me on a plate.' She took a breath and carried on, 'In fact, for an educated man, it was easy to have you fooled. How on earth did you ever think I would betray my friends, my family, to back you and your grasping, selfish, dishonest, warped ways in deceiving and robbing good people?'

'I'm your family!' shrieked Gemma.

'By blood, unfortunately.' Cathy kept her voice even and clear as she looked steadily back at the man standing on the other side of the desk.

The assistant knocked and the coffee was served, but once the door closed behind the woman, he bellowed at Cathy, 'Get out. I shall see that blasted place of your aunt's burn.' The words were hissed with sheer hatred.

She smiled as he realised his dreams were falling apart. 'The Law Society will be in touch.' Cathy turned and walked calmly out of the office.

• • • •

Mark had parked further up in the village. When Cathy got into his car, a long sigh escaped her, then she held her head in her hands and wept. Drained and exhausted, she sobbed it out. Never before had she said such nasty words or accused a person of ill doing. She had also hurt her sister and abandoned her in the office, no doubt to an onslaught of abuse from Roman.

Cathy's life was changing so quickly. From quiet, almost broke, and lonely living in the city, to co-homeowner of a beautiful plot, filled with drama and new friends. She knew which one she preferred.

Mark started the car and headed for Cregane. Once they were home, she would reveal all.

• • • •

'You said she would co-operate and was easily persuaded. Shows how much you know about your sister.' Roman's face with scarlet with anger, as he spat the words out.

Gemma sat in shock. *Had Cathy just cut her out of her life?* Her sister had never spoken to her like that before. She stood up, her decision made. This bloody country village had dislodged her thinking completely. She had to go home and be with her own kind. How had she got caught up with this angry, twisted man? 'She never behaved like that before.' Gemma found her voice. 'This is a new Cathy.'

'Fine fucking time she picked to change,' he scoffed. 'You sang to her like a lark with all my plans. I actually thought you had brains. I believed if I had you in my corner, I could get to her. Jesus, what a fool I've been. Well, if it's a fight they want, it's a fight they'll get.'

Gemma could see he was no longer talking to her. His eyes were wide, sweat beading on his forehead, his gaze on some distant thought.

'What is so secretive about the will?' she asked. 'Why so angry? You've handled it right, haven't you? Besides, she has no proof about the, you know, the objections and rumours.'

He turned to face her, as if he had almost forgotten her presence. He looked tired.

She knew he really wanted Cregane Court. He'd told her it was to be the beginning of his empire, a stream of apartments with his name on them. He'd shared his dreams with her, but now he was obviously worried that his plans were unravelling.

Suddenly he stood upright, as though he was trying to pull himself together. The charming smile returned, and his voice sounded calmer and more in control.

'Sorry for that episode of drama, Gemma. I've been under such stress,' he told her. 'A horrible week of court, to be honest. A nasty case where children were being taken from the mother. You know yourself, it's upsetting to be dealing with such horror each week. They, Mark and your sister, getting annoyed about a will is so trivial, don't you think, when others suffer such hardship?' He lowered his eyes in sympathy for those poor children.

'What? Oh yes, of course. I-I-I understand. But I don't think you and I can be friends any more, Roman.' Gemma had made up her mind. 'I don't like being shouted at and accused by friends or family. I wish you well, but I think I shall leave now.' Gathering up her coat and bag, she pulled on her gloves. The weather outside was freezing, and her warm home waited to welcome her. This meeting had been horrid, and she longed to be on the road and miles away from Ballybawn.

Chapter Forty-Six

The table was filled with food and drink, the fire blazed in the stove, Christmas music played in the background, and a happy, contented atmosphere filled the house. Luke and Sno had decorated the entrance porch with berried holly and lanterns, and the glow from the candles was welcoming and soft. The sitting room had Santas and snowmen dotted around the shelves, different costumes on each, some with Snowflake's own designs. It all looked fun and inviting. A large *papier-mâché* stag's head was hung on the chimney breast, a garland of greenery from the bushes and shrubs outside adorned its neck, with twinkling fairy lights woven through the shrubbery. Photo frames held more holly on top of them, and in the corner was a small tree decorated with baubles and lights of different colours.

'Sno, everywhere looks fantastic. You really have a great eye for design.' Cathy stood back to admire the home-made wreath the girl was placing on the front door. Their garden had supplied all the flora needed to make the decorations.

'Luke is amazing. I may have made these, but Luke's eye as to where to place them was the cherry on top.' Sno joined Cathy, standing back to admire her handiwork.

'Are you sure you're okay with all this?' Cathy gestured at the house and its festive dressing. Her friend's sorrow at losing her family was still raw at times, and Cathy didn't want her to feel uncomfortable about celebrating Christmas. None of them had mentioned the festivities until Sno herself had asked if they were going to make the place look pretty for Santa's visit.

'Oh yes, Cathy, this is wonderful. This is the best thing for me. I have you and the lads with me, and I know we all say it and think it, but really, although I will be sad a bit over the season, I must be thankful for what I actually have in my life. Now, what time is Gerard calling?'

Cathy blushed. Ever since reconnecting with Gerard, there had been a certain spring in her step – or so Mark teased her. But her old workmate's advice regarding Roman had certainly been invaluable. They had sent a formal letter of allegation with a copy of Cathy's recording to the Law Society, and were waiting to hear the outcome. Gerard was confident that Roman was nothing more than a crook.

The sound of a car engine outside announced the man's arrival, but then they heard chatter, indicating there was someone with him.

'Good evening, ladies, look at the stranger I met in the local shop.' Gerard stood back, and William appeared around the corner.

'William, you are so welcome. It's wonderful to see you.' Cathy hugged him warmly and so did Sno. When they had been preparing their evidence for the Law Society, Cathy and Mark had introduced Gerard to William for some of his local knowledge.

'See, I told you they would have been mad at me if I didn't bring you with me,' Gerard laughed.

'Well, if you were having a private event, I didn't want to impose.' The elderly gentleman smiled.

'You are always welcome, and it's not private, just dinner and chat.' Cathy linked her arm in his and they stepped inside to the warmth of the sitting room.

Mark and Luke were putting the final finishing touches to the meal as they all gathered in Cregane.

'Your news that Roman did not reply to the two letters sent to him dumfounded me, so the next step will now be taken against him,' Gerard informed the group during the meal. He was not officially working for Cathy and Mark, only assisting them in their dispute with Roman.

'What happens next then?' Mark enquired.

'Since he didn't engage with the committee, he will be directed to attend a hearing and produce all his files on the investigation. You will receive a copy of that request, Cathy and Mark, to keep you in the loop.' Gerard shook his head. 'He really is being stupid to ignore this, in my opinion. But if the guy is as arrogant as you all say, then it doesn't surprise me that he has not responded.'

'He probably thinks he's untouchable,' Luke chimed in.

'Actually, Gerard, there may be more trouble for him.' William set his knife and fork down on the table. 'It's a small village and news travels. The investigation has reached the ears of the locals and some are beginning to ask questions about their own dealings with the man. Up until now, no-one knew or maybe feared doing anything about their issues, but some are definitely wanting to know more.'

'Wow, looks like a right mess has opened up for him,' Luke spoke again.

'Any word from Gemma?' Mark looked at Cathy.

When her sister had contacted her after their meeting with Roman, Gemma said she was confused about everything that had happened and needed Cathy to explain exactly what was going on.

'I've arranged to meet her this Saturday,' Cathy told them with a grimace. She wasn't looking forward to it, and was still struggling with annoyance at her sister's behaviour.

'This Saturday coming, in the city?' Gerard asked.

'Yes, I'm getting the 10am bus in. I'll meet her for some tea, and then finish my Christmas shopping. I don't know what she expects from me. I honestly am beginning to think she's got nothing between her ears.'

Exasperation escaped in a huge sigh and the others smiled at Cathy's choice of words.

••••

The evening had ended in a pleasant way. After the meal, a game of cards was started up and there was plenty of fun and rivalry between them all. When the evening came to a close, the four friends decided to leave the clearing up until the morning. Gerard was going to drop William home on his way through the village, and Cathy walked out to the car with the two men and hugged William goodnight.

'Do I get one?'

Cathy glanced at Gerard. 'Sure.'

When she reached out to him in a warm embrace, he held her for a second longer than necessary, but she didn't object. It felt good being in his arms.

Pulling away gently, she smiled. 'Safe home, and talk soon. Thanks for coming out.' She curled her hair behind her ear and licked her lips shyly.

'See you Saturday.' He winked, and then they were gone.

Chapter Forty-Seven

The city was alive. Christmas music filled the streets from loudspeakers hung above buildings, with more spewing out from the busy shops. Lights of all colours dressed the city in sparkles and glitter. It was so crowded and busy compared to Ballybawn, but Cathy liked the buzz as she pushed her way down through the crowds. The treat of a hot chocolate with marshmallows waited for her, brightening her spirits more than the thought of meeting Gemma.

The air was cold and frosty, so she kept the beautiful rainbow scarf Sno had made her snuggled around her neck. Cathy felt cheerful as she heard Santa's 'Ho, Ho, Ho' shouted in greeting from every street corner.

'Over here!' Gemma waved at Cathy as she closed the door to the café behind her. The place was full, and Gemma had done well to grab a table. Taking her coat and scarf off, she looked around at all the packages and shopping bags lying on the floor around each table. Gemma had some at her feet, too.

'You've been shopping already?' Cathy asked her sister. There was no hug of greeting or kind word. It was plain awkward.

'I've the girls to collect from their friend's. They've a party with her daughter. I've ordered myself a coffee.'

Cathy nodded. Having her hot chocolate in this half-hearted atmosphere would spoil it for her, so she decided she would wait until later when she was on her own and have some mince pies and cream, too. She smiled at the thought.

'Well, good to see you happy.' Gemma must have spotted the smile. 'Care to tell me what the episode in Roman's was all about?'

'You were there; you heard,' Cathy replied, realising that her sister never asked her how she was any time they met.

'All I recall is you jumping down his throat for a copy of the will, like you didn't trust him. It was ridiculous when there are so many others out there with a lot harsher issues.' Gemma sipped her coffee.

'I see Roman's been tutoring you,' Cathy bit back. 'His words, are they?'

Gemma blushed. 'I can think for myself.'

'Why did you ask me here?' Cathy put her scarf back on, wrapping it around her for comfort. 'You seem to have all the answers you need.'

'You've changed, Cathy. Living out in that wilderness has not been good for you. Your *friends* certainly have tutored you,' Gemma lectured. 'Selling to Roman is a good idea. Maybe this nonsense of dragging him to the Law Society can still be stopped.'

'So, you are still in touch. I thought you'd have seen sense by now and cut ties with him.' Cathy sighed and shook her head. 'He used you Gemma. Yes, he's handsome, and I can see how he'd turn your head, but he only likes people so that he can see what he can get or how he can use them.'

'How dare you! Nothing happened between him and me.' Gemma stood up in disgust.

'I didn't say it did. Jesus, you are twisting everything. How are the girls?' Cathy tried to diffuse the tension that was gathering. 'Are they excited for Christmas morning?'

'Be there for about eleven. Dinner is at two.' Gemma ignored Cathy's questions and shoved on her jacket and gloves, preparing to leave.

'Where? Yours? I'm having Christmas in Cregane Court. I will drop the girls' presents in before the day itself.' Cathy stood now, too. There was no point delaying her sister when it was obvious she wasn't staying.

'No need. If we're not good enough, you needn't bother,' Gemma snapped haughtily. 'Enjoy your friends, Cathy.'

'Gemma, stop it. I never came to yours for Christmas Day before, so don't play the hurt sister now. In fact, I'm stunned to be invited.'

'It wasn't my idea. It was Roman's. He thought you might mellow, but it will all blow up in your face yet.' Gemma lowered her voice to continue, 'And when it does, I won't be picking up the pieces.'

Tears sprang to Cathy's eyes. Her sister was so cruel and bitchy. Shocked by Gemma's words, she stared at the woman, realising that her sister really meant what she said. It was like being a little kid again, when Gemma would threaten her if she didn't get the toy Cathy was playing with, or at school, when she'd ignore her on the playground, pretending they weren't sisters. A spark of anger lit within the Cregane Court woman. She leaned in close to Gemma, her blue grey eyes hardened, and her voice just higher than a whisper.

'I've put up with your shit all my life, but it stops here and now. You will never speak to me like that again, do you hear? Roman and you are cut from the same cloth; birds of a feather springs to mind. So have no worries about me ever coming to you to pick up the pieces of my life, should they need picking up. I have my own family for that – the bunch of misfits you loathe have supported and shown me a lot more love than you have ever done. You and I may be connected through blood, but in no other way. It's true that we can't always pick family. If we could, I would never ever pick you.'

She turned, tears flowing down her hot cheeks, her breath coming in gasps. It wasn't like her to be nasty, but Gemma had pushed the buttons on stored up anger and frustration, and Cathy had just let it go.

The cold air outside the café embraced her and she almost ran down the street to get away from the crowds. Turning down an alleyway to get some privacy, she leaned against a wall and cried. Great heaving sobs that rattled her. *How had it all come to this?* She had always tried to be civil, to overlook her sister's bullying ways, always the one to forgive and forget. But she knew she couldn't do it anymore, not with Gemma. Her phone vibrated in her pocket and she pulled it out, glancing at the caller ID. Gerard. Wiping her nose with her sleeve, she took a deep breath and answered.

'Hi Gerard, how are you?' She sniffled, her nose still runny from crying.

'You sound like you've a cold, are you okay?'

'Um, Gerard, I don't feel good right now. Can I phone you back? I'm—'

'Where are you? Have you finished meeting your sister?'

At the mention of her sister, the sobbing started again, and she slid down the wall and sat on her heels. 'I want to go home,' she cried. 'Can you take me home, please?'

'Where are you? I'll be right there.'

Cathy gave him instructions and her tired body remained crouched, waiting for the crying to stop. Happy shoppers passed her by, ignoring the young woman seated against a dirty wall. No-one stopped to ask, no-one noticed; all too busy with their own pressing issues.

Chapter Forty-Eight

The drive home held little chat. Cathy was still rocked at how she'd handled Gemma in a public place. She would never do that normally, but she had finally been pushed too far. Her relationship with her sister was over and there would be no going back there. It broke her heart that her nieces would no doubt be out of her life now, but maybe when they were older, she could explain why. Losing contact with them hurt her more than losing Gemma. The two little girls were adorable, but in truth, Cathy only saw them occasionally because their mother's company was so exhausting.

Gerard parked in Cregane Court, then came round to her side of the car and helped her out, keeping an arm around her. Sno, busy with her yarn, looked up to greet the couple with a smile then stopped. Cathy's face was swollen and pale, her eyes puffed, not a shopping bag in sight.

'What the hell has happened?' She jumped to her friend's side and wrapped her in a hug.

'I'll put the kettle on,' Gerard offered. A cup of tea was the staple that solved all of life's problems.

The women sat down on the large sofa, Sno remaining by Cathy's side, with her arm around her.

'It was awful,' Cathy whispered. '*I* was awful, Sno. I said some dreadful things to Gemma. I don't think she will ever speak to me again.'

'Is that such a bad thing?' Sno asked kindly.

'But... but I don't like conflict. But I'm tired of her slating my life, my friends, and her thinking it's okay.'

'So, she was in top form then. Please don't tell me Roman was there? One of us should have gone with you. Cathy, you are too soft and caring, always putting others before yourself. I'm sorry, sweetheart, I should have been there to support you.'

'Here, have this. I made a hot whiskey instead. I think you need it.' Gerard handed the glass to Cathy and sat opposite the women.

'Thanks, Ger. Roman wasn't there, Sno. Gemma just pushed the wrong buttons and all this stuff inside me just spilled out. In public, imagine!' Cathy's eyes were wide with wonder at her own behaviour. She laid her head on Sno's shoulder and smiled over at Gerard. *This is what it should be like, to be surrounded by people who care*, she thought.

'Thank you, Gerard, for bringing me home,' she told him between sips of her warming drink. 'I was so happy to see your name flash up on my phone.'

'Well, when you mentioned last week that you were going into the city, I thought I'd offer to take you for lunch after your meeting with Gemma. But another day maybe?' His smile lit up his chestnut brown eyes.

Cathy admired his strong jaw and set shoulders; the jumper he wore settled nicely on them. 'Definitely,' she replied.

• • • •

Mark and Luke had been busy shopping, and returned with their arms filled with packages. Once they'd unloaded the car, Mark went to collect some Chinese takeaway for them all for dinner.

'Are you going home to your parents for Christmas?' Gerard asked Mark, still not understanding fully the dynamics of the living arrangements in Cregane.

'God, no. They didn't really want children. I found that out after they had me.' He gave a hollow laugh. 'My grandmother pretty much raised me. She was Elizabeth's closest friend. Anyhow, my folks are probably off in the Bahamas and I will get a text on the big day itself, if they remember.'

'Wow, am I the only one who has family to go to?' Gerard asked incredulously.

'Looks like it,' Luke laughed.

'You are welcome to come here, too,' Sno offered.

Cathy glanced at Gerard. She would love if he accepted, but held her breath for his answer.

'Not this time, I'm sorry. My parents would skin me alive if I bailed now on such short notice. But I'd like to pop out to ye all if that would be okay, maybe St. Stephen's Day?' he looked at Cathy as he spoke.

'Great,' she whispered, and returned his warm smile.

• • • •

Christmas Eve brought light flurries of snowfall which just added to the magic of Cregane. Mark had placed lights on some of the trees in the drive and a large Christmas tree in the centre of the front lawn. Anyone driving by would see it twinkle through the trees. They were all in good spirits and looking forward to the main meal the following day.

Cathy had invited William to join them, but he declined, saying he had his own ways and memories, and he would like to be on his own. He thanked her profusely for thinking of him but promised to call in the New Year, when there would be a better stretch in the evenings. She gave him a bottle of whiskey – a special reserve malt that he'd mentioned once in passing during a conversation of theirs. He was totally taken aback that she'd remembered, and gave her a warm hug and kiss on the cheek.

• • • •

'What are you doing, Luke?' He sat at the kitchen table, rolling up what appeared to be a portrait. Cathy poured them both a glass of wine then pulled up a chair to join him.

'One of my gifts. For Sno, actually. Would you like to see it?'

She nodded excitedly. When he unfurled the cream paper, Cathy gasped aloud. 'Wow, that is beautiful, Luke. Really, really beautiful. She will adore it.'

'Thanks. I captured it one day she was on the couch, not long after losing her mum and brother. I thought she looked beautiful asleep. Maybe she could frame it,' he added quietly.

'Well, make sure you sign it. She is going to love it.' Cathy stood and yawned. 'I think I will take my wine with me to bed. Good night, and Happy Christmas, Luke.' She bent and kissed the top of his blond head. He winked in return.

Upstairs, Cathy thought about Luke's pencil sketching of Sno asleep. It got her itching to write, so she grabbed a pen and her notebook and started to scribble.

Snowflake,

When you are sleeping, we tuck the night darkness beneath your chin and sweep away the nightmares from your tangled hair. Only love and laughter enter your dreams.

When you are sleeping, we sit by your bed unseen, listening to the cries of the wild, recalling the stories we read when we were together.

Not just when you sleep, but with each breath, we breathe with you, encouraging and protecting you always,

For now that we are no more of this physical time,

We still live; on the next rung of the ladder. A ladder that stretches high to the Creator.

Know we are with you, Bolt and I, ever only a step away, within your shadow.

Cathy read it over a few times and then snuck downstairs and rolled it up, tying a ribbon around it, and placed it with Luke's gift beneath the tree.

Chapter Forty-Nine

The festivities were over and the late January winds blew cold. The weather plunged beneath zero and everywhere looked barren and sorry for itself.

When Roman O'Driscoll had still refused to show up to appointed meetings, Cathy and Mark were informed by the Law Society that the High Court had issued an order for him to reveal all files, and compelled him to attend. This meant he had no more chances to say no.

It also meant a day out for Cathy and Mark, to speak to their evidence. Thankfully, they had not met the Ballybawn solicitor on the day, much to Cathy's relief. Roman had disputed their allegations, but the committee had finally adjudged that there had been serious misconduct, so the matter would now go forward to the Solicitors Disciplinary Tribunal.

'That is serious stuff,' Gerard told them when he read the letter informing them of the decision. 'This is about being judged by your peers, and could see him struck off.'

'Well, since he has backed off from us, the locals have been asking if we are going ahead with the Centre, and it's all positive comments now. I think William was right when he said we weren't the only ones unhappy with his practice. I believe we got the ball rolling,' Mark offered, as he and Gerard stood inside the workshop.

Word had been getting around about Mark's carpentry skills – especially since the plaque was now in its rightful place – and orders were already starting to come in.

Cathy loved her gift. The carved edges with the black script looked fresh and new, and she felt a spark of joy every time she passed the plaque entering or leaving Cregane Court. When the local correspondent for a regional newspaper came out to interview them about their plans for the Centre, Mark and Cathy had been thrilled to have their photo taken standing next to the plaque on the wall.

'Cathy and you seem to be getting along fine,' Mark commented to Gerard while he fashioned some oak.

'I hope so. I like her,' Gerard admitted. 'Have done since we worked together, but office romances were frowned on, so I never did anything about it. Then I took off, because the place was toxic really, and Cathy took on a lot of extra work that others should have been doing. To be honest, I forgot about her – not intentionally – but I was busy with study and setting myself up. Who knows, it might have all been for the best back then.'

'She must have liked you, too, otherwise why would she have remembered you after all the years?' Mark laughed.

Gerard left Mark to get on with his work, but the comment about Cathy liking him, too, lingered on his mind.

• • • •

William and Cathy were sitting at the counter of the local pub with two hot ports with slices of orange before them. She was waiting for Sno to finish her knitting class in the local community hall.

'What are you going to do with yourself?' William sipped the warming drink and licked his lips.

'In what way?'

'Well, girleen, the lads are busy with their stuff, Sno is teaching and making stuff, so what are you doing to pass your time? Your plans for the future?' His soft eyes watched her, care and affection shining bright in them. She knew he was fond of her; he had said so many times.

'I don't know, William. I had thought I would do some life-coaching, to help people. But over the Christmas holidays, I started writing again.'

'I didn't know you wrote. What type of writing do you do?'

'Short stories and a few articles. Nothing major,' she shrugged, 'but I enjoy it, creating new worlds, having characters telling you their stories.'

'Well, why don't you do that then? I'm sure the regional paper would take some articles from you if you pitch to them. Am I right in saying pitch?'

'Yes,' she laughed, 'pitch is the correct term. Never thought of it before.'

'No, because you are too busy helping others to think about your own dreams. You know, Mark's grandmother was once the local correspondent. That paper has stood the test of time, but it's all online stuff now. You might be able to help them, though, so ask. Want another one?' He indicated to her half-filled glass and she nodded.

Time spent with William was always enjoyable.

Chapter Fifty

The first of the retreat's guests – two poets – arrived in Cregane Court on the last weekend of January, and were delighted with The Shed. Cathy welcomed them and invited them to dinner with the others that evening in the cottage, but they refused. They said they were there to work on projects that had deadlines looming.

Cathy asked them about their poetry, and felt a buzz inside her when she listened to them talk with such passion and self-belief. When she shared that she liked to dabble by writing short stories, they encouraged her to continue and shared information on courses and literary events she might like to go to.

'Well, why don't you?' Sno said, as the two women shared a pot of spaghetti bolognaise and a bottle of red wine that evening. 'The poem you wrote complimented Luke's portrait in a very personal way. I look at them both each night. Really, Cathy, think about it and also about what William said. Work with the newspaper would give you some income while you write the next bestseller.' The rich bolognaise sauce dripped down Sno's chin, and she grabbed some kitchen paper and wiped her face.

Cathy carried on eating without comment. She was absorbing her friend's words and thinking about what William had said. *She could give it a try, why not? If all failed, she could then still pursue life-coaching.*

• • • •

'What a great movie. I love Pierce Brosnan, he is the sexiest man I know,' Cathy gushed as they left the cinema.

'Excuse me, and what about your present company?' Gerard did a small twirl and she burst out laughing. She linked his arm, and they strode on to the car park. They had been dating for some weeks and

Cathy's life was happy once more. She had not heard from Gemma but didn't really miss her much now. As time had passed, she realised she no longer dreaded her phone ringing and hearing her sister put her down with comments that left her feeling low and unhappy.

• • • •

The allegations against Roman were proceeding, but the notebook was of no consideration, and there was nothing concrete contained in it. Archie had clearly given money to the solicitor, but there was no proof what for, and no evidence of Archie being forced to part with the cash. However, Roman's *'permissions for payment'* did disclose many brown envelopes changing hands. The council clerk that dealt with Roman and had accepted the payments sang like a nightingale when he saw he was facing jail time, and cooperated fully with the investigation into the allegations.

The biggest surprise of all, though, was Elizabeth's will, which had been doctored. Since she was elderly when she signed it and stated her wishes for Cregane Court, she had obviously not noticed the extra clauses that Roman had included.

'Are you telling me that you both inherited the house, but this living together and not selling it until after two years, was completely made up?' Luke asked, as he lay across Mark's lap on the sofa.

Cathy and Gerard were nestled together on an armchair, and Sno sat cross-legged on the floor.

Mark nodded. 'He will be struck off, I'm sure. The media has picked up on the story, and other wills he handled are being challenged. Families trusted him to be truthful, but unfortunately power does corrupt.' He played with his lover's blond hair, gently twirling strands of it with his fingers.

'How's your writing coming along?' Gerard enquired as he cuddled Cathy on his lap.

'I was going to tell you all later, but I've got a part-time job with the newspaper,' she announced, her eyes shining with happiness, 'and I sold my first short story to an Irish women's magazine.'

'Oh baby, that's terrific news. I'm so proud of you.' He kissed the top of her nose.

Sno jumped up to hug Cathy. 'How about we have an official launch of Cregane Court, send out invitations, and organise food and drinks to celebrate our success? What do you all think?' The cheers and laughter filled the cottage, and a date was set for the celebrations.

• • • •

The March weather was kind, and a pleasant afternoon with spring sunshine offered the launch of Cregane its blessing. The friends had worked hard, decorating with lanterns and chairs on the lawn for the expected visitors. And Gerard had brought a marquee to provide shelter. Irish weather was so unpredictable – the one guarantee in every Irish person's life, not just death and taxes.

Sno arranged flower pots filled with colour, scent, and beauty, while Elizabeth's own daffodils and tulips sprouted around the gardens and added to the happy occasion. A red and white ribbon hung from pillar to pillar in the driveway, with a small curtain framing the plaque Luke and Mark had created. The guest of honour would cut the ribbon and say a few words, then the food and drink would be served, and the music enjoyed.

Cathy stood for a minute in her bedroom to take it all in. Almost a year ago she had been on a downward spiral in life. Losing her father, her job, and her self-confidence, had been eating away at her. But now look at her. A new home, a new job, and a new love, and more importantly, a new family. People who genuinely loved *her* and who had her back at all times.

Her eyes teared up as she briefly thought about Gemma. Cathy had posted her an invitation to the evening's event, but her heart had shattered once more when the letter was returned unopened.

Gerard had put his arms around her and held her as she wept. 'Give it time, love,' he'd whispered into her ear.

The shouting of her name broke her from her thoughts, and she quickly checked her make-up in her dressing table mirror. 'Looking good, Cathy Reed,' she whispered.

••••

The paper she worked for was here to cover the event, and it seemed the whole village of Ballybawn had turned up. There was a carnival atmosphere with everyone chatting and laughing. Sno rang an old school bell to gain attention. She had borrowed it from the local drama group, some of whom were in her crafting classes, which had expanded to include crochet and cross-stitch.

'Ladies and gentlemen, family and friends,' she said, her eyes lingering on Luke, Mark, and Cathy, 'may I ask you to welcome our guest of honour to help us launch this wonderful celebration by cutting the ribbon and say a few words. Please put your hands together to welcome our very much-loved friend, William Sheehan.'

Applause swirled around the drive as William stood by the ribbon and cut it. Blown by a slight breeze, the coloured ribbon danced around before settling in the nearby shrubs. Cathy embraced Mark, then the two of them approached William with more hugs.

There were tears in the elderly man's eyes as he told them, 'I'm so proud of you both. Elizabeth and Diane are happy in their eternal reward this evening.'

'Speech, speech, speech' roused the trio to part, and William went over to stand by the plaque.

'I'll not keep you long.' Someone cheered in the crowd, and more laughter rippled through. 'Cheeky fellows nowadays,' William said with a smile.

Leaning on his stick and removing his cap, which he handed to Mark, he cleared his throat. 'I am very honoured and privileged to perform this great duty here this evening. As an old man, I've seen many changes in life, and in particular, in our own village. It has saddened me at times, but from the first day I met this girleen here, Cathy Reed, I got a good feeling in my stomach. There was a sparkle in her, a genuine, caring person who gave not just kind words to make you happy in yourself, but her time. When she said she would bring back Cregane to its former glory of being a happy place for people to call to, I believed her. Along with young Mark there, and the other two,' he pointed his stick at Luke and Sno, 'they have achieved it. It wasn't easy, with a few of our own turning against them with actions and bad words, but we shall let all that go today. Today, we are happy. And to Cathy, Mark, and friends, when I say we are here to support you in turning Cregane Court into the best retreat centre for arts of all kinds, I speak for the whole village of Ballybawn. Go on now with ye all, and party.'

A rousing cheer raised up into the sky, scattering birds from the branches in the grove. People clapped while others hugged Cathy and Mark.

• • • •

Sore heads and aching limbs from dancing were the main complaints the following morning. The locals had partied hard, and Cathy and Mark were exhausted from all of the night's celebrations.

'We did it.' Cathy's voice was a hoarse squeak. She had never talked so much before, but people had wanted to know all her plans and she had been inundated with offers of help.

Mark lifted his head from his hands, the pounding headache like ten drum kits playing in his brain. He could only nod through his pain. Luke joined them in the sitting room. The cleaning up still faced them, but it could wait. No-one was in a hurry to move.

'Is Sno okay?' Mark asked his partner.

'I checked in on her, she's just getting up, be here in a minute. Coffee or tea anyone?'

Luke went to fill the kettle. Following him to the kitchen, they gathered around the table, bringing their suffering with them.

Sno surfaced and groaned when she saw the sick-looking faces of her friends. 'Good, I'm not the only one who overdid it. Where's Gerard?' She sat next to Cathy.

'He left last night around eleven-thirty; he has work this morning in court.' Cathy placed her head on Sno's shoulder.

'What next, I wonder?' Luke commented, as he placed the mugs on the table.

'Get ready for a wedding, I suppose,' Mark replied.

'What? Cathy, has Gerard popped the question? Did he do it last night? Oh, this is so wonderful, I'm going to cry.' Luke grabbed some tissues.

'What? No, no, no!' Cathy shrieked.

'No, you goose.' Mark knelt down on one knee and took the young man's hand in his. He'd told Cathy he did not want to put off living in the shadows any further. He loved this man, and he wanted the world to know it.

'Luke, will you marry me?'

'Oh my God, yes. Yes, I will.' He pulled Mark up and kissed him, then they both turned and laughed to the women.

'Okay, folks, I propose a toast.' Luke took up his mug, while the others sat up straight and waited.

'Pick up your mugs, people, and say after me,' he paused, '*to us, The Misfits.*'

'To us, The Misfits.'

There was a clanking of mugs amid howls of laughter.

Cathy looked around the kitchen. This cottage had given her a new family, a belief in herself that she no longer doubted. Mark and Luke had found love while their talents for art and carpentry thrived plus Sno too had begun a new life. Cregane Court was once more a home, a home that brought them together with happiness. She raised her mug of tea once more and the others looked at her questioningly.

'To the real magic maker of all this, Ms. Elizabeth Sheldon neé Reed, to Great-Aunt Lizzy'

'To Aunt Lizzy' they chorused in unison.

The End

Acknowledgements

When writing a novel, there are always people who are willing to give time to help when needed. A good friend Adrian kept me on the right track when dealing with Roman O'Driscoll's corrupt antics. My editor, Christine is as always so giving with time and her expertise. My cover artist for this novel, Karina knew exactly what it was I was trying to describe to her and was so obliging.

My family and friends are always there encouraging me and it means a lot. To write a novel is hard work and exhausting especially when the characters want to go off and do their own thing and not what you had planned for them. This book is a special one for me and I really hope you enjoy the story.

The Author

Mary Bradford is an Irish author. Family and relationships are topics explored in her writing. She seeks to highlight the secret and often buried aspects that lurks behind closed doors. Our curiosity is a strong driving force when it comes to knowing about other people's lives. Mary likes to include a feel good factor for her reader, it may not all be rosy in her novels, but knowing life can come right after obstacles in its path, conveys promise.

Other books by this author

Novels

My Husband's Sin: Book 1, The Lacey Taylor Story

Don't Call Me Mum: Book 2, The Lacey Taylor Story

No More Secrets: Book 3, The Lacey Taylor Story

Available on Amazon, and wwwbuythebook.ie

Novellas

The Runaway (Western)

Destiny (Western)

One Night in Barcelona (Adult Romance)

Once Upon a Weekend (Adult Romance)

Available on Amazon

Leave a Review

If you enjoyed this book, please leave a review on Amazon, Buy The Book, or Goodreads, or tell all you know to buy a copy. A review can be as simple as one word or two – enjoyable, must read. Reviews help an author's work to be found. Thank you for your continuing support.

www.buythebook.ie[1] www.amazon.com[2] www.amazon.co.uk[3] www.goodreads.com[4]

1. http://www.buythebook.ie
2. http://www.amazon.com
3. http://www.amazon.co.uk
4. http://www.goodreads.com

Printed in Poland
by Amazon Fulfillment
Poland Sp. z o.o., Wrocław

81424276R00154